KILLER LEMONADE

"Look!" I whispered and pointed. We all held our breaths as a male ruby-throated hummingbird hovered over the red cups on the table, and stopped to sip one of the purple flowers in the centerpiece. He then headed for the end of the table, where he sipped out of one of the red cups.

His colors were brilliant. We were all transfixed.

Then, suddenly, he stopped hovering and fell to the table. Skye was closest to him. She touched his breast gently. "He's dead!" she said, looking at all of us. "And he was sipping from the glass of lemonade I poured for myself ten minutes ago."

"Are you feeling all right?" Patrick asked. "Do you want to sit down?"

She brushed him off. "I'm fine. But what just happened?"

Patrick shook his head. "Don't touch anything. I'm going to get someone from the police."

"That's really not necessary," Skye started to say. But Patrick was already gone.

Sarah and I looked at each other and the small still bird. I put down my own glass of lemonade. "I don't think we should drink any more lemonade . . ."

Books by Lea Wait

TWISTED THREADS

THREADS OF EVIDENCE

Published by Kensington Publishing Corporation

THREADS OF EVIDENCE

Lea Wait

KENSINGTON PUBLISHING CORP.
http://www.kensingtonbooks.com

KENSINGTON BOOKS are published by

Kensington Publishing Corp.
119 West 40th Street
New York, NY 10018

All Kensington Titles, Imprints, and Distributed Lines are available at special quantity discounts for bulk purchases for sales promotions, premiums, fund-raising, and educational or institutional use. Special book excerpts or customized printings can also be created to fit specific needs. For details, write or phone the office of the Kensington special sales manager: Kensington Publishing Corp., 119 West 40th Street, New York, NY 10018, attn: Special Sales Department, Phone: 1-800-221-2647.

ISBN-13: 978-1-61773-006-1
ISBN-10: 1-61773-006-8
First Kensington Mass Market Edition: September 2015

eISBN-13: 978-1-61773-007-8
eISBN-10: 1-61773-007-6
First Kensington Electronic Edition: September 2015

10 9 8 7 6 5 4 3 2 1

Printed in the United States of America

Chapter 1

Evil enters like a needle, and spreads like an oak tree.

—Ethiopian proverb

One black Town Car, one blue Subaru, and a dented red pickup were parked in the driveway of the old Gardener estate. The massive Victorian had been empty ever since Mrs. Gardener, who'd lived there alone after her daughter's death, had herself died back in the early 1990s.

I remembered hearing stories about the ghosts who lived there. My friend Cindy, who was Catholic, had crossed herself every time we passed it. Local kids challenged each other to trick-or-treat there on Halloween to see who—or what—would open the front door.

I'd never heard of a boy or girl brave enough to walk through the wide gates guarding the entrance to the drive, past the large cracked concrete circle that had once been a fountain, to approach the actual door of the house.

When I'd asked Mama about it, she'd just shaken her

head. Said some places drew evil or sadness to them. Someone should tear the old place down.

But no one had. And I'd never seen a FOR SALE sign there. The house seemed fated to someday collapse in on itself, keeping past secrets within its cracked walls.

A couple of times in my teens I'll admit I'd made use of a broken window in the carriage house, which had its own entrance a little farther down the road. For a few months, that window was an open invitation to the caretaker's apartment, which, while drafty and dank, was equipped with a bed. No caretaker had lived there for a while. Mice and bats—and teenagers in search of privacy—had made it their own.

After someone replaced that pane, no one was brave enough to break another window.

Today several people were walking through the uncut field of buttercups that had once been a manicured lawn. They were ignoring the blackflies and ticks, which lurked in tall grasses on early-June days in Maine, and were pointing at the old house.

I turned my small red Honda into the Winslows' driveway across the street and parked by their barn. During the first weeks I'd been back in Haven Harbor I'd borrowed Gram's car, but having my own wheels was really a necessity. I had to pay calls on the shops and decorators and private customers who'd commissioned work from Mainely Needlepoint, the business I'd taken over from Gram. And I couldn't leave her without a car. She had her own life to live, her own future to plan.

I'd never dreamed of me, Angela Curtis, becoming the director of anything, much less a company that did commissioned needlepoint for decorators and high-end stores. Turned out what I'd learned as an assistant to a private investigator in Arizona could be put to good use in Maine.

Although running Mainely Needlepoint had been both a surprise and a challenge, the business was now well on its way to paying its debts. So far, I'd had no trouble locating the business's customers, despite having inherited a motley and incomplete set of books from both Gram and my predecessor, the agent who'd driven the business into financial trouble.

That agent was gone, swallows had returned from their winters down south and were refurbishing their nests under the roof in our barn, and Gram was busy planning her wedding to Reverend Tom.

They'd set the last Saturday in June as their wedding date—only three weeks off. Gram and I had spent a day at the Maine Mall in South Portland and found her a pale blue silk dress and jacket to wear for the ceremony. I hadn't yet found a dress suitable to wear for my role as maid of honor, but I wasn't panicked. After all, I had three weeks to shop.

I picked up the package I was delivering to Captain Ob and his wife, Anna, glancing over one more time at the Gardener estate.

Without thinking, I touched the small gold angel on the necklace Mama'd given me for my First Communion. "To keep you safe," she'd said.

Since her funeral I'd worn it every day. Maybe for reassurance? Maybe to remind me no place was truly safe? *Mama, I'm okay. I'm home. Life is good.*

I took another look at the people across the street.

Whatever was happening there, I'd hear about it soon enough.

When anything changes in a small town like Haven Harbor, word gets around fast.

Chapter 2

Nothing is so sure as Death and
Nothing is so uncertain as the
Time when I may be to [sic] *old to Live,*
But I can never be to [sic] *young to Die.*
I will live every hour as if I was to die the next.

—Embroidered on a sampler by Lydia Draper,
age thirteen, born December 6, 1729

Anna answered my knock. Through the open door I could see Ob sitting at his computer in the kitchen.

"Good to see you, Angie," said Anna. Her long, dark hair streaked with gray was pinned up against the seventy-degree heat, and she was wearing faded jeans and a T-shirt. It was a basic outfit for anyone over the age of three. Anna was over fifty. She eyed the package I was carrying. "Is that the needlework kit I ordered?"

"It is," I said. "Gram says you're one of the fastest learners in her class." I glanced into the package, to be sure

I'd picked up the right one. "You ordered a marked canvas with symbols of Maine, right?"

"I did," she answered. "It was a patchwork picture. Maine, a lighthouse, a lobster, the date we separated from Massachusetts, a chickadee. Everything Maine."

I handed it over. "Have fun with it. Gram said to call or stop in if you had any questions or problems."

I might be the director of Mainely Needlepoint, but I was still in the early stages of learning the craft myself. Anna Winslow had picked it up enthusiastically. I suspected she spent a lot more time with her needle than I did. "And, Ob . . . ?"

Her husband, an experienced needlepointer himself, waved at me in acknowledgment and got up slowly to join us. His back must be bothering him again.

"Here's a check for the wall hangings you stitched this spring."

He grinned as he accepted it. "Always like a check coming in. I was just updating my website."

"For your fishing charter?"

"Reservations are down a mite this year. Still too early to predict how the season'll be, though. Some folks don't plan their vacations till the last minute. This summer I'm cutting the price for children aged eight to twelve. Seven hours of deep-sea fishing is a long day on the water for young'uns, and they need help, but I have Josh and a couple of college boys to help me. If we encourage families to come on board, it'll be good for the future of the business. Get kids interested in fishing when they're young, they're customers for life."

"I hope Josh is more help to you on the boat than he is to me around the house," put in Anna. "Takes me more time to remind him of his chores than it would to do them myself."

"He'll be fine," Ob said. "I'm looking forward to having him with me on the *Anna Mae.*"

Anna rolled her eyes.

"Makes sense to me," I said. "Sure you don't want to take on any needlework projects this summer, Ob?"

He shook his head. "Can't be bothered now. If the charters don't pick up, I might be calling you, though."

I glanced out their front window. "I noticed cars and a pickup over at the Gardener estate. Don't remember ever seeing anyone over there before."

"Exciting, isn't it?" Anna said. "Word is the place has finally been sold."

"*Sold?* I hope to someone who has lots of money for repairs. Or who's going to tear it down," I said.

"Jed Fitch's their real estate agent. He said the purchaser's name is being kept quiet until the papers are signed tomorrow. Whoever it is, they're planning to fix it up," Ob said. "We've waited a long time for this day."

Anna sniffed a bit. "That crazy old place has been there too long, so far as I'm concerned. It's an eyesore. I hope those new folks burn it to the ground and start over."

"Now, Anna, you hush," Ob said. "It was a beautiful house in its day. It would be a feather in Haven Harbor's cap if someone could restore it to what it once was."

"How did you happen to talk with the real estate agent?" I asked.

"He came to me for the key," Ob said. "I've been the caretaker there, at least when I was paid, for over forty years now."

"I didn't know that," I said, immediately thinking of that broken window. "So you knew Mrs. Gardener."

"He surely did. That woman was a pain in your 'sit-down,' and that's the truth. Just because she had more money than the rest of us, thought she could order Ob around as it suited her."

"Anna, she was an old woman when you knew her—an old woman who lived by herself. She needed help with the place. She was always good to me."

"Good?" Anna sniffed. "Paid you close to nothing, and kept you on call, day and night."

"You lived close enough," I said, looking out their living-room window. The roof and turrets of the Gardener place rose above the stone wall surrounding their property.

"He used to live closer still," said Anna. "Used to live right over there, in the carriage house."

"You did?" I said, turning to Ob and envisioning *that* mattress—Ob's mattress—in the carriage house.

"Moved in there after my folks died, when I was a teenager. Did errands for Mrs. Gardener after school and weekends. Picked up her groceries and mail and mowed the lawns and such. She insisted I get my high-school diploma. But after that, I worked for her full-time. When Anna and I got married"—he threw her a sly glance—"Anna wasn't comfortable staying so close to Mrs. Gardener. Living somewhere with the history that place has. I'd saved up a bit by then, since Mrs. Gardener never charged me rent, and she made us a wedding gift of the down payment."

"Right across the street," I added. "Giving you the down payment was generous."

He shrugged. "She and I got along. And being just across the street, I'd still be close enough so I could keep an eye on what happened there. After Mrs. Gardener died, I kept walking through the house and carriage house once every month or two. If repairs were needed, I called New York and Mr. Gardener's lawyer would send up a check to cover my time and materials. Mr. Gardener never came up from New York after Jasmine died, even though his wife was living here, but he kept paying the bills. My salary stopped when he died, about ten years back. I still check on the place once in a while on my own conscience, but now it's in serious need of repairs. At first, I called the Gardeners' lawyer in New York, but he didn't seem to care, and wouldn't pay me to do the work. Wasn't my responsibility to take that on for free. I'm glad somebody's finally taking an interest in the old place."

"Old rubbish heap, if you ask me," put in Anna. "Just sitting over there, decaying more every year."

"I wonder who's buying it?" I asked. "Someone local? Or someone from away?"

"I can't think of anyone local who'd have the interest and the money," Anna said. "All we know is Jed said it was someone from California." She paused. "No doubt someone with money. Someone new to lord it over us locals."

"Funny the name of the buyer is being kept quiet. Who would any of us know in California, anyway? Be interesting to see what the new folks plan to do with the place. It isn't decent for living now." Ob looked past me, through the window, to where the old house stood.

"We'll have to wait and see," Anna said, nodding. "I still think they should burn it down and use the land for something practical. A farm. Or a couple of new modern-type houses. After all, Jasmine Gardener died in 1970. Long enough ago for people to forget what happened there."

"Murder isn't exactly something people forget," Ob put in, speaking quietly.

"She was murdered?" I asked. "I remember hearing that rumor when I was a kid, but other people said she'd drowned. That it was an accident."

Ob shrugged. "Some said that. Mrs. Gardener was convinced otherwise. That's why she never left Aurora after

Jasmine died. Kept saying she wasn't going to die until she'd figured out who'd killed her daughter. Couldn't accept that death's as unpredictable as life."

I shivered a bit. "She was only seventeen, wasn't she? Jasmine, I mean."

Ob nodded. "Seventeen. Had big blue eyes and that shiny, long, straight hair girls had in those days. I always thought she looked like one of my sister's dolls that was too good to play with. Too perfect to dirty up."

"So you knew her?" I asked.

"I was ten when she died. But, yes, I remember her. My folks knew the Gardeners, and Jasmine was hard to forget." He shook his head. "It was real sad when she died. Nothing was the same after that. Not at Aurora, anyway."

"I'd forgotten they called the place 'Aurora.'"

"When the original Gardeners built that cottage, back in the 1890s, it was the fashion to name summer places. Some folks still do it, but not many. Anyway, story was the first Mrs. Gardener to live there loved to see the sun rise over the hills, east of town." Ob pointed. "She named it Aurora after the goddess of the dawn." He paused. "Pretty highfalutin', but they were from New York City, after all. A marble statue of the goddess Aurora, all naked except for her cape, stood in the middle of the fountain, right in the center of the front drive. Looked spiffy, all right, when that fountain was working."

"They tore the fountain down," I said, remembering the story.

"Mrs. Gardener said she couldn't stand to look out her window and see the place her daughter died. She hired men in town to break up the statue with sledgehammers and cart away the pieces." He shook his head. "I was too young to be a part of all that, but I remember my father coming home and telling my mother and my sister, Rose, and me. He was worried about Mrs. Gardener then—afraid she was going out of her head. But her mind was fine, so far as I could tell. She was stubborn, though. Didn't believe Jasmine had fallen and hit her head and drowned in the fountain. It made no sense to her. Years after that, when I knew her pretty well, she spent all her time thinking of what else could have happened. Talked about it all the time. That's about all she did, in fact. That and"—he pointed at the needlepoint kit his wife was holding—"doing needlepoint. The woman always had a needle and yarns in her hands."

"It's a sad story," I said, looking out the window as the red pickup pulled out of Aurora's driveway. "But maybe it will have a happy ending. Maybe whoever bought the house will fix it up the way it used to be."

"They may try," said Ob. "With enough money they might be able to bring back the house. But they'll never bring back Jasmine."

Chapter 3

With fingers weary and worn
With eyelids heavy and red.
A woman sat, in unwomanly rags
Plying her needle and thread.

—Thomas Hood (1798–1845)
The Song of the Shirt, 1843

I kept thinking about Jasmine Gardener on my drive home. She'd died when she was only seventeen. Today she'd be sixty-two. Thirty-five years older than I was. She might have been married and had grandchildren by now. Or had a great career as . . . what? I couldn't guess. All I knew about her was she'd been a rich girl and she'd died.

She might have made a major contribution to the world. Or she might have lived an ordinary life. Or a disastrous one. She didn't have a chance to choose. To die at seventeen meant all her possibilities were wasted. Canceled. Gone.

I'd been seventeen ten years ago. What had I accomplished with those years?

It was a depressing thought.

I'd felt like an average, ordinary girl, growing up not-rich-and-not-destitute in a harbor town in Maine until Mama disappeared, when I was almost ten. Then I became the subject of whispers; I was someone to be pitied. I was someone whose mother, many said under their breaths, was a slut. As a teenager I'd raged, followed in some of Mama's footsteps, and hated everything and everyone. I certainly hadn't made life easier for Gram, or for anyone else in Haven Harbor. Or, I was beginning to admit now, for myself.

Then I'd spent ten years in Arizona. Had I made a difference to the world? A difference, perhaps indirectly, to our clients whose spouses I'd tracked and who'd ended up winning in divorce court. No differences I was proud of, although my work had paid the bills.

And here I was, back in Haven Harbor. After all these years Mama's body had been discovered a month ago, and I'd been able to find her killer. I'd committed to staying in town six months. I wasn't ready to sign up for more small-town life than that.

Being back home opened some chapters of my life I'd tried to close forever. Meant confronting the memories and nightmares I'd grown up with.

But it also meant I was close to the rocks and sea I'd always loved. Back where the familiar screech of hungry herring gulls woke me in the morning, and the spring peepers kept me company at night. I could indulge in the seafood and fresh New England produce I'd missed in Arizona. For me, Mexican food would never replace haddock chowder, a lobster club sandwich, or, at this time of year, rhubarb crisp or strawberry-rhubarb pie, with vanilla ice cream.

I hoped Gram'd made something sweet today. Maybe her maple bread pudding. One sniff of her kitchen and I was back to my childhood. The good parts of my childhood. What would I do after she married Reverend Tom and moved to the rectory? I'd existed on fast food in Arizona. Someday I'd have to learn to cook.

I pulled into the driveway in back of Gram's car, opened the door, and inhaled. The smell and the taste of salt breezes were better than any tranquilizer or massage.

I wouldn't have minded a glass of wine or two, though. Or a gin and tonic.

For the moment I was living chastely, by chance if not by choice. But I hadn't given up all my vices. Wine, beer, cognac, gin . . . I didn't discriminate against any of them.

Those chairs Gram and I repainted last week looked inviting on the front porch. A glass in my hand, a copy of the *Portland Press Herald,* and a seat protected from strong sea breezes and overlooking Haven Harbor's Green—that's where I was headed.

"Gram? I'm home," I called into the front hall. Juno, Gram's enormous yellow coon cat, padded into the hall from the living room and greeted me with a yowl.

"In the kitchen, Angel," came Gram's response. "With Sarah. Come join us."

Gram and Sarah Byrne, the youngest member of the Mainely Needlework crew (except for me), were sitting at the table. I hadn't decided whether it was Sarah's blond hair streaked with pink and blue, her Aussie accent, or her frequent quoting of Emily Dickinson that made her the most memorable member of the Maine Antiques Dealers Association. Her excellent needlework made her a valuable member of our Mainely Needlepoint team. She and I also had agreed to establish a sideline to the business: identifying, conserving, and restoring old needlework. Was that why she was here today? It would have taken something important to convince her to close her antique shop on a June afternoon.

"Iced tea?" Gram asked. She and Sarah already had glasses. "I made a couple of pitchers this morning. They're in the refrigerator. Green pitcher's black tea. Clear pitcher's herb."

Iced tea wasn't exactly what I'd been thinking of. I poured myself a glass of the caffeinated variety. When I was growing up, Gram had only made that kind, complete with fresh lemons and mint from the garden and an amount of sugar I didn't want to guess at. Now she'd discovered green and herb teas and left both varieties unsweetened.

I added a packet of artificial sweetener to my glass and fleetingly wondered if it would be too obvious if I walked to the dining room and added gin. But I was still Gram's little girl. She did indulge in a glass of wine now and then—something she hadn't done while I was growing up—but I didn't think she'd be sympathetic to gin in iced tea.

I'd have to wait for a more serious drink.

In the meantime I joined Sarah and Gram at the old pine kitchen table.

"You were over to Ob and Anna Winslow's place, right?" asked Gram.

"Delivered that needlepoint kit Anna ordered, and gave Ob the last of the checks we owed him. He's hoping to fill his summer with fishing charters, not needlework." I took a deep drink. Gram did make good iced tea. "Seems to be something going on at the old Gardener estate. Ob said someone's bought the place."

Sarah and Gram exchanged glances. "That's what I was saying before you arrived," said Sarah. "Although that place gives me the willies. It reminds me of Emily's line—'I know some lonely Houses off the Road.' But if it's fixed up, it could be a stunner. Exciting to think of it, isn't it?"

"I've always loved it," I answered. "Never saw the inside, of course." (*Except for the carriage house,* I reminded myself privately.) "It's a shame it's been left to decay so long. No one can afford to build houses like that today."

"I don't know," said Sarah. "Maybe no one in Haven Harbor could, but there are wealthy people in the world." She looked from Gram to me. "People from California, for instance."

"Why do I have the feeling you know something more about it?" I asked.

"Last week, when I was having my hair done at Mane Waves, Elsa Fitch said she'd heard the old place was for sale. I didn't even think to mention it to you. We weren't going to buy it, and places in that condition can be on the market for years," Gram said.

Sarah grinned. "I know all about it. I was sworn to secrecy, but I have to tell someone! And I even have an excuse to tell both of you."

"So? What did you hear? Talk, lady!" I said.

Sarah was almost bouncing in her seat. It must be exciting news, or Gram had made the caffeinated iced tea a lot stronger than usual.

"Well," Sarah said in a dramatic whisper, leaning over, "Aurora, the old Gardener place, has been bought by Skye West!" She leaned back as though she'd just announced the Messiah would be dropping in for lunch.

"Skye West, the actress?" I asked hesitantly. Among the many areas of culture I didn't keep up to date with were

Hollywood figures. But I was pretty sure I'd heard of Skye West. "Didn't she win an Oscar a couple of years ago?"

"And a Tony last year." Sarah added.

Gram shook her head. "Sorry. Maybe I need to spend more time at Mane Waves reading *People* magazine. Can't say I've ever heard of her."

Sarah looked disappointed. We weren't as excited as she'd thought we'd be. "How'd you find that out?" I asked. Whether or not Gram knew who Skye West was, I was pretty sure. And no one but Sarah seemed to have heard she planned to buy a place in Haven Harbor. Sarah'd only lived in town a few years. I wouldn't have guessed she had an inside track to Haven Harbor gossip. Mainers took a while to welcome people from away into their inner circles, and Sarah had come from about as far away as you could get.

"That's even more exciting!" Sarah went on. "Late this morning I couldn't help spotting a fantastic-looking bloke in his early thirties looking through the stuff in my shop. I'd never seen him before. I sat in back of the counter doing needlepoint like mad and sneaking looks at him."

"So," I said, "a good-looking guy came into your shop. And . . . ?"

"A couple there at the same time was looking at my inventory as though it was a museum exhibit. Lots of looks and no purchases. When they left, the handsome hunk—"

"Hunk?" I asked. "Really?"

"Well, he wasn't Arnold Schwarzenegger, but I'll bet he lifts weights in his spare time." Sarah shot me a look that said, *"Let me tell my story, my way."* I shut up. "He asked me how long I'd been in business and where I came from. Then he asked me how much I knew about needlepoint."

"Yes?" Gram said, now paying closer attention.

"Of course, I told him about coming from Australia, and about Mainely Needlepoint. He said his mum's best friend was from Australia, too. I could have fallen through the floor when he said her best friend was Nicole Kidman!"

"And so who was this perfect man?" asked Gram. I suspected she didn't know who Nicole Kidman was any more than she'd heard of Skye West.

"I'm getting to that! He's Skye West's son, Patrick. And he's single and an artist, and he wants me to come and look at Aurora and appraise what's in there. He said his mum is buying the estate and plans to fix it up, and he's going to put a studio in the carriage house."

"So the place is being sold as is, with the contents?" asked Gram.

"Patrick says the place is a bit of a wreck, but they don't want to throw out anything valuable, so they were looking for an antique dealer to give it a walk-through. All I could think of was 'Mansions! Mansions must be warm! Mansions cannot let the tears in, Mansions much exclude the storm!'"

(Poetry isn't my thing. But I knew when Sarah said something odd, she was quoting Emily.)

"He said a lot of stitchery is in the house. Most of it's in poor condition, but his mother wants some restored."

"Ob mentioned Mrs. Gardener was a serious needle-pointer," I said. "It would be fantastic if they'd pay us to restore all of it! They must have tons of money to even attempt the work that cottage will need."

"That's what I thought. And I couldn't keep that possibility to myself. Plus, I'm a bit nervous about taking on such a large job. I haven't been an antique dealer for too long. So I asked Patrick if I could bring a friend when I do the appraisal—a friend who's an expert in needlepoint."

"Who're you going to bring?" I asked.

"You, of course!" Sarah grinned, brushing a strand of pink hair back from her face. "But remember, I saw Patrick West first!"

Chapter 4

I can be safe and free from care
On any shore, if thou be there.

—Words stitched on a sampler by an anonymous American girl, perhaps an immigrant, 1802

We were both nervous. Sarah had never done an appraisal of a whole house, and I was less experienced than that. I volunteered to photograph everything.

Camera taken care of, we got down to our most difficult decision: what we should wear. After several texts, balancing what we'd heard about the inside of the house with what rich people from Hollywood might expect appraisers to wear, Sarah decided on a preppie look, with navy slacks, a red blazer, and a white shirt. My wardrobe didn't present many choices, but I came up with tan slacks and an almost-matching sweater. Good thing June mornings in Maine were cool.

Focusing on wardrobe options took our minds away

from being nervous about what we hoped would be our biggest needlework preservation job yet. We had no idea whether we'd be looking at nineteenth-century (or earlier) samplers and stitchery, or the product of Mrs. Gardener's long years of living at Aurora with only her needlepoint to keep her company.

Plus, what else might be in a house empty for so long? I wasn't superstitious, but I shivered a little thinking about what might be inside.

"Hey, it isn't as though Jasmine Gardener's body is going to be there," Sarah assured me as we headed out to the estate. "Besides, if it were there, it'd be all dried up by now. A mummy, I'd think."

"That's reassuring?" I asked. "Besides, Maine's too damp to allow for mummification." I changed the subject. "Let's not think about Jasmine. Let's focus on what we have to do inside that house." I'd always been curious about the inside of Aurora, but today I felt as though those tiny Spring Azure butterflies were fluttering inside my stomach.

"Besides," Sarah continued, "I heard the fountain where Jasmine died was destroyed. There's nothing left to preserve evidence."

"Evidence? Of what?"

"Of whether she was murdered or died accidentally, of course." Sarah grinned as she turned and drove through the open iron gate in the gray stone wall surrounding the property. We parked on the oval pavement, now cracked and broken, in front of the house.

Up close the place was in even worse condition than I'd imagined.

Paint had peeled off once-white clapboards, leaving the mansion grayed from sea air and winds. Old shutters, which must have been collected after they fell, were stacked against one corner of the building. I suspected Ob had put them there years ago. Tall strands of witchgrass had grown up around and through the shutters' slats.

Sarah and I looked up at the precariously tilted balcony above the massive front door and the broken slate roof tiles littering the yard. Could we still back out of this job? Then two people walked around the side of the house and joined us.

"Sarah! Good to see you again," said the man.

Sarah was right. Patrick's loosely waved dark hair and deep brown eyes definitely put him in the "tall, dark, and handsome" category.

"And this must be your friend. Angie, am I right?" He had a firm grip and covered my hand with both of his, a strangely familiar gesture. His fingernails were stained with paint. "And this is my mother, Ms. West." He indicated the handsome woman with him. Her casually pinned-up hair was gray, with streaks of white. She was almost as tall as her son and walked as though she was a model. Maybe she had been. "Mom, these are the women who're going to appraise what's in the house."

"Please call me Skye. After all, we're going to be neighbors," she added, her smile taking in both Sarah and me. "Thank you for taking a look at what's left in the house." She wasn't what I'd expected a movie star to be. Her voice was low and calm and she wasn't wearing makeup. I guessed she was a well-preserved sixty and had spent a lifetime slathering on sunblock and antiaging creams.

I should give Gram a facial for a prewedding gift.

Skye's designer jeans and Haven Harbor T-shirt looked new, but she made no attempt to hide the streak of dirt across the front of the shirt. "I'll warn you—this place is a mess. We've already arranged for a couple of dumpsters. Most of what's inside the house will end up being junked."

She paused. "It's sad. You can still imagine what Aurora was in its heyday, but dampness, combined with cold winters and hot summers, has destroyed almost everything."

"Not to mention the birds and bats and various animals that have invaded it over the years," Patrick added. "And died there."

"Don't alarm Angie and Sarah even more than you have to," Skye put in, turning to us. "I assure you we've already removed the dead animals and birds. The damage they did, sad to say, wasn't as easy to do away with."

Sarah and I exchanged a glance. How bad *was* this place going to be inside?

"Sarah mentioned there's a lot of needlepoint," I said. "Are you thinking of having it all restored?"

She shook her head. "Sadly, no. You'll see. Some of it's in impossible shape. But I'd like to keep a few pieces, if you think they can be salvaged. Souvenirs of the history of this place."

While Sarah explained how we planned to divide the work, I got out my camera and lenses.

"I'll go with you," Skye was saying.

"Watch out for holes and rotten places in the floors. And some ceilings are on the verge of falling," Patrick added. "We're hoping the house will still be standing after we get all the ruined furnishings and torn wallpaper and chunks of fallen plaster into the Dumpsters. Taking the wallpaper off some walls will take the plaster down, too."

"I understand," Sarah said. "But an appraisal is going to take us a while. Why don't you give us a basic tour of the house, pointing out anything you want us to pay particular attention to, and then leave the two of us. That way we can focus on each room slowly. Make sure nothing is missed."

And not be distracted by either of you, I added to myself.

Skye hesitated. "That makes sense. Patrick, would you stay here?" She turned to Sarah. "The first two Dumpsters are going to be delivered this morning—one for the main house and one for the carriage house. I'm sure there's nothing worth saving in the carriage house, so you don't even have to look there. We're going to gut most of it so we can get a couple of rooms fixed up quickly. That'll be our home while work on the house is progressing. Patrick plans to make that building his studio eventually, but our priority now is moving out of our motel and onto the estate."

Sarah gave Patrick a quick glance. She would rather have had Patrick accompany us on our tour.

"I'll catch up with you if you're still in the house after the Dumpsters arrive," he assured us. "But I also have to deal with the construction crew due later this morning. They're going to remove the old plumbing and kitchen fixtures in the carriage house today."

I hoped they'd hired local people. People in Haven Harbor could use the work. And without even seeing the inside of this place, it was evident there'd be full employment here for builders, electricians, plumbers, painters, and wallpaper hangers for some time.

It would take a lot more than paint to make the house livable. And even fixed up, the carriage house wasn't a place I'd imagined show business celebrities would live. And now they were staying in a motel? Typical Maine, but way below Hollywood standards.

"Have you checked out the bed-and-breakfasts in town?" I suggested. "Several of them are quite luxurious, and you'd be closer to Aurora."

"Don't worry. For now, the motel is fine." She hesitated. "We're hoping Haven Harbor will be our summer home in the future. We didn't want to impose on the people who live here."

"When Mom stays somewhere, it often causes a bit of commotion," Patrick added. "We're staying south of here, out on Route 1, to try to keep our presence as quiet as we can for right now. We won't be there long." He headed toward the carriage house as Skye opened the wide front door and Sarah and I followed her into the large front hall.

No one said anything at first. I suspected Skye wanted us to absorb the beauty of the place and its potential. And the incredible task she—and we—had taken on.

We were facing a wide oak-paneled staircase, which climbed to an open-railed hallway circling the second floor. Above it, another staircase led to what I assumed was a third floor.

In 1970, the only year I knew much about the family, the Gardeners had been a family of three. This place must have been overwhelming then. Possibly earlier generations of Gardeners had been larger. And I suspected guests visited frequently. Also, I reminded myself, they'd had live-in help.

I was no expert on elegance, but the water-stained carvings on the oak staircase and woodwork must once have been spectacular. Elaborate scrollwork imitating rolling waves might have been considered simple when this house had been built. Today the dark oak overwhelmed the entrance hall.

"'Buzz the dull flies—on the chamber window—Brave—shines the sun through the freckled pane—Fearless—the cobweb swings from the ceiling,'" Sarah said, almost whispering.

"What?" Skye asked. "I didn't catch that."

"Emily Dickinson. But she was writing about the home of a woman who had died," said Sarah.

We were all silent. After all, this home, too, had held death. It smelled of mildew, as well as other scents I wasn't sure I wanted to identify.

If the rest of the house was like this, Sarah wouldn't have much to appraise. It would all have to go.

I started snapping pictures. I made sure to show the entire hall, and then focused on close-ups of damage to the floor, carpet, and woodwork.

The walls had once been papered in a gray blue scroll pattern, echoing the pattern carved in the woodwork. Most of that paper had peeled off, revealing large patches of mold. The enormous brass chandelier was now green, and a large hole in the floor blocked the entrance to one of the side rooms.

How could the family have let it decay so? I began to understand why Anna Winslow had suggested it just be torn down. Once, this place might have been a showcase. Today it was a disaster.

Skye West was the first to speak. "As you can see, she's a grand old lady, but she needs a little tender loving care."

I glanced over at Sarah, who was shaking her head. I couldn't imagine the amount of money and time it would take to return Aurora to its earlier glory. Or even to habitable condition. I took several pictures of each wall. "I'm going to photograph it all," I explained. "You'll have a record of what was here, and what condition it was in when you bought it."

"I'd appreciate that," said Skye. "I've already found photographs showing what it was like in the forties, fifties, and sixties. I'd love to put together an album of those, plus pictures of what the house looks like now, and how it will look after we finish fixing it up."

With all the money I assumed the Wests had at their disposal, why hadn't they bought one of the big modern homes being built along the coast? Those homes were clean, open, welcoming, energy efficient . . . and didn't reek of mildew and rotting boards.

"How did you happen to find this place?" I had to ask. "What brought you to Haven Harbor?"

As Skye turned toward me, a small piece of gray plaster fell off the ceiling onto her shoulder. "I like a challenge," she said, brushing off the plaster. "I'd seen pictures of what Aurora once was. It's always been my dream to restore an old home."

Maybe Aurora had been featured in a glossy decorator magazine years ago. Or in an article about the Gardeners. Wherever Skye had first seen it, she'd certainly picked a home with plenty of room for improvement.

"I wish I'd seen it in its heyday," said Sarah. She looked around once more and then opened her notebook and started to write. "The only thing in the hall worth appraising is the chandelier, and I'd need to see that closer to decide whether it was worth restoring."

"When the construction crew gets here I'll ask them to take it down. I don't expect you to climb a two-story ladder."

Sarah made a note. "Great. Where would you like us to start?"

Skye pointed to Sarah's right. "Let's begin with the living room. The first floor is in better condition than the second and third floors. The other floors protected it somewhat from leaks in the roof."

The large living room was filled with upholstered furniture that squirrels or raccoons had torn apart. Some of the pieces had once been covered with needlework. The animals hadn't cared. If any of the furniture was worth saving, all the upholstery would need to be replaced. I walked over to a large sofa with a carved oak back. Was it worth restoring? That would be up to Sarah and Skye. Victorian furniture wasn't exactly my area of expertise. I took some overall shots of the room and then started at the door to the front hall and began photographing the furniture, paintings, and decorations on the right-hand wall.

"This room is going to take some time to document," Sarah pointed out to Skye. "It looks as though everything is the way the Gardeners left it." She looked into a pair of glass cabinets, where blue-and-white china shared shelf space with rounded sea stones, shells, and sea glass.

I focused my camera on each shelf. I didn't know anything about china, although that blue color was relatively common in Maine. But were these pieces the then-inexpensive china used as ballast by sea captains returning from the Orient in the 1800s or modern reproductions? I knew more about the shells and stones. Shelves in my bedroom were filled with similar souvenirs of the sea. How long had these summer finds been here? Who'd collected them?

The house was over a hundred years old. I'd never thought of nineteenth-century "rusticators," as summer visitors to Maine were called then, searching beaches for the same treasures I'd looked for as a child. But perhaps they had.

"Your idea that we should walk through the house first to get an overview was a good one," said Skye, stepping over a hole in the floor and heading out of the living room toward the room across the hall. "Why don't you wait to take notes and pictures until after I've shown you the whole place? That way you'll have an idea of how much work you'll have to do. The dining room is this way."

Aurora's long mahogany dining table could have seated fourteen people easily, and I suspected a wall-length sideboard would contain treasures. But what I saw first were the three mounted heads hanging over the marble mantel: one moose, complete with antlers, one bear, and a five-point buck. Displaying hunters' trophies wasn't unheard of in Haven Harbor, but it was much more common in hunting lodges and homes farther Down East. Based on the condition of the heads, some Gardener from a while back must have been a hunter. When I was able to take my eyes off the animal heads, I realized there also were two large fish displayed over the sideboard: a cod, of a size not often seen off the coast of Maine today, and a striped bass. None of the preserved creatures were in good condition; the bedraggled animals were missing patches of hair, and one fish was missing a tail.

I wouldn't have chosen them for my dining room.

On the other hand, on the long outside wall, a series of framed needlepoint panels was hanging between the windows.

Sarah and I both moved toward them.

Chapter 5

Embroidery decks the canvas round and yields a pleasing view, so virtue tends to deck the mind and form its blissful state.

—Sampler embroidered by
Nabby Kollock Ide (1790–1813),
Wrentham, Massachusetts, 1804

I walked over to look at one of the large needlepoint panels more closely. "This is Haven Harbor Lighthouse," I said.

Skye nodded. "All the needlework panels in this room are places here at Aurora, or close by, in Haven Harbor." She pointed at the one closest to her. "That's the main staircase in the house. And I love the one of a moose in a field of flowers, over near the door to the kitchen."

Sarah walked to the other side of the room, looking carefully at each panel in turn. "Is this the fountain that used to be in front of the house?"

"Yes," said Skye.

The fountain Mrs. Gardener had destroyed after Jasmine's

death in 1970—I'd never seen a picture of it. Just as Ob had described it, the statue of a naked woman, partially concealed by a cape, was surrounded by plumes of water. The pool looked shallow—too shallow to have drowned someone. Maybe Jasmine had stumbled on the stone border and had hit her head.

"In old photos of Aurora, the fountain is beautiful," Skye went on. "And Millie Gardener did all this needlework. More of her stitching is upstairs, but these pieces are her best. Because she'd had them framed, they were better protected than a lot of her pillows and wall hangings. I'd like them restored, if possible."

I was still staring at the needlepointed panel of the fountain. Why had Mrs. Gardener chosen to stitch a picture of the place her daughter died?

"We can restore these," I said, focusing back on Skye's question. I took mental notes: a picture of Second Sister Island, one of the three islands in Haven Harbor; the Haven Harbor Town Pier; an eagle flying over the yacht club building; the Congregational Church building; a wide view of Haven Harbor itself, filled with small sailboats and lobster boats. Sarah didn't say anything, but pointed to mildewing in the stitching of some, to be sure I noticed it. Several of the pictures were also water-stained. I lifted one of those off the wall. The wall was stained, too. Strong winds must have driven heavy rain or snow through the clapboards onto the inside walls of the house.

"These panels are special, and were made for this house. They should stay here," I agreed. "We won't know how much work conservation and restoration will take until we remove the panels from their frames. We'll need to remove the backings and replace them with acid-free cloth. Some are mildewed, some have water damage, and the yarn in several has faded or broken. The work is lovely, but the panels aren't old enough to have value as antiques. If you'd agree, we could reinforce some of the stitching and perhaps replace some. Restore them so they'd look close to their original state." I hoped I was right. I was still learning about needlepoint restoration.

I must have sounded authoritative. Skye looked around the room and added, "And they should all be reframed with acid-free materials and sun-resistant glass. Can you do all that?"

Sarah and I looked at each other.

"We can," I said, sounding more confident than I felt. "We could have these back to you within a month, unless we find major problems when we take them apart."

"You'll let me know about that," Skye said. "Take them all when you leave today so they won't get mixed in with the items we're going to sell. I love these pictures. And if they take you a little longer than you think to fix, that's all right. The house won't be finished for more than a month or two."

A month or two? It looked to me as though the place would takes years of work. "We'll need you to choose new frames when the stitching is finished."

"I'll be here all summer," said Skye. "I'll be reading scripts, but I don't have any projects lined up until late in the fall. Restoring Aurora is my priority now."

We moved on.

The kitchen pipes had broken at some point; the floor there was so rotten we didn't dare examine the cabinets or their contents. I suspected Mrs. Gardener hadn't done much cooking in the years she'd lived here alone. Either she'd had a cook, or she'd eaten out a lot. When the family had been here, the cook probably had an assistant or two. The kitchen was as large as a small diner. Now it was unusable. And it looked as though it had been that way more than the almost-twenty-years since Mrs. Gardener had died.

Everywhere I looked, the house needed serious repairs requiring even more serious money.

I hoped Skye had some blockbuster scripts to read. Did she have any idea how much it would cost to restore this place? It would be cheaper to paper it with dollar bills.

"We have to be careful where we step on the second floor," said Skye, leading the way up the front stairway. "Patrick and I found rotten boards in several rooms. Some are under the carpeting."

I sniffed. Mildewed carpets. They would all have to go.

The only furniture in the second-floor hallway was a built-in window seat overlooking Haven Harbor. The clear glass windows were outlined in green-and-blue stained glass. Unfortunately, two sections of the glass were missing, so rain and snow had blown in. Ocean breezes filled the hallway.

"I can hardly wait to have this sitting area repaired," said Skye, looking at the damp seat cushion and the several needlepoint cushions on it. "I don't think these pillows are worth trying to save."

I agreed. The pillows were water-stained and mildewed; their threads faded. One had been torn apart. By a bird in the house? A squirrel? "They must have been lovely once," I said, looking at one of a puffin and another that might have been a laughing gull. "But I agree. I don't think we could reclaim them. What do you think, Sarah?"

She shook her head. "No. They're gone. Sadly." She picked up one of a chickadee. "We could reproduce them, though, if you were interested."

Good for Sarah! I hadn't thought of that.

"I like that idea," Skye said. "Let me think about it. In the meantime let's not throw them out."

Sarah followed her into the room on the right side of the hall. I stared at the window seat for a few more moments before following them. Had Jasmine Gardener sat on that window seat, looking out at the harbor? It would have been a perch hard to resist. If she'd been a reader, maybe she'd curled up with a book and leaned against those pillows. Or maybe the pillows had been done after Jasmine died, and her mother had sat here, watching the harbor, thinking of what might have been. The world the Gardeners lived in had been far from the Haven Harbor I knew. And yet they'd chosen to summer here. To look down at the harbor, instead of staying in what I assumed was a palatial New York City home.

What had it been like for Jasmine? Had she loved Maine? Had she missed her friends in the city? Nineteen seventy was so long ago. And why had Mrs. Gardener chosen to stay here after her daughter's death? Why hadn't she left this place and returned to her husband and life in New York? I looked down into the front hall. This might have been a beautiful home, but it also must have felt empty for one person living here alone.

I forced myself to come back to the present time and followed Sarah and Skye into the first bedroom. "This was the Gardeners' bedroom," Skye was saying. "Mrs. Gardener spent most of her last years in this room."

The bedroom was in better condition than the kitchen, but it, too, had been invaded by the mildew that seemed to have infected the entire house. A row of windows looked out over the harbor, as the window seat had. A high bed and several comfortable-looking chairs were arranged to face a small television set. One wall was covered by framed photographs, some of them stained by dampness or faded by time.

What images of her life had Mrs. Gardener chosen to highlight and revisit?

Sarah was looking at the large floor-to-ceiling bookcase that filled the far wall. The bookends were rocks that could have come from Pocket Cove Beach. "These are all books on needlepoint," she pointed out. "History of needlepoint, pattern books. It's an amazing collection."

"Are any of them worth anything?" asked Skye.

"I'd have to check their condition individually and their copyrights," said Sarah. "They might be. Because they're on an inside wall, I'm hoping they're not as damaged as the pictures and embroideries on the outside walls. They'll take a while to appraise."

"We don't have time for you to do a thorough appraisal of each book and magazine. Since you're both involved with Mainely Needlepoint, why don't you take all that stuff? Examine everything on your own time, save it, sell it, toss it out—whatever you decide is best. They're now all yours."

Sarah and I looked at each other. "Thank you very much," I said. "That's generous of you."

She shrugged. "I admire Mrs. Gardener's work, but I don't plan to take up needlepoint myself. I'd like to see her collection go to people who could use it."

"We could," Sarah confirmed. "Thank you."

Skye nodded. The subject was closed.

"I suspect Mrs. Gardener spent a lot of time in here stitching," I said. *And thinking,* I added silently to myself.

"Her wardrobe room is next. You'll see."

A bathroom, smaller than those in many homes today, but with marble walls and a large Victorian claw-foot bathtub, was connected to Mrs. Gardener's room. The room next to it held a dressing table and wide gold-framed mirror, a closet rod hung with clothing, and stacks of cardboard boxes.

"The boxes are full of embroidery yarns and floss and canvas and other materials," said Skye. "They may still be usable, but you'd know that better than I. Her clothing, unfortunately, is not in good condition. I hoped some of it would be wearable, because I love vintage clothing. But after Jasmine's death Mrs. Gardener must not have replenished her wardrobe often. Some of her sweaters and slippers are worn through, and the fabrics of her blouses and dresses are too fragile to be worn."

"Would you like me to check through them, anyway?" asked Sarah, making a note.

"Please. But if you find anything that won't go directly into the dumpster, put it aside and let me look at it before we decide to sell it."

We left Mrs. Gardener's rooms and crossed the hall to another large room. Jasmine's room was a time capsule of 1970.

Peter Max posters covered the walls. WAR IS NOT HEALTHY FOR CHILDREN AND OTHER LIVING THINGS. LOVE. Beatles posters. (She'd circled Paul in what might once have been red lipstick.)

Skye stared at the room. "She was only seventeen, you know. So young."

"'Left in immortal Youth On that low Plain That hath nor Retrospection Nor again—Ransomed from years—Sequestered from Decay Canceled like Dawn In comprehensive Day.'"

Sarah's words were appropriate, but Skye looked at her questioningly.

"Emily Dickinson," Sarah explained, for a second time. Her frequent quoting did take getting used to.

Skye nodded uncertainly.

Had Jasmine been an antiwar activist? I was pretty sure U.S. soldiers were still in Vietnam in 1970. Curling posters of the Beatles, Simon & Garfunkel, and the Beach Boys were thumbtacked to the wall. Like all teenagers, Jasmine must have loved music. A stack of LP records—33's—was next to a record player with detachable speakers: Joan Baez, Bob Dylan, the Beatles, and the Broadway cast album of *Hair.* Eclectic music. Unfortunately, the albums had been stored on top of each other rather than vertically. Most were bent.

Damp stuffed animals were piled on both beds in the room.

"Twin beds," Sarah pointed out. "Did she have a sister?"

"I'm told the second bed was so she could invite a friend to visit," said Skye.

Who had told her? But that made sense. Haven Harbor was a long way from the friends Jasmine must have had in New York. And with a house this large, it would have been easy for her to entertain friends from the city.

Her bureau was covered with bottles of long-evaporated scents, a box of loose powder, a few lipsticks, and a hairbrush with a few pieces of long brown hair still woven through the bristles. Interesting. Today the police investigating her death might have taken that hair, as a record of DNA. But, then, she'd died in 1970; before DNA had been important. And they'd known who she was, so they weren't concerned with identifying her body. I shuddered a bit, thinking of what this room must have meant to Jasmine's mother, since she'd never changed it.

Faded photographs of teenagers, maybe her New York school friends, were stuck in the mirror frame. I leaned over to look at them. Was one of the young men in the pictures her boyfriend? Had Jasmine been planning to go to college? All I knew about her was that she'd been young and she'd died.

This room was a museum about her. A shrine. I picked up one of the lipsticks. Tangee Natural. Makeup from the past.

"Two other bedrooms are on this floor. Guest rooms. The third-floor rooms are a total loss. They were for staff or other guests. You don't need to worry about those. I'll get someone to clean them out." Skye walked to the door. "Is there anything more you need to know from me now? I should check with Patrick about the Dumpsters and the construction crew."

"One question," said Sarah. "Are you planning to sell everything in the house that has any value?"

Skye hesitated. "I'd like to see your inventory list and appraisal before I decide. A few things, like the needlepoint panels, I know I'd like to keep. After I look at the inventory, I'll select anything else I want to keep before we fill the Dumpsters. Then I'll have a lawn sale. Invite everyone in town to come."

I had to concentrate to keep my mouth from hanging open. *"A lawn sale? Here?"*

"Exactly. I've heard the Gardeners always had a big party, complete with fireworks, at the end of the summer, on Labor Day weekend. They invited the town to come. It was a grand catered affair—a thank-you to the townspeople for hosting them during the summer."

Jasmine Gardener had died during the last of those parties. But what had those events to do with a lawn sale now?

"I've thought about it," said Skye. "I suspect a lot of people in town would love to see this house again. See what happened to it, and perhaps take home a souvenir of its past."

"People in town are going to think it's pretty strange for

you to have a lawn sale," I said bluntly. "Most folks have a sale when they need the money. They have stuff they've outgrown or inherited, or they want to unclutter their houses or barns. Your having a sale wouldn't be anything like that."

"It won't be intended to be anything like that. But the prices will be low, and people will come out of curiosity, don't you think? Curiosity about the house and about me. I'd rather have them come up with real answers to their questions than invent them."

"Then you're planning to be at this sale?" Sarah asked, looking from Skye to me and then back. "In person?"

Skye had said she was staying in a motel out of town to keep a low profile. Clearly, she was planning to change that profile in the near future.

"I will," said Skye. "And we'll serve punch and cookies." She looked at both of us. "I'd like you both to run it."

"Run the sale?" I said, thinking quickly through all that would entail.

"I'll pay you well," said Skye. "This will be my chance to meet people in town. Not a big fancy party like the Gardeners had. Something simple. I want to open the house to people in town. I don't want Aurora to be the subject of speculation and rumors. Anything that doesn't sell we'll dump."

"When do you want to do this?" asked Sarah, frowning a bit. I suspected she was thinking of the time it would take to do an appraisal, and then to tag things and run a sale. Time she should be at her shop. The summer season was just beginning.

"In about a week," said Skye. "I realize this is short notice, but I'll pay you each fifteen thousand dollars to organize and run it."

Sarah and I looked at each other. Fifteen thousand

dollars for one week's work? Even if we worked around the clock, that was more than anyone I knew made in a couple of months. Or longer.

"From what I've seen so far, you won't make near that amount of money from the sale," said Sarah. "Especially if you want everything priced cheaply."

"That's not a problem. I don't expect to make the money back," said Skye.

I wasn't worried about Skye West's money. Obviously, she had a lot of it. My budget, on the other hand, could sorely use an infusion. Car payments, warmer clothes, any work needed on Gram's house . . . "We'd be happy to run the sale for you," I said boldly.

Sarah stared at me. I'd decided quickly. I'd have to help her find someone to shop-sit while we were working here.

But she knew why I'd said "yes." She swallowed and agreed. "We'll need publicity about the sale, to make sure people know about it," she added, turning a page in her notebook.

"I have a friend who works at Channel 7 in Portland," I volunteered, thinking of Clem Walker. "Maybe they would cover it. 'Famous actress buys haunted house,' and so forth."

"I don't think that will be necessary. I want publicity centered here, in Haven Harbor. We won't be able to keep other people from coming, but this sale is for local people. Harbor residents. Understand?"

Sarah looked at me. "We understand."

"Good. I hoped so. Patrick and I will be close by to help out with whatever you want. If you need to hire anyone to carry furniture or set up, that's fine. That won't come out of your salaries. You'll need at least two large tents, with tables, in case of rain. Patrick's already arranged for someone with a tractor to mow the lawn tomorrow. As soon as that's finished, we can have the tents set up. And the Dumpsters should be here anytime now." She glanced at her watch. "In fact, they should already have been dropped off. I'm going to check on that. You ladies make yourselves at home." We heard her low heels heading down the front stairs.

Sarah and I looked at each other.

"Having a lawn sale is weird," Sarah said softly.

"She was clear about what she wanted us to do. And she's paying us well."

"More than well," Sarah agreed. "That's one of the strangest parts about it."

"I agree. Why go to the trouble to have a sale? To allow people in town to meet her? To buy souvenirs of Aurora?" I shook my head. "She has to have some other reason." A reason that was worth at least thirty thousand dollars to her.

"Whatever," said Sarah. "We agreed to be part of it. We'd better get to work. Get close-ups of the books and pictures. And let's not forget to check the drawers. I'll be following you. We can do the clothing and Mrs. Gardener's stash of needlepoint materials together."

Fifteen thousand dollars would pay a lot of bills. But we were going to work for it. And who knew? Maybe there were treasures left in this house. I pulled out my camera and started focusing on Jasmine's cobwebbed dresser.

Chapter 6

Give me a House that never will decay
And Garments that never will wear away—
Give me a Friend that never will depart
Give me a Ruler that can rule my Heart.

—Verse on anonymous American sampler, 1792

"I can take pictures of all the rooms, with close-ups of the larger items or those of special value," I suggested, bending to get a picture of a marble dog used as a doorstop.

"Okay. You start on that. I'm already thinking I'll inventory the place, but only include values for items that aren't junk. On those I'll suggest a lawn sale price."

"Sounds as though she wants to move almost everything out of here," I agreed. The house shook with a clash of metal. "The first Dumpster must have arrived."

"She'll need more than two," Sarah said, her tone getting serious. "We'll see how many rooms we can cover today. Tonight I'll work on valuations."

"When in doubt, throw it out," I said. "Most of the stuff

here is too damaged to be worth much. Who would buy a mildewed sofa?"

"You're right. But people might want the smaller items—posters, china, crystal. . . ."

"Watch out for rotten boards," I reminded her, sinking a few inches into the floor. "I think I just found one." I pulled my foot out of a hole between Jasmine's bedroom and bathroom.

An hour later we'd only finished one wall of Mrs. Gardener's room.

"The more we do, the more I see we have to do. I don't know whether to celebrate or cry," Sarah said softly. "Inventory this whole place, with values, and then set up a lawn sale? In one week?"

"Money," I said, rubbing my fingers together. "She has money, and she's used to getting what she wants. Right now she wants us to work our tails off."

Sarah grimaced. "And we bought in. Fifteen thousand dollars? No kidding, we bought in!"

"If we could finish the upstairs today, that would be major. Luckily, it's June. There'll be enough light to see and take pictures until about eight-thirty tonight."

"I could starve by then," Sarah put in, glancing at her watch. "Don't we get a lunch break?"

Patrick appeared in the doorway, as if on cue. "No starving allowed on my watch. Mom called down to Hogan's Sandwich Shop and had them send up provisions. We've already taken ours. All this is for you ladies. I hope you don't mind lobster and crab rolls. Mom and I love all the seafood here, but you probably get tired of eating lobster."

"Not really," I said drily. Hogan's didn't usually deliver. Money made a difference. But as to the food . . . I'd had clams and haddock and mussels in the six weeks since I'd moved back to Maine, but hadn't tasted lobster yet. Spring prices were higher than summer. But it definitely was time. Especially when someone else was footing the bill. "This all looks delicious. Thank you!" I reached for a bottle of water to wash down some of the dust I'd inhaled.

"Yum!" said Sarah, taking the basket. "Potato chips, strawberries, water, and . . . is that fudge?"

"Made locally," said Patrick. "Guaranteed evil, with no artificial ingredients, and lots of chocolate, cream, and sugar."

"You're the best," Sarah agreed, choosing a lobster roll. "We heard the Dumpsters arriving."

"Yup. They're here. We have several men coming in about an hour to start filling them with everything from the carriage house. I doubt they'll finish that today, but if they do, we'll have them start on the third floor here at the house."

"We're still working on Mrs. Gardener's room," said Sarah.

"That's fine. We won't disturb you. But if you need something, or want help lifting anything, just yell. Mom and I'll be supervising over at the carriage house, but it's not far away."

"Any problem if we stay until dark tonight?"

"No problem for me. But don't exhaust yourself the first day. After all, Mom says we have a week to get ready for the sale."

A week! Had Patrick any idea of how much work there was to do before then?

"Thank you so much for the food," Sarah said again. I was pretty sure she was batting her eyelashes.

"Not a problem. Don't want the help to be hungry," he said, winking at me. *Or maybe at Sarah?* He headed down the long front steps again.

Sarah looked after him. "He's gorgeous. And he came bearing gifts."

"No complaints in the food department." I put down my bottle of water and looked through the basket. "And brownies. He didn't say there were also brownies!"

"Yum," said Sarah, her mouth full of lobster. "My kind of comfort food. Shellfish and chocolate."

All was silent as we chewed and drank.

"I'm curious about Jasmine's room," Sarah said a few minutes later. "It's spooky that Mrs. Gardener left it exactly as it was when she died."

"Maybe she went in there to feel closer to Jasmine," I suggested softly. Gram and I'd done that after Mama disappeared. I'd cleaned her room out just last month, seventeen years after she'd left. Our newly immaculate guest room was still painful to look at. We kept the door closed most of the time; although Juno, Gram's enormous yellow coon cat, had declared her intention to make Mama's comforter her own.

Sarah sighed. "Well, we're here for the duration. I guess my store won't be open for a few days."

"Is there anyone you could ask to sit there for you?" I said. "Someone who could at least take money and reach you on your cell?"

Sarah started shaking her head. Then, "Ruth! I wonder if Ruth Hopkins would shop-sit for me. She knows a bit about antiques, and she stops in about once a month to see my new finds."

Ruth was near eighty and used a walker, but her mind was as sharp as ever. She'd been one of the first Mainely Needlepointers, but the arthritis in her hands prevented her from doing much stitching now.

"Why not ask her?" I agreed. "It's only a week. Maybe

she'd like the chance to get out of her house and talk to people."

Sarah pulled out her phone. I did the same, hoping Gram would pick up. She'd expected me home for lunch.

"Gram? I'm still at Aurora. This job is going to take a lot more time than Sarah and I thought."

"So you won't be home for lunch?" Gram's voice was as calm and caring as ever. "Anything I can do for you?"

"Probably not for dinner, either." I looked around the room again. "You go ahead on your own. I'll tell you everything when I get home."

"I may drive to Camden," Gram said. "I've been thinking I'd like a new dress and a pair of dressy slacks for my honeymoon. I heard a couple of stores there are having preseason sales."

Gram shopping in Camden boutiques? She wasn't the penny-pinching grandmother I remembered from my childhood. We'd both changed.

"Go have fun," I agreed. "Treat yourself to a late lunch while you're there." Camden had a selection of good restaurants, as well as dress shops. Retirees with money kept the town buzzing twelve months a year. Camden was the sort of town I'd have expected someone like Skye West to move to: elegant, well populated, and a scenic harbor complete with schooners. Not quiet Haven Harbor.

"I'll go, then," said Gram. "And remember everything about Aurora to tell me tonight. I haven't been inside there in years."

"You've been *inside*?" I asked. She hadn't mentioned that before.

"At the end-of-season parties," she said. "Everyone used to go."

"I'd like to hear about that," I said. "I'm taking pictures, so I can show you what the place looks like now."

"I'm sure it's not the same," said Gram. "It used to be such a beautiful home. I'm not sure I want to see it now. But we can compare notes."

"Have a good shopping trip," I said. "See you tonight."

"All set?" asked Sarah.

"All set. Gram's going honeymoon clothes shopping."

"Lucky her."

"What did Ruth say about shop-sitting?"

"She'll do it! I always leave a key at The Book Nook in case of an emergency. I called to tell them it was okay to give the key to Ruth. She said she'd take a book and shop-sit for the whole week if I needed her."

"Great! Now," I said, looking around, "let's take a look at Jasmine's room. Clockwise or counterclockwise around the room?"

"Clockwise. If I see anything we'll need a close-up of, I'll let you know." She moved toward Jasmine's dressing table. "Don't forget the inside of the drawers and closets."

"What about the photographs?" I asked. "Not mine, the ones in the house."

"Skye said she was going to make an album. Why don't we collect any photos we find to give to her?" Sarah reached for an over-the-shoulder bag made of now-faded Mexican embroidery of red and blue, which was hanging on the wall. "This seems pretty clean. And it's dry. Let's put all the photos in here."

She started taking the pictures off Jasmine's mirror. "I wonder who these people are and where they are now."

I picked up one and turned it over. "It says, 'Mary and I at Miss Pritchard's.'" I looked at the picture of two pretty girls, both with long, straight hair. One wore a peasant blouse and a short skirt and boots. The other one wore a short, loose caftan. "Which one is Jasmine?"

"And who is Miss Pritchard?" Sarah said. "But we don't

have time to worry about that now. Jasmine must have been popular. Most of these pictures are of boys. Skye can worry about who they are, if she cares. It was a long time ago." She put a handful of the pictures into the Mexican bag. "Start clicking! I'd like to get home to sleep tonight."

Chapter 7

Death's terror is the mountain Faith removes
'Tis Faith discovers destruction.
Believe and look with triumph on the Tomb!

—Sampler stitched by Elizabeth Greenleaf, age ten, Newburyport, Massachusetts, 1768

"Fifteen thousand dollars? For one week's work?" Gram looked thunderstruck. "Are you sure you heard her right?"

It was after ten at night. I was exhausted and covered with dust, dirt, cobwebs, and quite possibly other things I didn't want to think about. I could still smell the mildew, even though I was now home, a couple of miles away from Aurora. All I wanted was a long drink and then a hot shower and bed. Gram, on the other hand, had spent the day peacefully enjoying a successful shopping trip to Camden and had finished supper without me.

I was starved. (Sarah and I had laughed when Skye asked whether there was some local place that would deliver pizza or Chinese. The only thing delivered in Haven Harbor was mail.)

Thankfully, Gram had ignored my instruction to forget about dinner. She'd made my favorite macaroni and cheese with Swiss and Gruyère and sharp Vermont cheddar. I poured us each a glass of wine. I gulped my wine, poured another glass, and stuck my plate of mac and cheese in the new microwave I'd bought for her as an early wedding present. I suspected I'd need to buy another one for her to take to the parish home she'd share with Reverend Tom. This microwave was going to stay where it was—in the kitchen that would soon be mine alone.

I couldn't imagine the kitchen without Gram.

She looked pointedly at me, and then at my wineglass, with a silent *"another glass already?"* expression. Tonight I was too tired to care.

Soon she'd be married. No one would be here to care how many glasses of wine I'd poured. I'd enjoy that freedom, but I'd miss having someone care about when, or whether, I got home and what I ate. Or drank. I'd lived on my own for ten years. I was twenty-seven. But it still felt good to be taken care of.

"She really said fifteen thousand dollars. We're going to work for it, though," I said, taking a bite of my pasta, and then adding a bit more cayenne. "We were there almost twelve hours today. Sarah's still working tonight. She's checking current prices for the items she identified as being worth something."

Gram smiled. "And what will you do with all that money?"

"I haven't decided. I could pay off my car and have a few hundred left to buy some new clothes," I said. "Most of what I wore in Arizona won't work here in Maine. But I'll put some aside in an emergency fund, too."

"I'm assuming the house is in awful condition now."

"Lots of water damage from the roof leaking. Mildew. Wallpaper peeling. One ceiling has fallen in, and several are threatening to collapse. Squirrels and a raccoon got in at some point, and at least one crow. Everything is in bad shape."

"So Sarah won't have too long a list to work on."

"Longer than we thought. Fabrics are in horrible condition, brass and silver needs to be polished. Some may be beyond reclamation. But much of the glass and crystal and china is just dirty."

"Sad. It used to be such a beautiful place. So full of light and color," said Gram.

"You told me you'd gone to those end-of-the-season parties the Gardeners used to give?" I'd definitely need more mac and cheese. And wine. While she talked, I got up to make a deeper hole in Gram's casserole.

"Most folks in town went. Every year in the fifties and sixties, the Gardeners gave a party the Saturday night of Labor Day weekend. They headed back for New York after that, and the place would be closed up until spring," Gram remembered aloud. "They'd have a big barbecue and lobster bake, catered and all. An open bar. And music. Usually, a local group, although I seem to remember their having a disc jockey one year. Children brought balls and Hula-hoops and kites and played on the hill in back of the house. Men sometimes started up a softball game. The party would start at four in the afternoon and end with fireworks."

"If everyone in Haven Harbor went, it must have been crowded."

"Well, not *everyone* went. But a couple of hundred guests showed up each year. Little kids were everywhere, and romancing couples found dark corners. It wasn't only the yacht club set, who knew the Gardeners best. Everyone in town was invited, so you never knew exactly who would turn up there. It was a wonderful, friendly way to end the summer. Until the last party, of course."

I put down my fork. "The night Jasmine died."

Gram nodded. "I was dating Henry, your grandfather, then. I remember that night especially because he was leaving for college in a few days. He was a senior at the University of New Hampshire, and he'd just given me my ring." Gram looked down at her naked left hand. "At my age I don't need an engagement ring. I told Tom that. But I was only twenty then, and thrilled to have a diamond, no matter how small. I was on top of the world that night. The only sad part was that Henry would be leaving for school soon. But we were young, we were engaged, and we had our whole life together ahead of us. The world was ours." She smiled, remembering. "It was a beautiful evening. Not cool, the way it sometimes gets in early September. A bit of wind came up about eight o'clock, though. I remember Henry went to his car to get me a sweater before the fireworks started."

"Did you know Jasmine?"

"Know her? Not really. Oh, of course, I knew who she was. Everyone knew the Gardeners. But she had her own friends. She loved to sail, and she spent a lot of time at the yacht club."

"Where the rich kids were," I added.

"To be fair to Jasmine, she didn't seem to care much about where someone came from. In those days some of the locals worked at the yacht club or taught classes there. Or even were members. Haven Harbor was never like one of those ritzy places down the coast, where you practically had to own a yacht to belong to the club. Plenty of people in town were members."

"But you weren't one of them."

"No. I waitressed in the dining room there. That's where I saw Jasmine and her friends."

"I didn't know you'd worked at the yacht club!"

Gram smiled. "You don't know everything about me. I never thought those couple of summers were very important. Everyone in town worked somewhere, the way they do now. After a couple of years at the yacht club, I moved on to other jobs. Henry and I got married after he graduated. You've seen the pictures of our wedding."

Gram and her Henry had been married in the Congregational Church—the same church where she'd be married again, in three weeks. My grandfather had died before I was born. Would I ever be as happy with someone as Gram had looked on her wedding day? Not that I was looking to get married soon. But sometimes I wondered.

"What was that night like—the night Jasmine died?"

"It was lovely. Wonderful and fun, as always. I'll admit Henry and I weren't paying much attention to other people. We danced and we ate clams. We both loved fried clams. People kept coming up to us and congratulating us on our engagement. I only remember seeing Jasmine a couple of times. Before the end, of course."

"So you were there when her body was found." *Why have you never told me this?* I thought.

"We were sitting on the hill in back of Aurora, overlooking the harbor, watching the fireworks. I was feeling wild, sipping a beer, even though the legal age to drink in Maine had been lowered from twenty-one to twenty the year before. Some people were smoking pot. This was 1970, after all. It was all very relaxed. Then the fireworks ended, and everyone picked up their blankets and headed back to their cars. Mothers and fathers were calling to their children, gathering everyone to leave. A few people had had a little too much to drink, and the local cop—I can't remember his name—rounded them up. The police sometimes drove home people who needed help after the Gardeners' party.

"Henry and I had just started toward our car when we heard screams. At first, we thought it was teenagers being rowdy. But then the screams got louder, and people started to run toward the front of the house."

"Did you see her?"

"No. We were in the back of the crowd. We'd wanted the night to last as long as it could. By the time we got close, everyone was saying it was Jasmine, and that she'd been in the fountain. Someone had pulled her out. The police held everyone back and an ambulance came. Then we all went home. The next morning we heard she'd died."

"What do you think happened?"

"At first, everyone said she'd fallen and hit her head on the fountain. Then some people said she'd drowned." Gram shook her head. "It was so sad. She wasn't perfect—no seventeen-year-old is—but she was so full of life." Gram looked at me. "It doesn't matter how she died. What's important is that her life was ended so early. And her mother's life ended that night, too."

"Her mother?" Mrs. Gardener had lived years after her daughter died.

"Oh, Mrs. Gardener didn't die, but she stopped living. She hardly left her house after that. I heard she'd convinced herself Jasmine had been murdered. She spent the rest of her life trying to prove it." Gram paused. "She didn't go back to her husband, or to whatever life she'd had in New York. And she was never really a part of Haven Harbor, either—even though everyone knew she was there, at Aurora, by herself, all those years. However Jasmine died, her death was the end of her mother's life, too."

Chapter 8

From Rocks, Shoals and Stormy Weather
A Rainbow At Night
O God Protect the Potosi ever. Is a Sailors delight.

—Sampler, including ship *Potosi,*
stitched by Susan Munson, 1824

"I almost forgot," I said. "Ten needlepoint panels are in my car. They're scenes of Aurora and Haven Harbor that Mrs. Gardener stitched. Skye West wants them preserved, restored, and reframed."

"Bring them in and let me look at them," said Gram. "I'd love to see what she did."

It took me three trips to bring all the framed stitchery into the house. Each panel was fourteen by twenty inches, matted, and then framed in heavy mahogany, probably to match the dining-room table.

Years of work.

I leaned them against pieces of living-room furniture so

we could both see the series. Gram stopped at the picture of the fountain. "That's just the way it looked," she said. "Water flying up and catching the sunlight. I'm sorry Mrs. Gardener had it destroyed, but I understand why she did."

"But then she took the time to design a needlepoint picture of it, and work the picture," I said. "I wonder what she was thinking when she was doing it."

Gram shrugged. "One of those things we'll never know." She moved on, looking at the other embroideries. "I love her moose. I think he's in the back meadow at Aurora, where we sat to watch the fireworks over the harbor. And she's pictured the yacht club. And the church."

She turned to me. "Did you know Jasmine's funeral was there, right here in Haven Harbor?"

"I didn't."

"Everyone thought her body would be taken back to New York, but it wasn't. That church was full for Jasmine. I remember someone saying it was her last party."

We stood and looked at the framed embroideries around our living room.

"What are you doing tomorrow?" Gram asked.

"Sarah and I are meeting at seven at Aurora to show Skye how far we've gotten on the contents of the house. We'll need some help removing furniture and taking it either to the Dumpster or to the tents for the lawn sale."

"It's too bad the high school is still in session. Dave Percy could have suggested some young men to help." Dave was the Haven Harbor High biology teacher—and a Mainely Needlepointer. Gram thought a minute. "Ob Winslow's son, Josh, is back home. He might have some friends who could help, too."

"That's a good idea. I'll call him. The Wests had a few local men there today, but we may need more than that."

"If you'd like, I could take these out of their frames tomorrow," Gram volunteered, looking closely at the lighthouse panel. "Then we could see how much work needs to be done on them."

"That would be a help," I said. "Thank you. Some are mildewed. And I can see a water stain on the one of the harbor. I'm not sure what we'll do about that."

"Sunshine might kill the mildew," Gram said. "I'll do some research on that tomorrow. Some of these will need overstitching if Ms. West wants them restored. We'll know better when they're out of the frames. If you need to divide these between the needlepointers, we might as well get started now. I have a feeling Skye West isn't used to waiting for what she wants."

"You're right. But tonight I'm going to bed. It's been a long day."

I took another glass of wine upstairs with me.

My bedroom window was open so the sea breezes could blow in. It was a beautiful night, with a hint of crisp air. Like the night of that last party at Aurora.

I pulled my comforter up around me. What had happened to Jasmine Gardener that night? The estate was full of people, from what Gram had said. Had anyone seen her fall into the fountain?

Exhaustion, wine, and sea breezes lulled me to sleep before I had time to think more about it.

Chapter 9

Nothing is so sweet and beautiful as a flower
But yet it blows and fades all in an hour.
For life as fairest flowers soonest fades
So God takes home the most beautiful maids
Therefore in blooming youth pray now be wise.

—Unsigned New England sampler, 1767

The next week was a blur.

Sarah and I were at Aurora early each morning and worked until dark. Every night Sarah refined her appraisal list, checking current values online, in valuation guides and in auction catalogs.

Although Patrick brought us lunch every day (only in Maine could you get tired of lobster rolls), we didn't see him as often as Sarah hoped. He spent his days at the carriage house, supervising the gutting of the building. The first two dumpsters were replaced by two others, and a third arrived to hold window frames, tiles, wallpaper, and decayed furnishings from the third floor of the house. Skye had been right; nothing on that floor was salvageable.

She chose to keep a few things besides the panels: the Meissen china stored in the dining room, a carved oak Victorian chair from Mrs. Gardener's room, and, to our surprise, the twin beds from Jasmine's room and some of Jasmine's phonograph records. She loved Victorian art glass, so we set aside Mrs. Gardener's collection of end-of-the-day baskets. (Sarah explained they were handblown ruffled glass baskets originally made as pink or green or yellow gifts for brides. However, at the end of each day, the glassblower would combine the colors he'd been using, and the result would be one or two multicolored baskets. These were considered less valuable at the time, but more valuable today.)

We saved all of the photographs we found, no matter their condition.

We didn't have time to guess the rationale for each item Skye asked us to save. We just knew anything she decided to keep was to be put in the storage trailer she'd rented and moved onto the property. We put the needlework seabird pillows, which she'd said she might want reproduced, in there.

Patrick arranged for two large tents to be delivered. One contained lines of tables for "smalls" (five dollars per item, seven dollars per item, and so forth). The other tent was for furniture.

Aurora was more alive than it had been in years, but this time not with vacationers and guests. This time it was filled with people determined to pull down the old and replace it with new.

Restoration? Perhaps. But in some areas, like the carriage house, reconstruction was more like it.

Gram carefully removed the needlepoint panels from

their frames; on every sunny day she left them in direct sun. She also dabbed the most persistent areas with a mild solution of vinegar and water. She was gambling the mildew would disappear before the threads faded any more than they already had.

Ruth Hopkins, true to her word, sat behind the counter at Sarah's shop for the duration. Sarah stopped worrying about her business after Ruth sold an entire shelf of early Belleek china to someone who merely admired it.

And although Ob Winslow couldn't lift anything heavy because of his back problems, he and his son, Josh, were there almost every day. Ob worked with the construction crews, advising them about what might need to be checked on the property. I wondered how much Ob was being paid. The *Anna Mae* sat in port as he worked at Aurora.

Josh and a friend of his lugged furniture, drapes, and boxes of books and pottery and even decorative rocks. ("Someone might find it amusing to buy one that had been in Aurora," Skye said. Sarah and I didn't argue.)

Who'd pay money for rocks and shells you could find down on Pocket Cove Beach? But Skye was the boss. What she said was what happened.

Even Patrick stayed out of her way, especially in the mornings, when she gave out instructions for the day. She and Patrick were still living in the motel, but they'd be living on the estate sooner than I'd assumed. The first floor of the carriage house had been gutted, and Patrick had scouted the area for both old and new wicker furniture and Adirondack chairs to be used as informal living-room furniture as soon as the walls were replaced and painted. The Wests planned to move in the day before the sale.

To ensure his future studio would be warm enough, Patrick had its walls insulated. He hired a mason to build a chimney for the woodstove he'd chosen. Electric heat was being installed on the second floor.

It was amazing how fast work could be done when you were willing to pay overtime.

After our first day at the house, I forgot about looking elegant. Jeans or shorts and old T-shirts worked fine. My arms were scratched from all the trash and treasures I carried from the house to the Dumpster or the trailer or the tent. Sarah, on the other hand, appeared every day with makeup in place, wearing a coordinated outfit. Corporate casual, I suspected it would have been called in Phoenix.

"Patrick talks to us," she confided, concerned. "But we have so much to do, there's no time for real conversation. I'd hoped to really get to know him. Maybe once the lawn sale is over?"

Once the lawn sale was over, I saw no reason we should be at Aurora, unless we were discussing the needlepoint panels. But I didn't point that out to Sarah. She was besotted. And having checked the man out myself, I could hardly blame her. Although when tall, dark, handsome, and charming also came with money . . . I didn't trust it.

Truthfully, I wasn't so sure about trusting men on general principle. Or on specific principle, either. I had a history. It might not be as checkered as some people in Haven Harbor imagined, but I hadn't exactly behaved like a nun in a convent.

Gram's intended was more interesting than I'd imagined a minister would be. Better-looking, too. Although I hadn't had any personal experience with ministers, I'd imagined they saw life a little differently than the rest of us. They were more rarefied—more head in the heavens, less feet on the ground.

Reverend Tom broke all my imagined rules. He'd even introduced me to Ouija boards. (He collected them, and he and Ruth occasionally spent an evening with spirits. And, I suspected, with a glass or two.)

Bottom line: I liked (and trusted) him. So maybe Patrick would break all the rules for tall, dark, handsome, and the world at his fingertips. I hoped so, for Sarah's sake.

It would be nice to know a couple of good guys under the age of sixty. (Even if they were other women's guys.)

Skye had set the date of the sale for a Saturday.

"More people should be able to come on a Saturday," she declared.

I didn't point out that most people in Haven Harbor worked several jobs, especially between Memorial Day and Labor Day. Weekends were work days here.

Word spread quickly: A famous actress had bought Aurora and was going to restore it. People wondered if it was to be a summer home or a full-time residence. How bad was the house's condition? How long would it take to fix up? How much money would it cost? How much of that money would be spent in Haven Harbor?

Sarah and I arrived at six the morning of the sale. Dozens of people were already in line outside the closed gate. Wisely, Skye had decided to discourage early birds and dealers arriving predawn to scout the merchandise.

Sarah called Patrick. He appeared quickly and let us in.

The sale was to start at seven. We'd set up two tables, one in each tent, where Sarah and I would play cashier. We each had stacks of "sold" stickers to hand out, and Ob's son, Josh, and a friend of his were at another table to arrange to pick up any heavy furniture and deliver it. For a fee, of course.

Tables and chairs were set up between the large tents. Free iced tea or water or lemonade or coffee and piles of cookies awaited early-morning customers there. I walked through "my" tent (the one with the furniture). There'd be more questions about the "smalls," as Sarah called them, and she was better equipped with answers.

Then I got a cup of coffee and a cookie or two before the hordes descended. After the past week's work, I could use all the caffeine and sugar I could get.

Skye was checking coolers of water and cartons of cookies still to be unpacked. She'd bought some from the patisserie in Haven Harbor, but I also noted boxes marked: STANDARD BAKING COMPANY, PORTLAND. The local patisserie might have been overwhelmed by the size of her order.

I poured my coffee as Skye looked at her watch. "It's almost six-thirty. I called the high school to find several girls there who'd come to help with the refreshment table. They should be here at any time."

She'd thought of everything.

"I have to ask," I said, between munching a molasses cookie and taking sips of coffee. "We've been racing so fast to get all this set up. But . . . why? Why not take anything of value to a local auction house and throw the rest out?"

She smiled as she added sliced lemons to an enormous punch bowl of lemonade. "Because I want people from Haven Harbor to come to Aurora the way they did when the Gardeners entertained. I want them to see I'm an ordinary person, not a pompous celebrity from California." She paused and looked out toward the gate. "And because I'm hoping people who were at that last party in 1970 come today."

"Why?" I blurted. "That was years ago! I'm sure the majority of people who were here that day don't even live in town anymore." *If they are even still alive,* I thought.

"Some do," Skye said knowingly. "And those who don't may hear about the sale and decide to come."

"My Gram was here that night. She'll probably stop in today. But who knows exactly who was here that night?"

"I've heard many people in town talking as though they were here," Skye said. "Maybe it's like everyone who was young in 1969 claiming they were at Woodstock. But I think those who need to come, those who knew Jasmine best, will be here today."

"And?" I couldn't help feeling that wasn't a complete answer.

"It will be the first time most of them have been back since that night." She leaned toward me and lowered her voice. "I don't believe Jasmine drowned accidentally. I believe someone killed her."

I stared at her. I hadn't expected anything like that. This lawn sale was about Jasmine Gardener?

"If no one comes forward today to share information, then I'll talk with them later. But I'm going to find out what happened that night. I'm going to find out who killed Jasmine."

Chapter 10

While beauty and pleasure are now in their prime,
And folly and fashion expect our whole time,
Ah, let us not these phantoms our wishes engage.
Let us live so in youth that we blush not in age.

—Sampler stitched by Mary Ann McLellan
(1803–1831), Portland, Maine, 1807
(Collection of the Portland Museum of Art)

Patrick opened the gate at seven o'clock on the dot, and the long line of potential customers flooded in.

"Here they come!" Sarah said, watching with amazement. "We'd better get to our posts. Skye was right. Everyone in town is coming."

I raised my cup of coffee in her direction and headed for the furniture tent. I suspected Sarah would need reinforcement at some point. More people would be interested in small items they could take with them than would be fascinated by pieces of furniture that needed refinishing or reupholstering. Or both.

To my surprise, Patrick followed me.

"You did it!" he grinned, looking around the giant tent sheltering all the motley pieces of furniture that one week before had been inside Aurora. "And the weather's on all of our sides. Mom was worried rain would keep the crowds down."

I looked out the end of the tent. "You're right. It's a gorgeous June day," I said, glad I'd worn a sweater. "The sun should warm us all up in a few hours."

The stream of people coming through the estate's gate divided. Guided by signs we'd printed by hand the night before, some people headed to the "smalls" tent, some walked toward the house itself (to get a peek at the inside), and a very few (dealers, I suspected) raced toward us.

"This tent won't be the first stop for most people unless they're looking for a specific piece of furniture. Or,"—I watched as two men turned a table upside down, shook their heads, and left it on the ground—"they're people who know old furniture and are looking for a bargain."

"Mom and I've been impressed with how hard you and Sarah worked to get this ready so quickly. We know it wasn't easy. We'll eventually end up with a spectacular new home. You guys just get to collapse."

With large checks in our pockets, I thought. "Collapsing will sound pretty good by the end of today, I suspect," I said. "Setting this all up has been an experience."

One I wouldn't want again. But, then, if the money was equally as good, who could say?

"For all of us," he acknowledged. "Mom's bought other places before. She has a home near L.A., a place in New York City, and for a while she had a retreat in Aspen. But she usually hires someone to direct any construction or decorating she wants. She keeps in touch by phone.

Sometimes she asks me to go and check on the work. I've never seen her as involved as she is here."

"You live with her, then? All the time?" Not to be nosy, but shouldn't a thirtysomething guy have his own place?

"It's not what you're thinking. First of all, Mom's often on location somewhere else in the world, so all our homes are empty. I can use them—however I choose, whenever I choose. In L.A. I have a studio nearby. That's where I spend most of my time, working. When I'm really involved with a project I sleep there. If I want to entertain, I invite a friend or three there, or I can be more formal at the big house. It's good to have options." He smiled, almost shyly. "Mom and I get along pretty well. I have my own friends. I don't get involved with all the Hollywood parties and gossip. Being an artist is convenient. People tag me 'creative' and I have a built-in excuse for not doing what I don't want to do."

"And you'll have a studio here."

"Exactly!" He nodded. "When we finish it, the carriage house should be perfect for what I need. It will be a place to paint and store my work, a place to sleep, a small kitchen for any cooking I feel in the mood to do. I'm a genius at pasta dinners and pancake breakfasts, and I can even turn out a mean frittata." He looked at me and winked. "Sometime I hope you'll let me demonstrate."

He glanced at me. . . . He did have dark eyes! And he continued talking before I thought of an appropriate response. What would Sarah think of his invitation? But maybe Patrick was just being friendly. Maybe he'd invited Sarah for frittata, too.

For more than a moment, I wished she hadn't seen him first.

"I'm tired of Southern California, and was never into the Aspen scene. But here?" He threw open his arms. "A beautiful location, quiet for most of the year, and, from what I've heard, an active art community. Before Mom bought this place, I made a scouting trip to check out galleries in Boston and Portland. I have no time this summer, with all the work that needs to be done here, but next fall I plan on visiting more of the galleries, checking out their openings, and introducing myself."

"So you plan to spend the whole year here."

"I do," he answered, nodding. "Although I'll reserve judgment on the word 'whole' until I've lived here awhile. I can see making a trip to the islands, or the Mediterranean, or even back to L.A., in January or February, if the snows get too high to see out the windows here."

A woman came up to my table holding a gold-framed Victorian mirror. The mirror itself was damaged, but the frame was fabulously elaborate, with cupid faces peeking out from a vine pattern.

"This is marked fifteen dollars. Is that right?" she asked a little cautiously.

I checked. "Yup. It's fifteen dollars."

"Then it's sold!" She grinned. "A new piece of mirror and it'll be perfect for my downstairs bathroom." She rested the mirror on the ground while she dug a ten and a five out of her wallet. "This is a fantastic sale! I'll put the mirror in my van, but I'll be back! I see other possibilities, but I have to measure them. And I haven't even been in the other tent yet."

"Great," I said, tucking her money into the tin cookie box I was using as a cash box. "If you're interested in any larger pieces, we have people who can help get them to your vehicle."

"At your service." Patrick bowed toward her.

She looked him up and down and actually giggled as she picked up her mirror. "Now I'll definitely be back."

"First sale from this tent!" I said. "Hope everyone is as pleased as she was."

"The tent will be empty by noon," Patrick promised optimistically. I wasn't as sure.

"So, how hard *are* the winters here?" he asked, getting back to our earlier conversation. "Seriously."

I laughed. "Contrary to popular wisdom, it doesn't get that bad here. We're on the coast. We don't get as much snow as inland. But, sure, we get our share of cold and ice."

"I'll be disappointed if there isn't a lot of snow," said Patrick. "I was looking forward to a classic New England white Christmas. In fact, Mom is already planning to be here for the holidays."

"Could be a white Christmas," I agreed. "Certainly a better chance of it than you'd have in L.A.! I'm kind of hoping for snow then, too. I've been away a lot of winters, and December twenty-fifth never really seemed like Christmas when temperatures were over seventy degrees."

"Where were you?" he asked.

"In Mesa, Arizona. Just outside Phoenix," I said.

"School?"

"Briefly. Mostly, I was working."

"As what?"

"For a private detective." I didn't say I was used to carrying. Or that I'd only come back to Maine after my mother's body had been found.

He raised his eyebrows. "Interesting work."

"Sometimes."

We watched Skye greeting people at the side of the house. She was signing papers—autographs, I guessed—and posing for pictures.

"Doesn't she ever get tired of smiling?" I asked, changing the subject from my past to our present.

"She likes acting. She likes the money she earns. Being

photographed and talked about is one way she pays for doing a job she loves. By now, she's used to it. Her idea was that by inviting everyone here for the sale, she could establish herself as a new member of the community. *A contributing member.* Not someone you might invite for dinner once a week, of course, but someone who's accessible."

And she wants to learn more about Jasmine Gardener, I told myself, thinking of my earlier conversation with Skye.

"I'm glad you had the construction crew put boards over the weak spots in the floor of the house," I added. "Most people are heading inside before checking out what's for sale."

"Last night we closed off the third floor," Patrick said. "We put up a sign saying it wasn't safe and there was nothing up there. The old guy who used to be the caretaker—Ob Winslow?—is up on the second floor, making sure no one heads farther up into the house."

"Your mother seems fascinated by Jasmine Gardener's story."

He shrugged. "She does. It's a little spooky, but she loves stories. She's made several movies about ghosts, you know. Jed Fitch, the real estate guy, told her all about Jasmine. Not a lot of people want to buy a house where there was a mysterious death. But Mom wanted this place, despite all the work it'd take. She's been thinking about getting a place in Maine for years. Several of her friends have places along the coast . . . John Travolta, Patrick Dempsey, Stockard Channing, and probably some others I don't remember, or don't know about. I remember Tony Shalhoub praising the state, too. I think he went to the University of Southern Maine. They all said Mainers were good at maintaining the privacy of well-known people. That meant a lot to her. She'd visited here a long time ago and loved it then. That was what encouraged me to check out the art scene. I didn't have anything to do with her choosing to buy this property. However, when I heard it had a carriage house, I was sold."

"Why do you think she's so fascinated with what happened to Jasmine?" I asked, keeping my eye on a couple checking out chairs that had been in Mrs. Gardener's bedroom.

Patrick shrugged. "All she ever said to me was that she and Jasmine were about the same age, and she didn't like to see a murder go unsolved."

"Maybe she's been in too many crime movies, where all the answers are tied up at the end," I suggested. "Unfortunately, life isn't like that."

"Philosophy from the needlepoint queen," said Patrick. "But you may be right. I think it's just a phase, in any case. How could she solve a murder forty-five years old? If it even was a murder."

"She told me she's convinced Jasmine didn't die accidentally," I said quietly.

"That's what she believes. I don't know why. Somehow she thinks she'll be able to solve a possible crime the police and townspeople and Jasmine's mother, all of whom tried for years, couldn't even definitely determine was a murder." He leaned over and lowered his voice. "Truthfully, I hope she forgets the whole thing. Once, she decided to raise prize Dalmatians. That only lasted a year or so. She didn't have the time to get as involved as she wanted, so she lost interest. She ended up giving all the dogs to a shelter." He shook his head. "This Jasmine Gardener thing is probably like that. A passing interest. As soon as she gets back to work, she'll be researching a new role and forget all about it."

"I wish her the best. Maybe it is just a hobby. But as

long as she's fixing up the house, that's fine." I grinned. "Maybe Jasmine's ghost will appear to her and tell her what happened."

"Who knows?" Patrick said, putting his hand lightly on my shoulder. "For the moment, though, I'd better go and see whether Mom or anyone else needs help."

I watched him walk confidently across the grass toward where his mother was surrounded by fans and curiosity seekers.

"The price tag on that glass-topped rattan coffee table says twenty dollars. Is that right?" a young woman was asking. I had to get to work. There were no ghosts in the furniture tent. At least none I could see.

Chapter 11

Needlework: a generic and comprehensive term, including every species of work that can be executed by means of the Needle, whether plain or decorative, and whatever description the Needle may be. From the most remote ages the employment of the Needle has formed a source of recreation, of remunerative work, and no less of economy, the useful occupation of time and charity, amongst all classes of women, in all parts of the world.

—*The Dictionary of Needlework: An Encyclopaedia of Artistic, Plain, and Fancy Needlework,* London, 1882

As the day wore on, I found myself both selling furniture and answering questions. A good percentage of those coming to the sale were as curious about the dark history of Aurora as Skye West was. And those that didn't mention Jasmine Gardener's death wanted to know about Skye herself. Since I was working there, they assumed I had an inside track to all Aurora, Jasmine, and Skye-related information.

"Why did a famous actress buy this house? Why Haven Harbor?"

"Was it true Jasmine died of arsenic poisoning?" (I hadn't heard that before, but a number of Haven Harbor residents had, because several people asked me.)

"Where was the fountain where that girl died?"

"Is the house going to be torn down?"

"Is the Gardener girl's murder investigation going to be reopened?"

"Was any new evidence in Jasmine's murder found when the house was cleaned out?"

"Isn't all this talk of murder ridiculous? No one in Haven Harbor would kill anyone. Mrs. Gardener was too embarrassed to admit her darling daughter had been drunk and hit her head when she passed out."

Several people asked which pieces of furniture had been in Jasmine's room. Unfortunately for those macabre types, Skye had decided to keep those pieces. I discouraged people looking for "the bed she died in" or "pictures of the crime scene." I sent them to the tent where, I suspected, Sarah was being kept even busier than I was. She was selling the records Skye hadn't wanted to keep and Jasmine's faded posters.

Women were even buying damaged needlepoint pillows, partially completed canvases, and other remnants of Mrs. Gardener's handiwork. Sarah and I had gone through her needlepoint stash and removed any threads or yarns or floss we might need to use in restoring the panels. The bird pillows Skye liked were safely put away. But the rest of

Mrs. Gardener's work and supplies were for sale—complete with mildew.

About noon Sarah arrived at my table. "Patrick's taking over for a while in the other tent.

He's sending someone to cover for you, too," she said. "I'm exhausted and need a break. You?"

"Absolutely." As soon as one of the young men who'd been helping take furniture to trucks, cars, and vans appeared with the news that I had an hour off, I closed the cash box and stretched.

"Patrick said there's lunch in the carriage house for us," Sarah shared as we headed away from the crowds. A lot of people were still walking through the grounds; they were chatting and examining what was left of the merchandise.

"How much have you sold?" I asked her.

"I haven't had time to add it up," said Sarah, "but I'd guess about four thousand dollars. The silver and crystal went fast. But people are even buying the rocks Mrs. Gardener used as bookends, and the shells and pieces of driftwood that decorated the house, too." She paused. "I don't know if they're looking for souvenirs of Aurora, of the Gardeners, or just want to buy something a famous actress has owned, however briefly. It's crazy."

"Skye was right. People aren't buying things. They're buying memories. And souvenirs. I saw people carrying out the needlepoint we decided wasn't worth restoring."

"A lot of people asked about Millicent Gardener's embroideries. They've pawed over even the ratty, mildewed pieces. Pillow covers, wall hangings, chair cushions, even pieces only partially finished. They've all disappeared. Local folks knew Mrs. Gardener did a lot of needlepoint. They see her work as a fitting souvenir of Aurora. Perhaps some of them will end up coming to us to help restore them. 'Don't put up my Thread and Needle—I'll begin to Sew When the Birds begin to whistle—Better Stitches—so.'"

"Emily?"

"It's the first part of a poem she wrote about a dying woman who wished she could sew again."

I shook my head. "Amazing, although you're right. Selling all this old needlepoint could mean more business for us down the line. I've even sold those awful animal heads."

"Those moth-eaten monstrosities?" asked Sarah.

"A man from Waterville bought the moose, and Elsa Fitch, who owns the beauty parlor, bought the others."

"Why? I mean, why would she want them?"

"I have no clue. But she seemed excited."

"No wonder it's hard to buy antiques that will sell," Sarah added. "You never know what idiotic thing people will buy."

"Are you getting lots of questions about Jasmine's death?"

"Almost as many as about Skye West's next film, and whether or not she's had face-lifts."

"Only a few more hours to go," I declared. "I can hardly wait. What a week this has been! Almost everyone connected to Haven Harbor has been here today."

"I saw your grandmother," Sarah agreed. "She and Reverend Tom bought a set of embroidered pillowcases. Maybe for her trousseau. All the Mainely Needlepointers have been here except Ruth, who's down at my store. Dave Percy bought one of the incomplete pillow covers—one with herbs on it."

"Sounds like Dave," I agreed. "If anyone can finish the pillow, he can. And it'll go with his garden."

"And, of course, the whole Winslow family was here—

Ob worked in the house, Josh was helping you with the furniture, and Anna bought two crystal tumblers."

"I saw Pete Lambert a few times. He and another cop are helping direct traffic."

"Oh . . . and Elsa Fitch, who bought the heads? She looked through all the needlepoint and then asked if we had any of the local scenes Millie Gardener stitched. She must have heard about the panels. Her brother, Jed, and his wife were here, too. He's the real estate agent who sold the place, right?"

"That's right. Maybe he mentioned the panels to her."

"Maybe."

"Elsa's sister, Beth, bought four small wooden chairs for her kitchen. She's planning to paint them in bright enamel colors."

Sarah frowned. "I haven't lived in town as long as you have. Is Beth Fitch the one who teaches second grade?"

"She was my second-grade teacher," I admitted.

"Then I do know her. She's come into my shop a few times looking for nineteenth-century schoolbooks or merit cards, or other educational collectibles." She paused. "Patrick's invited us to stay after the sale closes at four o'clock. He mentioned champagne and tasty goodies, to thank everyone who's helped out today."

"I was thinking more along the lines of a hot bath at that point," I admitted. "But for champagne? I could stay a little longer."

"Patrick's been wonderful, hasn't he?" Sarah asked quietly as she and I picked out sandwiches (roast beef or chicken or vegetarian) from the coolers in the carriage house. I added a bag of barbecued chips to my plate and a few carrot sticks.

"I've had at least one cup of coffee every hour since dawn," I said, choosing a bottle of soda. "I don't need any more of that. But I still need caffeine to get through the next few hours."

"Sounds good," Sarah agreed, following my lead. "I can't believe we won't be back here tomorrow again. They've hired boys from the high school to dump everything that's left."

"I could sure use a late morning, and a quiet day," I said. "And I suspect you have accounts to do at your store."

"You're right. Ruth just makes out the sales slips. I'll have to do the final accounting." Sarah took a bite of her sandwich. "I'll miss seeing Patrick every day. Do you think it would be too forward to ask him to dinner?"

"I'd wait a few days. He's got to be as exhausted as we are."

"Right. And we're not really finished with Aurora, are we? We still have to talk with Skye about the needlepoint panels."

"You know, someone else asked me about them today. I can't remember who it was. But it wasn't Elsa Fitch. They said they'd heard Mrs. Gardener had done a series of pictures of the town as it was in 1970."

Sarah added potato chips to her sandwich. "Sounds like the ones hanging in the dining room, all right," she said. "But they're not for sale, so it doesn't matter."

"No. What matters are the checks for fifteen thousand dollars we'll be pocketing," I added. "And whatever it will cost to restore those ten pictures. I've had no time to talk with Gram about them, but I'd like to get them farmed out to the needlepointers tomorrow or the next day. Gram's wedding is two weeks from today. She and I have a lot to do between now and then."

"Is she getting excited?" asked Sarah. "I'd sure be excited if it were my wedding. I don't think I'd be able to sleep the two weeks before! June has certainly turned out to be a lot more interesting than we'd thought."

"And lucrative," I agreed. I'd never made fifteen thousand dollars carrying a handgun and a camera around Mesa, Arizona. There were a lot of different ways to make a living. But it helped to work for someone who didn't mind writing large checks.

Chapter 12

Let virtue prove your never fading bloom
For mental beauties will survive the tomb.

—Sampler stitched by Mary Chase (1816–1832), Augusta, Maine, 1827

At three-thirty, Patrick and a few of the other men helping with the sale walked through Aurora, checked to make sure everyone was out, locked its doors, and announced that the gates would be closing at four o'clock. Everyone should complete their purchases and leave.

A crowd of last-minute townspeople gathered around the refreshment area and helped themselves to glasses of lemonade and cookies while thanking Skye for a wonderful day. Several children (and more than a few adults) left with pockets loaded down with cookies.

At four o'clock the men made another round of the tents and grounds to make sure no one not working was on the property. A few people lined up to make last-minute purchases, and then, finally, it was over.

Relief.

An amazing amount of stuff had been sold, but the Dumpsters would be full again tomorrow. Sarah and I added up our sales, checked the cash and check totals, and brought them to Skye, who was sitting by the refreshment table.

She'd taken her shoes off and stretched out her legs. She looked as tired as we felt. It had been a long week, followed by a long day.

"What were the total receipts?" she asked.

"Both of our tents together . . . a little under nine thousand dollars," I answered. "We added quickly, so we may be a few dollars off, but that's pretty close."

"Wonderful. That will make a nice contribution to the Haven Harbor Hospital," she said. She handed Sarah and me our checks for fifteen thousand dollars each. "You've both done a great job in the past week. It took a lot of work to pull this off so quickly. We couldn't have done it without you."

"So now the house is empty, and we can begin the construction," said Patrick, joining us. "It's so beautiful outside I asked the caterer to bring the champagne and hors d'oeuvres here, instead of leaving them in the carriage house."

I looked over and saw two men carrying a large cooler in our direction.

"Before I indulge in any champagne, I'd like a last glass of lemonade," I said, filling one of the red plastic cups stacked on the table. "I don't think I've talked so much in one day for months. And in this heat . . . I'm thirsty."

"I sympathize," said Skye. "I just had a glass myself. And I never want to see another cookie! If you or your grandmother would like some, please, *please* take them. After everyone takes what they want, I'll have one of the boys drop the rest off at the assisted-living center and the nursing home next to the hospital. I've already told them any goodies left would go to them."

Skye had thought of everything. I sipped my lemonade and looked around. Suddenly a flash of red caught my eye.

"Look!" I whispered, and pointed. We all held our breaths as a male ruby-throated hummingbird hovered over the red cups on the table. He stopped to sip one of the purple flowers in the centerpiece. He then headed for the end of the table, where he sipped out of one of the red cups.

His colors were brilliant. We were all transfixed.

Then, suddenly, he stopped hovering and fell to the table. Skye was closest to him. She touched his breast gently. "He's dead!" she said, looking at all of us. "And he was sipping from the glass I poured for myself ten minutes ago."

"Are you feeling all right?" Patrick asked. "Do you want to sit down?"

She brushed him off. "I'm fine. But what just happened?"

"Don't touch anything. I'm going to get someone from the police," Patrick said with authority.

"That's really not necessary," Skye started to say. But Patrick was already gone.

Sarah and I looked at each other and at the small, still bird. I put down my glass of lemonade. "I don't think we should drink any more lemonade," I said.

"But we've been drinking it all afternoon," said Skye. "Everyone's been drinking it. No one's been sick or complained about anything."

"Maybe the bird was sick before he drank it," Sarah suggested.

We all stood around the table, feeling helpless, until

Patrick reappeared. Pete Lambert was with him. "I told him what happened," said Patrick.

"You're sure the bird sipped from the cup?" asked Pete, nodding at me. I hadn't talked to him in the past couple of weeks, but we'd gotten to know each other a month ago when I was trying to find out how my mother died.

"We all saw the bird," I confirmed. "He sipped from one of the purple flowers in the centerpiece," I explained, pointing, "and then he sipped out of that cup."

"Everyone feels all right?" Pete asked, looking around at the few of us who were still there. "Hell, I even had a glass of that lemonade earlier this afternoon. But I'd better check it out."

He pulled a pair of plastic gloves and an evidence bag out of his trousers. "Never investigated the death of a hummingbird before, I'll admit." He took the dead bird and the cup the bird had sipped from. "I'd better take the punch bowl, too," he said, looking around. "I have some sterile containers in my car."

"I'll help you," said Patrick, "if that won't mess up any evidence."

"*Evidence?* Of a hummingbird's death?" Pete grinned a little. "I doubt anyone else is in any danger."

"But the bird just dropped dead!" said Sarah.

"Birds die," said Pete. "No one else's died here this afternoon, have they?"

Skye smiled, but I had the feeling she wasn't as amused as Pete appeared to be. "Everyone else is healthy. But that was my cup the bird sipped from."

Pete looked down at the cup, now in his hand. "It looks pretty full. Had you drunk anything from it?"

"No. I had a glass a little while ago, and then poured another. Several people stopped to talk with me, and I left that cup on the end of the table. I was about to go and get it when . . . the bird got there first."

Pete frowned. He sniffed the cup. "Can't tell anything now. Was anyone near this cup?"

We all shook our heads. The table had many red cups on it. Several dozen people had dropped off empty or partially full cups as they left. We'd started to clean up. Someone would have had to watch Skye closely to know that particular red cup was hers.

"I'll have the cup and what's in it tested," Pete promised. "I'll let you know if we find anything unusual. In the meantime no one drink any more lemonade or touch any of the cups on the table! I doubt there's a problem. But to be sure, we'll need to test all the glasses. Does anyone remember who drank from the other glasses?"

None of us had been paying attention. People had been dropping cups off all afternoon. Most of them had ended up in the two large trash barrels on either side of the refreshment table.

Pete took pictures of the table and the glasses. He called his office to ask that someone come and bring more evidence bags and containers.

The rest of us stood around and watched.

Pete finally looked at us. "I heard you were planning a bit of a celebration after today's sale. I suggest you all go and have your party. I know who's here, and one of my fellow officers will be arriving anytime to help me. Why don't you all go back to the carriage house and leave me to this?"

"We'll do that. And you'll be sure to let me know what you find?"

"I will," said Pete. "It won't be a secret. But I doubt anyone here is in danger."

The guys picked up the cooler they'd brought out and

we all trooped back to the carriage house. But the mood was broken. Despite the champagne and French bread and shrimp toasts and salmon pate and other goodies, no one seemed hungry.

After a glass or two and a few bites, we all headed home.

It had been a long day. A long day with an odd ending.

The death of a hummingbird.

Chapter 13

This work in hand my friends may have
When I am dead and in my grave
And which when'er you chance to see
May kind remembrance picture me
While on this glowing canvas stands
The Labour of my youthful hands.

—Sampler wrought by Elizaetta Wray,
age fourteen, 1752

Gram's note was on the kitchen table, along with her purchases from the lawn sale:

Tom and I've gone out for dinner. Thought you might be eating at Aurora tonight. If not, baked beans and coleslaw are in the fridge. See the treasures we found at your sale? Fun day, thinking back over the past.

The only one home to greet me was Juno, who meowed her greeting, and stood plaintively by her supper dish. Gram always left dry food for her, but opened a can of wet food for Juno's dinner. She must have left without filling Juno's expectations.

Feeding a cat was about all I had the energy to do. I opened a can of mackerel and liver. Juno expressed her appreciation by ignoring me and happily slurping her way through every ounce. She was not a deprived cat.

Then it was my turn. Despite the two glasses of champagne I'd had at Aurora, I poured myself a serious shot of vodka, adding an olive to turn it officially into a martini.

Baked beans and coleslaw. The classic Maine Saturday-night supper.

I put the pot of beans in the oven to heat and started nibbling on the coleslaw. Gram varied the traditional dish by adding thin slices of red onion and horseradish dressing. I was hungrier than I'd thought. The coleslaw disappeared before the beans heated, but not before I'd poured myself a second drink.

I worked hard this week, I told myself. *I deserve it.*

Besides, no one was here. I wasn't driving. And I definitely planned to sleep in tomorrow.

I found a box of chowder crackers in the cabinet and started nibbling those before the beans were ready. A strange supper, but it filled my stomach. Couldn't drink on an empty stomach. While I was snacking, I looked over what Gram and Tom had purchased at Skye's sale.

Sarah had told me about the Waterford vase—a treasure for their new home together. The pillowcases delicately embroidered with daffodils and lilies of the valley were lovely, but not my style. I smiled to myself, wondering if Dave Percy had seen them.

Dave's hobby (aside from needlepoint) was his poison garden, which he used to interest his students and warn them of the dangers local plants could hide. He'd begun to teach me some things, too. That was why I knew daffodil bulbs and lilies of the valley were both beautiful, but poisonous.

I decided not to mention my newfound knowledge to Gram.

I used to see the world that way, too. Beautiful and full of hope and promise. But that was before Mama disappeared.

Of course, now I knew that wasn't exactly what had happened.

But I couldn't change history.

I'd also learned a lot about the rotten side of human nature in Arizona. Back here in Haven Harbor, I'd been able to put my gun away and focus on Gram and her custom needlepoint business. And now Gram's wedding.

Domestic issues I hadn't thought would be part of my life ever again.

Finally the smell of molasses and maple syrup filled the kitchen. I took the bean pot out of the oven, spooned out a plate full, and dug in. Worth waiting for. I could have microwaved them, but that wouldn't have felt authentic.

One of my high-school friends had loved cold baked beans; she'd eaten sandwiches of cold baked beans for lunch every Monday. But although I didn't insist on my beans sizzling, I did prefer them warm.

I should have bought something for myself at the sale. Something other than the cartons of needlework books and magazines that now filled the luggage compartment and backseat of Sarah's car. I hadn't even thought of choosing something for myself. Soon this house I'd grown up in would be mine. The parish house was already furnished. What would Gram take with her to her new life? In Arizona I'd furnished my tiny apartment from Goodwill, and, with the exception of a desert painting I'd bought and asked my neighbor to ship to Maine, I hadn't taken anything with me when I'd left. The painting now hung in my bedroom. It looked a little out of place in Haven Harbor, but it represented part of my life. It would stay there.

I looked at the check Skye had given me. Fifteen thousand dollars. I might never see another check that large. How much money must she have? I couldn't imagine.

Not the kind of money private investigators or directors of needlepoint companies earned. That I knew for sure.

I filled another plate with beans and sipped my vodka. Not gourmet, but tonight it worked for me.

I still needed to find an outfit to wear to Gram's wedding. No question I'd be able to pay for one now. And I should find something to give her. I'd already given her a microwave. But I wanted to find something more special. More lasting. Maybe fancy wineglasses? Gram and Tom both drank wine.

And tomorrow I needed to spend some time with Gram, figuring out what to do with those needlepoint panels for Skye. It was time to assess the damage and figure out whom to give the pieces to for restoration.

I finished the vodka and the beans and headed upstairs to bed. My stomach was bloated (I had overdone it with the beans) and my head and feet were aching.

The next week would be a full one: a trip to Portland, and getting caught up with the paperwork and calls for Mainely Needlepoint.

At least, except for those panels, I was through with Aurora. I needed to get on with the rest of my life.

I took two B12 tablets to help combat any effects of the vodka, as well as an aspirin, just in case the B12 wasn't enough.

What I needed most was sleep.

Chapter 14

And what is friendship but a name
A charm that lulls to sleep
A shade that follows wealth and fame
But leaves the wretch to weep.

—Lines stitched by Elizabeth Keyes on her sampler, 1806, taken from Oliver Goldsmith's (1730–1774) "The Hermit," 1765

The sound of my cell ringing woke me Sunday morning at eight o'clock. I pulled my pillow over my head and pretended I didn't hear it. Who would call so early? Sunday was supposed to be a day of rest. And I needed one.

I'd left a note telling Gram I wouldn't be making it to church this morning. I had a quiet day planned. Laundry. Sorting through Mainely Needlepoint messages that I'd postponed dealing with when I was at Aurora. A quiet walk to the beach to indulge in some fried clams and a view of the harbor. Sea breezes to blow the cobwebs and dust and mold of Aurora out of my brain.

The phone kept ringing. I groaned, sat up, and answered it.

"Angie? Good. I was about to hang up. I thought you might be in church this morning." I glanced down at the caller ID. "Patrick?"

"Yeah. It's me. Sorry to call you so early on a Sunday morning. But a few minutes ago, we got a call from the Haven Harbor Police. Pete someone?"

Patrick usually sounded smooth. In control. Sophisticated. This morning his voice was like sandpaper. A late Saturday night? When Sarah and I'd left the carriage house last night, there'd been a lot of unopened champagne bottles on the table.

"Lambert." I filled in. "Sergeant Pete Lambert."

"Right." Patrick paused. "Well, he didn't say exactly why, but he wants to see Mom and me. On a Sunday morning!"

As though those sworn to protect and defend our towns could take Sunday off.

"About the hummingbird?" I asked.

"Probably. But Mom's all excited. She thinks his wanting to see us might have something to do with Jasmine Gardener."

"I suspect it's about something more current, like traffic problems with the construction trucks around Aurora. Or the hummingbird." Mainers took traffic jams, especially traffic jams during tourist season, seriously. And if the wildlife folks thought anything untoward had happened to that hummingbird, that news could make the local paper. Maybe even the *Portland Press Herald*. Mainers cared about their wildlife.

Patrick sighed. "I know. But, still, Mom's all uptight about it. How well do you know this guy Pete?"

"A little. We've worked together. Shared lunch. He's pretty sane," I said.

"So you know him. And you're a Mainer. Would you mind being here when he comes to talk with us? It would relax Mom, and that would make me feel better. Especially since I told Mom that you've been a private investigator."

"But I wasn't! I said I worked *for* a private investigator," I corrected quickly.

"Same thing. You understand about investigations and questions and all. Mom talks a lot about Jasmine Gardener, but I don't think she has a clue about what a real police investigation is like." Patrick hesitated. "It's not like in the movies. I don't want her to make a fool of herself. Please. We need your help on this one."

"I really don't think I can do anything," I said.

"*Please.* As a favor."

I still had Skye West's check in my pocket. She'd certainly been nice to Sarah and me. What choice did I have? "All right. I'll come over. When did Pete say he'd be at your place?"

"Eleven o'clock."

"I'll be there a few minutes before then. But don't tell him you asked me specially to be there. I've happened to stop in."

"Fine, fine. Just so you're here. I owe you! And"—Patrick's voice lowered—"don't tell anyone about this. People gossip. We don't want anyone knowing the police were here."

The phone clicked off.

Don't tell anyone? Patrick didn't know small-town Maine. Before noon everyone in town would know there was a police car at Aurora.

I found a pair of relatively clean jeans and an unspotted T-shirt, set the percolator to brew, and paced the living room, waiting for the coffee and wishing I could at least call Sarah. Sarah had been at Aurora as many hours as I had been, and she'd probably talked with both Skye and Patrick more than I had. But she didn't know Pete Lambert well. And she hadn't worked for a private investigator.

She'd gone out of her way to talk with Patrick. She'd be gracious, but not happy he'd called me.

Remembering the expression in his eyes stirred more than a desire for breakfast.

Stirrings I dismissed. Instead, I scrambled two eggs with a few leaves of spinach and a little grated Parmesan. Feeling indulgent, I sprinkled a piece of buttered toast with cinnamon and sugar. Being in the kitchen where I'd spent a good part of my childhood reminded me of so many little details I hadn't thought of in years. Did anyone still put cinnamon and sugar on toast? It had been one of Gram's standbys. The sweet taste and aroma took me right back to being six or seven years old.

When Mama was waitressing, Gram and I would have tea and scones or cinnamon toast or sometimes cookies as our afternoon snack. I'd tell her what had happened in school, and she'd show me how much needlepoint she'd done that day, and remind me to put away the clothes she'd washed, or we'd plan what to have for dinner. Mama was seldom home for meals, so menus were up to Gram and me.

In those days, before Gram started watching her cholesterol, and we both knew too much sugar or fat was bad for us, butter was always in the kitchen, and a jar of bacon fat stood in a covered jar on the stove. Baked beans were ready every Saturday night, as they had been last night—as they were in most Haven Harbor homes—with enough left over for Sunday dinner or supper. Molasses and raisin cookies were more common than chocolate chip, and there were no Chinese or pizza or Thai places that delivered then. Actually, as Skye and Patrick had discovered this past week, there still weren't.

I spent the rest of the morning examining the ten needlepoint panels Skye wanted preserved. Gram had removed them from their frames and spread them on our dining-room table.

She'd successfully sponged the surface dirt off them, and the three invaded by the most mildew were now in much better condition. Putting them in the sunshine seemed to have stopped the mildew's progress and killed it, I hoped.

If Sarah didn't know what we should do next, I'd call the Museum of Fine Arts in Boston. Their textile division should be able to head us in the right direction. And they should know where to get antiacidic backings for the needlepoints, and tell me whether the stitching itself should be treated in any way.

Skye had said, "Restore and preserve . . . but also repair." I separated those panels that needed repair work on broken stitches, or stitching over sections that had faded or torn. I'd confirm with Gram, who'd already looked at the pictures closely, but it looked as though four of the panels (those of the Haven Harbor Lighthouse, the eagle flying over the yacht club, the staircase at Aurora, and the Haven Harbor Town Pier) were in good-enough condition to be carefully lined and reframed. Of the remaining six, two had major problems and four needed minor repairs and adjustments.

All in all, the pictures weren't in as bad condition as I'd initially assumed.

Who would be free to work on them, though? Gram had

already done more than her share. I couldn't ask her to take on anything else.

Ruth Hopkins's arthritis would keep her from volunteering. Ob Winslow was focusing on his charter fishing this summer. Sarah might be able to do one or two, although she was coming up to the busiest time of the year for her store. I wasn't experienced enough to take on any of the repair work myself. That left Dave Percy, whose classes at the high school should be over this week, and Katie Titicomb. Katie was a careful stitcher, no doubt. And she'd said she was ready to take on new projects. It looked as though she and Dave would be handling these pieces. But Sarah would want to be involved, I thought, since she'd been a part of this from the beginning. I'd give her the two with the fewest challenges.

By a little after ten-thirty, I was in my little red car, headed back to Aurora, hoping my visit would be short and simple.

Chapter 15

Thine eye my bed and path survey
*My public haunts and privit [*sic*] ways.*

—Verse stitched on American sampler, 1769

Pete arrived at Aurora's carriage house at eleven o'clock. Right on time. His uniform was pressed and his thin brown hair slicked down. His back was straight. Even though he'd worn the same uniform when directing traffic around Aurora or collecting information about the hummingbird's death yesterday, this morning he looked much more official.

His eyes widened when he saw me, but he wasted no time in announcing why he was there.

"Arsenic. The crime lab guys said that hummingbird died of arsenic poisoning. That cup the bird sipped from contained four or five grains of arsenic." He took a breath. "That's more than enough to kill someone."

Skye and Patrick looked at each other.

I pointed out the obvious. "Hundreds of people drank

lemonade yesterday. It was a hot day. I drank some. You did, too."

"Yeah. I did. There's no trace of arsenic in the punch bowl or in any of the other cups we took back to the lab."

"Then . . ."

"I'll admit, when you asked me to have lemonade tested because a bird died, I thought you were all a little—"

"Crazy?" asked Skye. "Paranoid?"

"I didn't say that. But, considering the situation . . ."

Meaning, I suspected, *"because you're rich and famous."*

Pete continued: "We did check. The only arsenic we found was in your glass, Ms. West. Either someone was trying to kill you, or they staged the scene to look as though someone wanted to kill you."

"'Staged the scene'?" repeated Patrick. "As in 'cue the hummingbird'? That's ridiculous!"

"You tell me," said Pete. "All I know is there was enough arsenic in that cup to kill at least a couple of dozen people. We in Haven Harbor don't take kindly to that sort of a joke."

"*Joke?* Pete, you can't believe putting arsenic in a cup where anyone could have picked it up was a joke," I put in.

"But no one else did pick it up. Ms. West identified it as her cup. And yet she didn't drink from it. That's quite a coincidence, considering there was a table covered with identical glasses."

True, there were Mainers who rejected those from away, especially those who had money. But Skye was trying to do everything right: hiring locals—or mostly locals, contributing to local charities, and fixing up one of the town's eyesores. What was Pete getting at?

"Someone tried to kill me yesterday," Skye said, her voice amazingly steady. "What are you going to do about it?"

"Ms. West, we don't know that someone tried to kill

you. All we know is there was arsenic in that one cup. The state crime lab says it isn't officially an attempted murder unless we know for sure who the glass was meant for and who tampered with it."

"It was my glass. Someone tried to poison me," Skye repeated.

"Well, if someone wanted you dead, they failed. You're still alive," said Pete. "I'll be blunt. I've only met you once or twice. I don't know you, or why you're in town. You could choose to live anywhere in the world." Pete paused. "You're an actress. I've heard about people like you. Celebrities. You play roles. You need attention. You like to be the center of gossip." Pete stared at Skye. "I'm wondering if this is all a setup."

"I've been working with Ms. West for the past couple of weeks," I put in. "She's very sensible. Not the type to get hysterical, no matter what the movie magazines say. Why would she want you to think someone was trying to kill her? She'd want to avoid gossip, not encourage it."

Pete looked sidewise at me, but backed up a little. A very little. "Ms. West, if you didn't set this up yourself, I can understand why you'd be nervous. Scared. But if someone wants to poison you, there must be a reason. What could that be?"

Onstage and onscreen, Skye West had probably dealt with worse, but in her own backyard?

How would anyone react?

And, yes, gossip might certainly be involved. But not gossip Skye or Patrick would have started.

Pete had asked a reasonable question—the same one I had. Why would anyone want to kill Skye West?

Chapter 16

I live in a cottage and yonder it stands
And while I can work with these two honest hands
I'm as happy as those that have houses and lands.

—Sampler worked by Nancy Chadwick,
age thirteen, 1811

"For right now, let's accept the supposition that you didn't stage anything. You didn't poison the cup. Then . . . who did?" Pete looked from Skye to Patrick and back again. "Do either of you have any enemies? Any problems you brought with you to Maine? Some of those paparazzi types who follow celebrities around?" Pete wasn't smiling.

"Mom must have signed a hundred autographs yesterday," Patrick answered. "She wasn't anything but gracious." Patrick smiled proudly at his mother. "She's good at her job, onstage and off."

"No matter who poisoned the cup, it was lucky that hummingbird tasted the lemonade before you did. One sixteenth of a teaspoonful of arsenic would kill someone.

Your cup contained many times that amount. And your cup was the only one tampered with," Pete pointed out again.

Skye's lips pursed. "And you have no idea who did that."

"We were hoping you'd have some suggestions. Yesterday you said you'd poured the glass, but then stepped away to talk to some people and sign a few autographs. During the time between your pouring the cup and the hummingbird's sipping from it, someone added the arsenic. We'll need a list of everyone who was near the refreshment table during that time."

Skye shook her head. "Sergeant Lambert, almost all of the people here yesterday were strangers to me." She threw up her hands. "Can you help, Angie?"

"I'll try to remember who else I saw in the area." Pete handed me a pad of paper. "But I wasn't there for the whole time period you're talking about."

"Write down everyone you can remember," he said. "If you don't know their names, then a description of them."

Skye stood up. "You're absolutely sure it was arsenic in my cup?"

"It's not something we see every day, but it's easy to test for. We're certain."

She nodded decisively. "I don't know who wanted to poison me, but I can guess why."

I looked up. Skye was calmly sipping from a pottery mug of coffee. She knew? And she wasn't panicked or fearful?

"Yes?" Pete asked. "Why?"

She turned to face him. "Because I bought Aurora to find out who killed Jasmine Gardener. Any police records about her death should include the fact that her mother was convinced Jasmine was poisoned by arsenic before she fell in the fountain. I believe whoever poisoned her is still in or near Haven Harbor. Was here yesterday. And either wanted to kill me the same way, or frighten me so I'd leave town. Convince me not to investigate." She put her mug down decisively. "But I'm not leaving."

Pete looked as though Skye had slipped into another reality. "Pardon me, Ms. West, but Jasmine Gardener died almost forty-five years ago. I'm not an expert on the case—it was definitely before my time—but I know that although there was some local gossip about arsenic, the police ruled Miss Gardener's death accidental. You've bought a house with a past. It might seem amusing to you to assume Miss Gardener was murdered, and to solve that murder. But forty-five years is a long time. The chances of anyone knowing something about her death that we don't already have in our files seem dubious."

"I understand you don't believe me," said Skye. "But the reason I held that sale yesterday was to encourage Haven Harbor residents to come here, to Aurora, to revisit what happened here in 1970, and to talk about it again. Many of them did. I asked questions, and I overheard comments. I believe Jasmine Gardener's murderer was here at Aurora yesterday, and that he or she decided it would be safer for them if I disappeared. Luckily, as you can see, I've neither died nor been scared out of town."

"But why would anyone connect you to what happened all those years ago? Excuse me, Ms. West, but you're just an actress who bought an old house with a history. You'd never even been in Haven Harbor before a few weeks ago."

Skye smiled, her lips tight. "There I'm afraid you're wrong, Sergeant Lambert. I have been in Haven Harbor before. I was a guest here at Aurora the entire summer of 1970. Jasmine Gardener was my best friend. I was here the night she died."

Chapter 17

Beauty and virtue when they do meet,
With a good education make a lady complete.

—American Colonial sampler, 1724

Patrick crossed the room to stand next to his mother. I assumed it was a show of family solidarity. What she'd just announced came as a shock to Pete, and certainly to me. Had Patrick known? I wasn't sure.

Pete's voice was calm, but questioning. "I don't know what you're trying to do, or who you are, lady. But I grew up here in Haven Harbor. I never heard anything about an actress being at Aurora that summer. And although you're right that there've been rumors about Jasmine Gardener's being poisoned by arsenic, I've never seen proof."

"There was proof," Skye stated precisely. "True, the first medical examiner said Jasmine was drunk, fell into the fountain, and hit her head. But if you read his report carefully, it doesn't say Jasmine drowned, although that was what most people in Haven Harbor believed."

"There's a long step between hitting your head on a marble fountain and arsenic poisoning," Pete pointed out. He'd taken out his notebook, but hadn't written anything down. I recognized his tone. He'd used it with me when I'd insisted on finding a motive for my mother's killer.

Pete was putting up with someone he thought was foolish . . . or crazy.

Skye didn't strike me, now or ever, as either foolish or crazy.

She kept talking. "Millicent Gardener, Jasmine's mother, suspected something else was involved besides alcohol, so she had Jasmine's body tested privately after the ME was through with it. Those tests showed her daughter had a high alcohol level, but she'd also ingested a fatal dose of arsenic shortly before she died."

"And how do you know that?"

"Because Millicent Gardener became a close friend, a patron of mine, after Jasmine's death. She knew I'd cared about Jasmine. She sent me a copy of the two reports. But I'm not the only one she told about the arsenic. She gave a copy of her report to the Haven Harbor police. I'm certainly not blaming you, since you probably hadn't even been born then, but the Maine medical examiner hadn't tested for arsenic. Giving him all due credit, there was no reason for the ME to have done so. And the police didn't believe the private report Millie Gardener had done later."

"So you're saying you've known about this for almost the whole forty-five years since Jasmine died, and you didn't do anything about it?" Pete was taking notes, but he didn't look convinced.

"As you said earlier, I'm an actress, Sergeant. I was in touch with Millie Gardener when she was living here. She was very alone, living by herself, believing that her daughter had been killed by someone. Most likely by someone she knew, right here in Haven Harbor. And yet no one listened to her." Skye's voice was calm and convincing. "She telephoned me, and she wrote to me. She encouraged me in my career. I can assure you it was the sorrow of her life that no one believed her when she said Jasmine was poisoned. Not even her husband believed her. But I did. And I promised her that someday, when I could, I'd carry on her efforts to find Jasmine's killer. That's why I'm here in Haven Harbor. I'm keeping my promise to an old friend."

"Ms. West, even if everything you're saying is true, 1970 was a long time ago. People have moved in and out of Haven Harbor. There's no new evidence. I'll accept that you were Jasmine's friend. I believe you want to do the right thing. But there's no reason to open a case now. It isn't even a cold case. Jasmine Gardener's death was ruled accidental."

"What about the arsenic you found in my cup? Was that an accident? Doesn't that say there's someone else in town who wants this case to stay closed?"

"I can't explain the arsenic. It's not something most people have around their homes or barns today."

"It could have killed me."

"Yes, it could have. But it didn't. You're the only one I've heard recently talking about Jasmine Gardener being poisoned by arsenic." He leaned forward and looked at her closely. "Why should I believe anyone else put that arsenic in your cup?"

"You're suggesting that my mother poisoned herself?" Patrick asked angrily.

"I'm pointing out that she didn't drink from the poisoned cup. And that she and maybe you were the only people thinking about arsenic poisoning before this happened." Pete stood his ground. "Your mother knows how to put on a darn good show. What could be a better show than staging an attempt on her own life? Maybe she thought it would draw attention to Jasmine Gardener, and even get us to open a case on her death."

"I never," said Skye.

"I assure you we are paying attention to you. Our crime scene unit was up most of the night testing all those cups from your refreshment table yesterday. We found nothing other than the arsenic in your cup. We'd need more evidence before we're convinced your life was in danger."

Skye threw back her shoulders. "I am insulted and appalled. You think I'd go to the trouble of pretending to poison myself? I'd planned to contact the local authorities as soon as I'd found new evidence in Jasmine's death." She walked to the door, dismissing Pete. "I can see that would waste my time and yours."

Pete stood, visibly relieved. "Welcome to Haven Harbor, Ms. West. I hope you and your son are happy here. And should you have any genuine emergencies, I'd be happy to assist you."

"Don't worry," she said. "I won't be bothering you from now on. Millie Gardener warned me about how obstinate local law enforcement people were in Maine. She said that because she was from New York City they never took her seriously. I thought she'd exaggerated. I'm sorry to say she didn't."

I hesitated. I had to admit, Skye being the victim of the same poison she believed killed Jasmine Gardener did sound far-fetched.

But I'd seen the expression on Skye's face when that hummingbird dropped dead on the white tablecloth. I had no idea what was in that cup, or how it had gotten there. I didn't think Skye had poisoned her own drink.

She deserved to be taken seriously.

Pete looked at me as he left. "Angie, don't get trapped

into believing everything you hear about this place and the people who lived here. Or who live here now." He slammed the door after himself.

Left alone, Skye sat down again. "Thank you for staying, Angie. Do you believe me?"

"I believe someone put arsenic in your cup yesterday. Maybe it had something to do with Jasmine Gardener's death. Maybe it didn't. But arsenic doesn't appear in a cup by itself."

"Thank you for giving me credit for the intelligence to know that," said Skye.

"You said you were here at Aurora that summer," I said. "How did you know Jasmine and the Gardeners?"

"Jasmine and I were classmates at Miss Pritchard's School in New York City. We came from different worlds—I was a scholarship student—but we became best friends. That year Jasmine didn't want to come to Maine for the whole summer. She didn't want to leave her friends in New York. She begged her parents to at least let me come with her." She smiled, remembering. "Jasmine usually managed to get what she wanted. At first, when the Gardeners said they'd love to have me as their guest, I refused. I said that no, I needed to stay and work at the deli where I'd worked weekends in the winter. To convince me to come, Millie Gardener arranged for me to get a grant from a private foundation that covered more than I would have earned that summer. I had a choice—stay in the city in a hot apartment with my mom and her current boyfriend, and whoever else happened to need a place to stay, and work long hours in a deli . . . or spend the summer hanging out with my best friend in a gorgeous house on the coast of Maine. It wasn't a hard decision."

I grinned. "I imagine not."

"Jasmine and I shared her room and her clothes, and she taught me to sail and play tennis and eat lobster. For Jasmine, it was the way life was and always had been. For me, it was magical, even though Jasmine was coping with a lot of issues. She hid what she was doing and feeling from most people, but she couldn't hide from me. I knew about her life in New York City, even if it wasn't mine. And I could see her life in Maine. More than once, I wondered how it would all turn out. Until, of course, the night of the party. Then Jasmine's life—her death—became a nightmare." Skye paused. "That night her problems were solved. But not in any way she'd imagined. Or would have wanted."

Chapter 18

Now in the morning of my days
Let me acquire deserved praise
And well improve my mind.
Soon will those happy hours be gone
And loaded years with pain come on
Unlike to those behind.

—Sampler stitched by Phebe Garretson, age nine, Springboro, Ohio, 1825 (Phebe married at age twenty-three, moved to Indiana with her husband and his parents, and was the matron at Earlham College, which all five of her children attended. She died shortly before her eighty-second birthday.)

"What was Jasmine like?" I asked.

"She was pretty and she loved dancing and singing folk songs. She always said she wanted to learn to play the guitar. She was planning to take lessons in the fall." Skye paused. "When you're seventeen, you think you have the rest of your life ahead of you. Years and years and years, stretching so far you can't imagine them. Jasmine didn't think much about her future. She used to laugh at me because I studied like crazy. I needed to keep my scholarship at Miss Pritchard's and then get a college scholarship. Jasmine wasn't even sure she wanted to go to college. Her grades were good enough, and her parents had the money to send her, but she didn't look forward to four more years in school. She certainly wasn't worried about college." Skye paused. "She didn't worry about much, until that last month or so. She'd never had to. She'd always had what she wanted, from clothes to friends to boyfriends. I found her fun and fascinating . . . a bit like that poor hummingbird who died yesterday. Bright and flashy and reflecting the sun, and then . . . gone."

"And you're convinced she was murdered."

"I am. I suspected it at the time, but she died so suddenly, and no one else seemed to consider that possibility. She'd been drinking, and she'd been found in the fountain. People assumed she'd drowned. But her mother never believed that was the whole story. And even in the midst of the horror of her daughter's dying, Millie Gardener was kind, so kind, to me." Skye spoke softly. "She and her husband even paid for the two years I went to Vassar. And when I dropped out to study at the American Academy of Dramatic Arts, they were still cheering me on. Millie Gardener saw every one of my movies, and Mr. Gardener attended the plays I did in New York City. I stayed in touch with Millie until a few weeks before she died. Not every day, of course, but maybe every week. She wasn't feeling well the last few months of her life. She had serious stomach pain. I tried to convince her to see a doctor. I should have flown up here and taken her to the doctor myself. But I was on location in Singapore, and she kept saying she'd be better soon. I wanted to believe her. I think she thought of me as another daughter. She was my biggest fan." Skye's eyes filled for a moment. "And I was hers. She was a second mother to me."

"Do you suspect someone in particular?" I asked. "Do you have any ideas about who might have killed Jasmine, or why?"

"Why do you ask? The police weren't interested." Skye's voice hardened. "I don't want Haven Harbor laughing at me. Or angry because they think I've accused someone unfairly."

"I wasn't even born when Jasmine died. But Gram—my grandmother—was at that party in 1970. She was celebrating her engagement. She said it was a lovely evening. Until, of course . . ."

"Until the fireworks were over, and Jed found Jasmine," Skye finished.

"Jed?" I said. I hadn't heard anyone refer directly to who had found Jasmine. "The same Jed Fitch who's now a real estate agent in town?" When I was growing up, he was the guy people called when they needed a minor plumbing problem fixed, or wood split, or a shed painted. He'd changed professions since I was a teenager.

"The same Jed Fitch. He sold us Aurora. He wasn't the way I'd pictured him." Skye smiled a bit sadly. "Of course, after all these years, none of us look the way we did then. He's lost most of his hair and doubled his weight. I wouldn't have recognized him if I hadn't known his name."

"What was he like then? When you knew him before?" I asked.

"Then? He was the pride of Haven Harbor. Almost a cliché. Going to be captain of the football team. Lobstered with his dad, which bleached his hair whiter and kept him tan and fit." Skye smiled. "In those days only athletes went to gyms to work out, but pulling lobster traps six months of the year certainly built muscles. And everyone wanted to be tan. No one thought about skin cancer."

"Sounds as though you had a crush on him," I said, teasing.

"Not me. My type was not as gorgeous . . . and more serious. Interested in the arts and books. Jed dated Jasmine that summer."

"Did he remember you when he sold you Aurora?"

"No," she said wryly. "Of course, I've changed, too."

"But he didn't remember your name? 'Skye West' is a memorable name," I said.

"That's what my agent thought," said Skye. "Which is why I chose it. When I was here with Jasmine that summer, my name was Mary North. That's the name Jed might have recognized."

Chapter 19

On the breast of her gown, in red cloth, surrounded with an elaborate embroidery and fantastic flourishes of gold threads, appeared the letter A.

—Nathaniel Hawthorne (1804–1864), Chapter 2 of *The Scarlet Letter,* 1850

"'Mary North?'" I asked.

She laughed. "Now you know all my secrets. Or at least one of them."

"Of course, I knew actors and actresses sometimes changed their names. I just never thought . . ."

"Most people don't," she answered. "And some people keep their 'real' name for various purposes, and only use their stage name when they're in the public eye. But I legally changed mine, and I never used any of my husbands' names."

"Which is why I'm Patrick West," added Patrick.

"So even those in Haven Harbor who remember Jasmine Gardener and her friend in 1970 might not recognize you."

"If they remember she had a friend visiting that summer, they'd think of a quiet brown-haired girl named Mary," said Skye. "Which actually works toward my purpose. I knew a lot about Jasmine's life that summer. Certainly, more than either of her parents did. And some of what I knew might be relevant to her death."

"Her murder," Patrick corrected softly. Clearly, he was a believer.

"Her murder," Skye repeated.

"For example?" I asked.

"When she died, Jasmine was a little over two months pregnant," said Skye. "She knew, and I knew. But I don't know whether she'd told the father of the baby, or anyone else. Certainly, her mother didn't know." She looked into the distance for a moment. "Millie found out when the autopsy results came in, but that part of the report was never released. The police and the family felt it wasn't necessary for anyone to know. Privacy was still important back then, especially if it was the privacy of a family that made large annual donations to the Haven Harbor Police Department."

"But she'd been drinking heavily that night," I said. "If she was pregnant—"

"Back in 1970, the connection between drinking alcohol during pregnancy and birth defects or fetal alcohol syndrome hadn't been established. Certainly, it wasn't a connection a seventeen-year-old girl would have made. So, yes, she was drinking that night. She'd actually been drinking all summer and getting high. Usually with her friends, and sometimes in her room at Aurora. Not out in public as she did September fifth."

"Who was the father of her baby?" I asked.

Skye shook her head. "Truthfully, I don't know. It had to have been Jed Fitch or Sam Gould."

"'Sam Gould'?" That was a new name.

"She'd been dating Sam in the spring, in New York. He went to college there. But he came from Maine, and he was around that summer, too."

"She was dating both of them?"

"She was seventeen. I'm not sure she was serious about either of them."

I remembered being seventeen. I certainly hadn't been serious about anyone then. "So she might not have known who the father of her child was."

"I think she knew. But what she was going to do about it? That I didn't know. You'll remember, this was before *Roe* v. *Wade.* But she wouldn't have been in danger from an illegal abortion. She wouldn't have had to use a coat hanger or sneak into an illegal clinic. Jasmine's parents could have afforded to send her out of the country, to where abortions were legal and relatively safe. But she hadn't told her parents. I tried to get her to talk with her mother. She refused. She told me she was planning to tell the baby's father and hope he stepped up. I'm not sure what she meant by that. I don't think she wanted to be married. But for a year or so, to give the baby a father and a name . . . she might have done that. Whoever the father was, her news was certainly going to mess up both their lives."

Suddenly I was in another place. Mama had been seventeen when she was pregnant with me. She'd never told anyone who my father was. I'd never heard Mama or Gram mention the possibility that she might have ended her pregnancy. Ended me. And Gram hadn't thrown her out. Mama hadn't been the best mother, but she and Gram had taken care of me. I wasn't a perfect citizen. But Mama had given me a chance.

Jasmine and her baby hadn't had that chance.

Skye was still talking. "Jed Fitch's real estate office is right here in town. I thought that was ironic. I'd left word with a local real estate agency to let me know if Aurora ever came on the market, and Jed was the one who called. Sam Gould is still around, too. His company builds yachts in Camden."

"You're suggesting one of them might have had a motive to make Jasmine and her baby disappear," I said.

"It's possible," said Skye. "It's even logical, although they're not the only ones who might have had motives. I was only here that one summer. I didn't know everyone in town. It could have been someone with a grudge against the Gardeners, or against wealthy people in general." She shrugged her shoulders.

"So?"

"So I want to figure out who had the best motive. And then prove they were responsible for Jasmine's death."

I kept thinking of that flighty, pregnant seventeen-year-old. How scared she must have been! Scared to be pregnant. Scared to tell her parents. Scared of how having a child would change her life. Scared of telling the man—the boy—who was the child's father.

I kept thinking of Mama.

"I'll help you," I blurted. "I know a lot of people in town. They'd be more comfortable talking to me than to you. Pardon, Skye, but you're a famous actress from California. People might ask you for your autograph. They might smile a lot. But I don't think they'd tell you their secrets." Had I just volunteered to jump off a twenty-foot diving board into an empty pool? But I kept talking. "If you'd like me to help find out what happened that night, whatever it was, I'm willing."

Patrick, who'd been listening silently, came around from in back of his mother's chair. "That's a wonderful idea, Mom. You wanted to have someone from local law enforcement helping you. That doesn't sound as though it'll work out. Someone with private-investigator experience is the next best thing." He looked at me. "Angie's already proven she's a hard worker. Plus, I don't think you could find a prettier investigator in the whole state of Maine."

What? I turned crimson. "It was just an idea. I've always been fascinated by Aurora and its stories. . . ."

"How much would you charge?" Skye asked.

"I don't have an investigator's license. It would be illegal to charge you. And, besides, you've already paid Sarah and me so generously. I would help because it's the right thing to do."

"I'd want to pay you. I don't care what we call the payments. We could figure that out later. So, yes, I'd love to have your help," said Skye, glancing at her son. "We'd both like that. We should sit down and go over the notes I have. Lists of people who were here that Saturday night, and who might have been responsible."

"That would be a good start," I agreed. "But today I need to get caught up with some needlepoint business. Tomorrow morning?"

"That would be fine," said Skye. "I'll have everything here in the carriage house."

I did have a lot of work to do—not counting getting ready for Gram's wedding.

What had I volunteered to get myself into?

Investigating a forty-five-year-old death that the police didn't think was a crime?

It wasn't the craziest thing I'd ever done. But it certainly wasn't the sanest, either.

And what would Gram think?

Chapter 20

May I with innocence and peace
My tranquil moments spend
And when the toils of life shall cease
With calmness meet my end.

—Sampler stitched by Mary Ann Moore,
Wilmington, Ohio, 1835

"You agreed to do *what*?" asked Gram. She'd come home to change from her "go to meeting" clothes into her gardening attire.

She'd decided to put in several tomato plants, lettuce, and zucchini—enough so I wouldn't starve—and after she moved out, she could come and pick what she needed. Already the early black-seeded Simpson lettuce was sprouting. I wished she'd put in peas for the traditional salmon-and-peas Fourth of July dinner. I'd have to buy peas at the farmers' market. By then, Gram and Reverend Tom would be (somewhere) on their honeymoon.

Maybe I'd invite Sarah to join me for dinner before the

fireworks over the harbor that night. Did she even know salmon and peas were the New England version of Fourth of July barbecue in the South? What would be the equivalent in Australia? I should ask her.

It would be strange living in this house without Gram.

Juno sprang into my lap and meowed her welcome. I scratched behind her ears. Between my work at Aurora and Gram's wedding planning (everything was now set, she'd assured me . . . except for whatever I planned to wear), Juno was feeling neglected. She accepted her rightful scratch and then leapt up to the kitchen windowsill to oversee the bird feeder. A pair of goldfinches and three chickadees were enjoying their Sunday dinner beyond Juno's reach.

Juno wasn't thrilled about Gram's ruling, but she was an inside cat. Birds took priority outside.

Juno, at least, wouldn't be moving until the honeymooners were back. So, technically, I wouldn't be alone until then.

I'd told Gram I'd agreed to help Skye investigate Jasmine's death.

"What exactly do you plan to do? Sounds to me as though that Skye West has a few screws loose. She seemed nice enough yesterday at the lawn sale. But I don't remember her being around in the summer of 1970." Gram tied on her apron. "Tuna salad for lunch? I picked up some young spinach leaves and scallions at the farmers' market yesterday to mix into it. And I saved us a couple of the strawberry muffins I made up for the ladies' reception at the church this morning."

"Sounds good. Thank you. And I don't know exactly what information Skye has. I'm going to talk with her tomorrow morning. She implied she has a couple of possible suspects in mind."

"Suspects? And she hasn't thought to mention this for forty-five years? If the woman was even here in 1970! My memory isn't perfect, but I would have remembered someone with a name like that, even if I didn't know the Gardeners well. And what has she been doing all this time that she didn't think to contact anyone if she had proof?"

I wasn't sure I should say anything about Skye's change of name, but this was my Gram. I could certainly trust her. "In 1970, her name wasn't Skye West. It was Mary North."

"'Mary North'?" Gram thought a minute before saying, "I don't remember anyone named Mary North. No Wests and no Norths." Gram tore spinach leaves in half as though they were Skye's ideas. "Phooey. That's what all this fuss is. And nonsense. Who comes back forty-five years later and has a brainstorm about a possible crime?"

I opened a large can of tuna (Juno reappeared and rubbed around my ankles, to make sure I hadn't forgotten her) and got out some salad dressing. "I have no clue. But first I want us to figure out who we're going to ask to work on the needlework pictures. I looked at them last night. You managed to get rid of most of the mildew."

"I did, yes," Gram said as she chopped a little red onion to add to our salad. "Sunlight's the best cure for that, I've found. If you leave the work in the sun too long, of course, it fades. But sun does kill mildew. Before we hand the pictures over to anyone else, I'll double-check. A couple of pieces might need a bit more treatment with a mild vinegar solution to make sure they're clean. All in all, the panels are in pretty good shape. A couple could be backed and reframed now. I called one of those archival houses and ordered nonacidic backing. It came in Friday. You've been so busy I haven't had a chance to tell you."

"Thank you. We've both been racing about. I was thinking of giving a couple of the pictures to Dave Percy to work on, since school will be out in a couple of days, and perhaps one or two to Sarah that she can work on at the store. I'll give the rest to Katie Titicomb."

"Good thinking. Sarah's been in this since the beginning. Dave's finished the work we gave him in May and said he'd like some other assignments, and Katie's bored stiff with her daughter and grandchildren down east for the summer. If she visits them, she can take her work with her."

"Skye doesn't seem in a hurry to get the panels back, but I'd like to get them finished as soon as we can, before gift shops start asking for more of the pillows and sachets and wall hangings we stitched last winter."

"I'll look over the pictures to be sure they're ready to be farmed out, then," Gram said. "I noticed you dropped off some silk threads and yarns last week. Are they for the panels?"

"If you think they'd work," I agreed. "They came from Millicent Gardener's needlepoint stash, and looked as though they might have been matches for those she used in the panels. Of course, the ones in the pictures have faded, so the colors won't be exact."

"Close enough, though. The fading we can leave, but in some sections threads have rotted or are broken. They'll need to be stitched over, and bright colors wouldn't go with the rest of the picture. We'll divide any of the threads you brought, and any we have in stock, and send them along with the panels when you deliver them to our needlepointers."

"Thank you for helping with this, Gram. I know you used to do this all by yourself. I'm still on a steep learning curve." And, of course, I'd been cleaning out an old house for the past week. Not exactly stitchery work. When Gram and the other Mainely Needlepointers had asked me to become their director last month, I'd assumed I'd be focused on sales and accounting. When it came to reclamation and knowing how long a specific project would take I had to lean heavily on Gram and the others.

"Skye wants me to talk about the people who were at the party in 1970. You said you were there."

"I didn't kill Jasmine Gardener. And I didn't see anyone else do it, either," Gram declared, putting our plates of salad on the table. "If I had, do you think I'd have swallowed hard and not told anyone for forty-five years?" She took two glasses out of the cabinet. "Iced tea or lemonade?"

"Lemonade," I said. I'd already had too much caffeine today. (And, to tell the truth, lemonade now reminded me of arsenic poisoning.) "You said maybe two hundred people were at Aurora that night."

"I wouldn't be surprised. But none of them would be spring chickens now—that's for sure," said Gram, settling into her salad.

"Ob Winslow said he was there."

"He must have been a babe in arms, then."

"He said he was about ten."

"That would make sense. There were a lot of children there. Fireworks and hamburgers and music. People of all ages were there. And, of course, Ob's family knew the Gardeners well."

"He said he lived in the carriage house there when he was a teenager."

"After his family was killed—an awful accident, when a storm came up and their boat went under—Ob was the only survivor. Lost his parents and his sister, both. He was in high school then, as I recall, and state family services weren't exactly on the ball about such things back then. The Gardeners had known his parents, and they told Ob he could live in their carriage house. Stay the winter and do odd jobs that needed to be done around the estate, open it up in the spring and close it in the fall. He was on his own there, but he must have managed fine. After he graduated, he stayed on and officially became their caretaker. Did that, in addition to his woodworking, for a few years before he and Anna married. By then, he'd inherited a bit from his parents. A trust of some sort. Enough to buy himself the fishing boat he still takes folks out on. And he and Anna bought the old Thompson farm across the road from Aurora. They're still there."

"So you and Ob were at the party. I wonder how many other people still in town were there."

"No idea. Some people who were summer folks then moved here permanently when they retired. Old folks died off. Young folks moved away. Hard to say who was around that long ago." She paused. "A fair number, though."

"Maybe Ob remembers some," I said. "And Skye seemed to have some ideas."

"Pshaw. Sounds like she's got too many ideas. No one remembers her, but she not only remembers people she hasn't seen in decades, but she thinks she can nail one of them for murder?" Gram looked at me. "I know she was real generous to you for helping with her house. But don't get too involved with that woman, Angel. You got your check. Now you've got a business to run and things to do for the wedding."

"You and Tom seem to have the wedding under control," I said. "Everyone in the congregation's invited to the church. Reception will be hosted by the women's group in the church hall. The way I figure it, all I have to do is find a decent dress to wear and show up."

"You definitely have to do that," Gram said. "But . . . you are my maid of honor."

"Yes?"

"Would be real nice if I had a shower. Never had one the first time I was married. And some of the women at the church this morning asked when you were planning to let them know when the shower would be."

Gram was sixty-five years old. She wanted a bridal shower? All the showers I'd attended (I'll admit there hadn't been many) had involved lingerie or kitchenware. Not the sort of things Gram and Tom would need. (Although I wasn't sure I wanted to ask her about the lingerie.)

"I was thinking, a little party, with cupcakes and punch, you know," said Gram. "Nothing fancy. Just a fun afternoon to talk about the wedding."

"What sort of gifts did you have in mind?" I asked. "I shouldn't have to ask you, but several people have wanted to know what to get you and Tom for your wedding. I haven't had many ideas."

Gram, as usual, had it all figured out. "We'd like the beginning of a wine cellar," she said. "Some bottles for special occasions. Tom fancies himself a connoisseur, at least of wines on the low end of the price scale. And I'd like to learn more. If not now, when?"

Wine cellar? My Gram? I swallowed hard. "If you're sure."

"We are," said Gram. "We're starting a new life together. Why not plan some hobbies we can share? Indulge a little."

"The wedding is in two weeks. That means a shower would have to be—"

"Next Saturday," said Gram. "But don't tell me any more. I've never had a surprise party. It's time." She drained her glass of lemonade. "Now let's take a look at those needlepoint pictures. Tomorrow you can deliver them to the needlepointers."

"I'll do that right after I meet with Skye," I said. And find out who she thought had murdered Jasmine. And make a list of people to call about a bridal shower. I had a sneaking feeling that decorations, as well as cupcakes, would be called for.

Sarah, or one of the other needlepointers, might have some ideas.

When did twenty-seven-year-old independent women (that would be me) start giving bridal showers for their grandmothers?

The world was changing, and I was right in the middle of an earthquake.

Chapter 21

Sickness may strip you of
The bloom of the rose
But the beauties of
The mind will endear
Beyond the grave,
My young friend
Prepare to meet
Your God.

—Sampler worked by Susanna (Sukey) Merrill in 1793. She was 14 years old and lived in Newburyport, Massachusetts.

When I arrived at Aurora the next morning, I could hear hammering from the house, but all was quiet at the carriage house end of the property. Patrick opened the door. "Salutations," he said, gesturing that I should enter. The navy blue sweater he was wearing was probably cashmere. My orange T-shirt was cotton.

His jeans fit well, I noted as he headed back to the kitchen.

"Coffee?" he called back to me.

"Please. Black," I answered.

Skye was sorting through papers scattered over the coffee table. "Thank you for coming. That scene with the policeman yesterday was humiliating. I can't believe he thought I tried to poison myself."

I sat down across from her. "There was arsenic in that cup. Even if the police had doubts about what happened in 1970, they should have paid more attention to what happened here Saturday."

She picked up her coffee mug. "Thank you for believing me. For not thinking I'm crazy."

"No one said you were crazy, Mom," said Patrick, handing me a steaming mug and joining us at the table. "I just don't think they expected to connect two events so far apart. That cop had probably never even read the file about Jasmine's death."

"That's possible," Skye acknowledged. "But it doesn't explain why he wouldn't be willing to consider what I said a possibility. Arsenic isn't as easy to get hold of today as it was years ago. Don't you think it was strange not only that my cup was poisoned, but poisoned with the *same thing* that might have killed Jasmine?"

"I do," said Patrick. "But I suspect I know a lot more about the history of this house and Jasmine Gardener's death than that policeman does. Now at least we have Angie to help us investigate. She'll listen," he added confidently.

"I'll do what I can," I said cautiously, "but I can't do it full-time. I have my business to run, and a wedding to prepare for."

"You're getting married?" asked Patrick, glancing at my

naked left hand. Maybe I imagined that he looked a little taken aback. "Congratulations!"

"Not me," I answered his look. "My grandmother, actually."

"Well, good for her," said Skye. "You're never too old for love, I always say."

"You do indeed, Mom," Patrick said with a wry smile.

"My grandmother was here at Aurora, at that party in September 1970," I added.

"She was? How wonderful! Maybe she'll be able to help us put the pieces together," said Skye. "Have you asked her what she remembers? Who she talked to? Who was here? Maybe we met."

"She was newly engaged to my grandfather. She didn't mention talking with anyone else. But I can ask her again," I added, seeing Skye's face drop. "I told her you were here. She knew Jasmine. Not well, but she knew who she was. She didn't remember you."

"I'm not surprised," said Skye. "Not many people will remember me." She paused. "Although a few might. So, for now, please keep what I'm going to tell you to yourself."

This wasn't my first investigation. Everyone had secrets.

"Remember, I wasn't Skye West then," she continued. "I was Mary North. I was here all summer, but I spent most of my time at Aurora. Skye had friends here in town, and they weren't interested in me. She was rich and fun-loving. I was quieter. I stayed at home, reading and writing poetry." Skye grimaced. "I was a bit of a nerd in those days. Jasmine would go out with her friends and then come home and tell me about her adventures—what they'd done, and what they shouldn't have done, and how they'd get in big trouble if anyone found out."

"I see," I said.

"Oh, I went sailing with her sometimes, and to the beach. And I went for long walks by myself. I loved Haven Harbor. Although, of course, it all ended horribly, and I went back to New York. At first, I was surprised Millie—Mrs. Gardener—kept in touch with me. But maybe she felt safe talking with me because I was an outsider. By then, she realized there was a lot about her daughter's life she hadn't known until after Jasmine's death." Skye sighed. "I promised her I'd try to take the pieces of the puzzle she'd found, and what I knew that summer, and put them together. It's taken me years, I know. I was working long hours in different places, and it never seemed the right time. After Millie died, I called a real estate agency here in Haven Harbor and asked about Aurora. I was told it wasn't for sale. Mr. Gardener wanted to leave it as it was. He could never stand to come back to it, but he didn't want anyone other than a Gardener living here. And, of course, I wasn't a Gardener." She looked at Patrick. "Every year or two, I'd check to see if Mr. Gardener was still alive. After he died, I contacted the agency again, but the estate was tied up in trusts. I left word that if the house was ever free for purchase to let me know. About two months ago I got that call. That's how I ended up here."

"Mom's talked about this place as long as I can remember," said Patrick. "We had no idea the Gardeners had let it get so run-down."

"When I first saw Aurora the way it is today, it was so awful. I knew I had to bring it back. Restore it. Make it at least close to the way it was when Jasmine and I were two very different teenagers who somehow balanced each other. The way we were in the summer of 1970. The house should be a memorial to happy times. Not to death."

I needed more details. "You and Jasmine sound very different."

"We were. Her parents donated a wing to the school and sponsored several scholarships. I didn't live on the Upper East Side like Jasmine and most of the other students. I lived in Greenwich Village. The East Village, to be precise. In those days it wasn't a great neighborhood. My mom was an artist, and so were most of her friends. Or . . . that's what they called themselves. They were aspiring artists or writers or musicians or singers or actors. We had a two-room walk-up apartment. Fifth floor, in the back. I never knew exactly who'd be sleeping there when I got home from school every day, but I was sure the place would smell of grass and wine and paint. Not necessarily in that order. On good days someone would buy a pizza or a box of sugary cereal."

"Grandma was a hippie," summarized Patrick.

"True," said Skye. "She loved me, but she had interesting ideas about parenting. Our world was the city. She didn't want me to grow up in what she termed the 'ticky-tacky suburbs.' But she'd get involved with her friends or her painting and forget details, like having food in the refrigerator or paying the electric bill. When the power would go off, I had to ask her friends for donations so I could go to Con Ed and get the lights and stove turned on again." She shook her head. "Mom wasn't embarrassed when that happened. She was proud of me. She called me 'self-reliant,' which was high praise. I was on my own from the time I was old enough to walk to school. And I loved school. It was quiet and I could focus there. And sometimes the lunch I got there was all I ate. When I was in high school I spent a lot of time at the Jefferson Market Library doing my homework. It was too crazy and noisy at home for studying."

"I'm guessing not many students at Miss Pritchard's came from backgrounds like yours. How did you end up there?"

"My sixth-grade teacher was impressed by what she termed my 'self-motivation.' She submitted an application. By some miracle I got it. You're right about my life being different from those of the other students. From the time I was twelve, I took the subway every day to another world. Miss Pritchard's changed my life." She paused. "In so many ways. I'd always wanted to act. But where I lived, that was a common ambition. I joined the drama club at school, and I saw productions—Broadway, as well as the off-Broadway previews, filled with those of us who could get free tickets."

"Did Jasmine want to act, too?"

"No, no. Once I convinced her to try out for a small part in the school's production of Lorca's *The House of Bernarda Alba,* and she kept forgetting her lines. She talked about singing or playing the guitar or acting, but she didn't need to look for a job or a career. She partied instead of focusing on her future."

"I saw the peace posters in her room," I said. "Was she anti–Vietnam War?"

"Of course. By 1970? We all were," said Skye. "College boys weren't being drafted, and most of the young men Jasmine knew in New York weren't as worried about the war as were boys in other places. But she had friends here in Maine who'd been drafted, or were about to leave. She talked and sang a good story about getting out of Vietnam. She believed in the peace movement. But she wasn't a political activist. She was upset about the war because it changed the lives of people she knew."

Jasmine sounded pretty selfish, but she'd been Skye's friend. And it had been a long time ago.

"I suspect one reason I was invited here that summer was because the Gardners thought I'd be a calming influence on Jasmine. We were going to be seniors that fall. I'd already chosen several schools to apply to. Jasmine hadn't even taken her SATs junior year. She'd had a headache that day."

"Would she have gone to college, if she'd lived?"

"Probably. Somewhere. But she might have graduated and she might not have. I sometimes wonder what would have happened to both of us if Jasmine had lived. It's impossible to know."

Skye looked off into a distance only she could see, and then down at the papers on the table. "I've made a list of people I remember our being with that summer. People I know were at that end-of-season party. Some of them were locals—Haven Harbor young people. Some of them still live here. I'll add your grandmother to the list. She might think of other people who were here then, and are still here now. What was her name then?"

"Charlotte Owen. Soon to be Curtis," I said. "I'll ask her if she remembers anyone else. Ob Winslow was there, too, with his parents."

"That's a start," said Jasmine, writing down the two additional names. Then she handed me her pad. "Do you know any of these other people?"

I looked at the list. "I do. I definitely do."

Chapter 22

Now in the opening, spring of life
Let every flowret bloom
The budding virtues in thy breath
Shall yield the best perfume.

—From sampler worked by Charlotte Clubb,
age twelve, Washington City (D.C.), 1813
(Charlotte never married. She died in 1846.)

Skye's list now included Gram and Ob.

Some of the others on her list were interesting. She'd done her homework:

Ruth Hopkins
Linda Zaharee
Elsa Fitch
Jed Fitch
Beth Fitch
Carole Simpson
Sam Gould
Ned and Patsy Fitch

I read the list over again. "I don't know all these people. Ned and Patsy Fitch, for example."

"They were the parents of Elsa and Jed and Beth," Skye said.

"I'm pretty sure they both died a while back." I read the list again.

Skye added, "Sam Gould lived in Camden then, and I checked. He's still there. Took over his father's shipbuilding business."

I made a note. "Ruth Hopkins is still in town. In fact, she's one of the Mainely Needlepointers. Elsa Fitch owns Mane Waves, the hair salon in town."

Skye nodded.

"Elsa's brother and sister are Jed and Beth. Beth Fitch was my second-grade teacher. She's still teaching second grade. You've already talked to Jed. I don't know Carole Simpson."

"She's now Carole Fitch. At least she hoped to be the last I heard of her. She had a real crush on Jed that summer." Skye looked a bit amused. "But Jed was definitely more interested in Jasmine."

"So, which guy did you like then?" said Patrick.

Skye shrugged. "None of them, really. I listened to Jasmine talk about them. Maybe because of all the men in my mother's life, I kept my distance from most boys. From what I'd seen, they didn't stay around long. And most of the boys Jasmine and the other girls at Miss Pritchard's dated weren't interested in a girl from the Lower East Side."

"I thought the sixties and seventies were supposed to be a time of freedom. Love. Acceptance," he said.

"Maybe downtown. Or in San Francisco. But on the Upper East Side people's expectations hadn't changed that much," said Skye. "In any case Jed wasn't interested in me or in Carole. He was interested in Jasmine."

"You said she was also dating this Sam Gould guy from Camden," I said, looking down at the list again.

"Oh, she was. Hot and heavy. But that was in the city. Here in Haven Harbor it was another world. Sam was working for his father and wasn't free to play with Jasmine. Jed was here in town, though. So even though he worked long hours, he was available."

"And both Sam and Jed were here for the party?"

"They were," Skye confirmed.

"Do you mind if I take this list and ask my grandmother about the people on it?" I asked. "See if she remembers seeing or hearing anything else. She waitressed at the yacht club that summer, and says she remembers Jasmine and her friends there."

"That would be a good start," Skye agreed. "I'd like to put together a patchwork picture of what happened at the party that night. Different perspectives. Millie Gardener wrote to me, just before she died, that she'd finally figured out who'd poisoned Jasmine, and that the killer was still in Haven Harbor. If she was right, then we can eliminate anyone who died before then."

"I'll talk to Gram," I promised. "And this afternoon I'm going to see several of the Mainely Needlepointers. I'll ask them."

Could we really solve a forty-five-year-old crime, even if, as Skye believed, the killer was still in Haven Harbor?

I wasn't convinced, although I was willing to give it a try. People who live in small towns often know a lot more about their neighbors than they volunteer to the police. Or to people from away.

Luckily, my family credentials dated back a couple of hundred years.

Folks in town knew me. Maybe knew too much about me. But they also knew Gram, and she was about to marry the minister at the church most of them attended. If they'd talk to anyone, they'd talk to me.

I hoped.

Thinking of which, I remembered I'd better start inviting people to that surprise bridal shower Gram wanted. A wine shower for the minister's intended.

This week was getting more interesting by the hour.

Chapter 23

N *was once a little needle,*
Needly
Tweedly
Threedly
Needly
Wisky—wheedly
Little Needle!

—Edward Lear (1812–1888), British artist and author known for his nonsensical poems, *Alphabet of Nonsense,* 1871

I might know most of the residents of Haven Harbor, and they might know me (at least by reputation or relation), but I didn't have close friends in town. My best friend from Haven Harbor High, Clem Walker, now worked for a TV station in Portland. We texted and talked sometimes, but our current lives were very different. Clem had pulled Cindy Titicomb (now Bowers) into several lunch dates we'd managed to have, but Cindy lived in Blue Hill now.

She was married with three young children; she'd moved on, although her parents were still in Haven Harbor. Her mom, Katie, was a needlepointer.

I could usually confide in Gram, but in light of her forthcoming nuptials, I didn't think this was the right time. And right now, early on a Monday afternoon, I wanted to talk to someone not connected to the Gardener family.

Sarah was a new friend, but she and I had been working so closely together in the past couple of weeks that I felt comfortable texting her: Lunch? Now?

Her answer came back almost immediately: The Gardeners addicted me to lobster rolls. The co-op?

I'd spent long summer hours at the Lobsterman's Co-op when I was a teenager. Some young people worked the take-out counter or fried clams or chicken, or they put together peanut-butter-and-jelly sandwiches for desperate parents of kids who refused both seafood and chicken. I'd always ended up working long, sweaty hours on my feet at the steamer. I steamed lobsters. Bagged and steamed clams and mussels. Shucked and steamed corn.

Clem had worked at Harbor Lights Gift Shop, where she'd worn a skirt and blouse every day. She'd even managed to keep her nails manicured. I'd pinned my hair back and pulled on jeans and a long-sleeved T-shirt, no matter the temperature. The first day of the first summer I worked at the co-op, I learned burns from steam or dripping seafood direct from the steamer were more painful than the sunburn I got from working outside every day.

I suspected Sarah, who'd spent her teen years in Australia, had no idea what a place like the co-op meant to me.

I texted her: See you there.

The place had improved in one way since I'd worked there: They now had a bar, which served wine (from boxes) and bottled beer. A lobster roll and a Samuel Adams

Summer Ale sounded good. And maybe Sarah would have some ideas about the bridal shower.

I pulled my car into the lot on Water Street. Sarah was walking down the hill from her shop.

"Good timing!" I called to her.

"I was about ready to forage for lunch," she answered, catching up to me. "With the hours we've kept for the past two weeks, I never made it to the grocery store. I was about ready to share the cat's food. So glad to get your text! 'Undue Significance a starving man attaches To Food—.'"

"Not sure I'll have a lobster roll," I said, sniffing the air on the pier and immediately going back to summers when my clothes and I had smelled like lobster 24/7. I glanced at the board listing the day's choices and prices. "A crab roll. Want to share a bloomin' onion?"

"I'm definitely having the lobster roll, on a toasted roll with butter. But, sure, I'll share the onion. Do you believe I'd never heard of such a thing before I got to the U.S.? I think Outback Steakhouse invented them."

"Really?" I said as we lined up to give our orders. "They're a staple of lobster piers in Maine. A lot better than the limp fries some places serve."

"Which didn't originate in France," Sarah said, nodding. "I love the States! They encompass the world. Are you having beer or wine?"

"If you order my crab roll and the onion, I'll stand in line at the bar for both of us. What do you want?"

"Glass of white. They don't give you much of a choice here."

"True." I nodded. "I'll get our drinks and save us a table."

The tables were picnic style, equipped with large trash cans every two or three tables, umbrellas which kept the sun off at some times of day, and a large sign: BEWARE! GULLS ARE THIEVES! DON'T LEAVE FOOD UNATTENDED!

The sign looked identical to the one that had been here years ago. Greedy gulls didn't change. Every year tourists took pictures of the sign and laughed. Then they complained when their clams or lobster or fries disappeared while they were getting a second beer or visiting the men's room.

Gulls living close to outdoor restaurants tended to be well fed. I took a deep sip of my beer. Eating here was part of Haven Harbor I hadn't revisited before now. I wasn't as uncomfortable as I'd thought I'd be.

Sarah slid onto the bench opposite me. "We're number seventy-nine." She raised her plastic wineglass in my direction. "To us! To surviving two weeks of total chaos and dirt and emerging with checkbooks comfortably bulging."

I'd have to tell Sarah. I didn't want her thinking I was hiding anything. "I was back at Aurora yesterday. And again this morning."

"Whatever for?" asked Sarah.

"That poor hummingbird that died Saturday? Turns out there was arsenic in Skye's cup. Pete Lambert went to talk with her yesterday. Skye wanted me there because of my investigation experience in Arizona."

"I don't get it. She wanted you there as a witness? A voyeur?"

I shrugged. "Pete's somehow convinced Skye poisoned her own cup to show that she's in danger from the person who killed Jasmine. I think he's crazy, but I'm not sure what actually happened. Skye thinks Jasmine Gardener's killer is still here in town."

"She's not buying the drunk-and-drowned story?" Sarah asked.

"Nope. Mrs. Gardener believed Jasmine died of arsenic poisoning. Turns out Skye was a friend of Jasmine's."

"She never said that last week."

"No. She just told me yesterday."

Sarah took a deep drink of her wine. "What did Pete say?"

I decided to simplify the story. After all, I'd told Skye I'd keep it quiet. And I'd already told Gram that Skye West was really Mary North. I hated not telling Sarah the details, but this was an investigation. "Pete didn't buy it. So Skye asked me to help her find Jasmine's killer."

"You?"

"Sometime I must have told her or Patrick I'd worked for a private investigator. And she feels that since I grew up here, people will be more likely to talk with me than they would with her."

"She's right about that. I don't hear half the gossip you do. I open my mouth and people close theirs."

"Number seventy-nine!" blared the loudspeaker.

"Luckily," Sarah said, "the locals have no trouble taking my orders. Or my money!" She headed toward the pickup window to retrieve our lunches.

"So I assume you agreed to help her?" Sarah said a few minutes later, handing me my crab roll and putting the onion on the table between us.

"I did," I said, breaking off a piece of onion and dipping it into the cup of horseradish dressing. "I said I'd talk to some of the people I knew. I'm not very optimistic about the whole thing. But she's been so generous to us, I felt a bit obligated."

"Jasmine died in 1970, right?"

"Right. Year of hippies and 'Make Love, Not War' and long hair and miniskirts."

Sarah shook her head. "Good luck even finding anyone who was at that party, much less getting them to talk with you."

"Gram was there. And according to Skye, Ruth Hopkins was, too. And Elsa Fitch, over at Mane Waves."

Sarah took another bite of her lobster roll. "Okay, so some people may remember. I'm glad Skye didn't ask me to be involved. I'm glad to be back in my shop. Ruth was a big help, but I have tons of accounting to do. And dusting. You can't imagine what two weeks of no dusting can do to a shop, and with Ruth using her walker, I couldn't ask her to clean."

"Can I ask you a favor about something else, though?"

"You can ask," said Sarah. "No guarantees, though. My work is really backed up."

"Gram announced this morning that she'd like—rather she expects—a bridal shower."

Sarah looked at me and giggled. "Charlotte said that?"

"She did. I assure you."

"What does she think two totally adult people need? Or is she expecting sexy lingerie?"

That had been my exact thought. But now this was too serious and close to home to kid about. "She wants a wine shower. Seems she and Tom have always wanted a wine cellar. My job is to make that happen."

"Why do I sense you're not thrilled?"

"Because we have only two weeks until the wedding. Which means the shower would have to be next Saturday. And I'm not an expert on flowery, romantic bridal showers."

"Okay," said Sarah. "This can be done. Since they're not exactly blushing teenagers, why not make it a bride-and-groom shower? Call Tom and ask him about it. If he agrees, you're golden. Then get a list of all his parishioners. The church secretary probably has e-mail addresses and can send everyone an invite."

"To a wine shower?"

Sarah shrugged. "If that's what they want. You could have it at your house, or, better yet, why not in that community room at the church?"

The room we'd gathered in a little over a month before for Mama's funeral reception. But Sarah was right. That space would work.

"I'll bet the women's organization at the church would love to get involved. There's always someone in groups like that who likes to hang crepe paper and umbrellas."

"'Umbrellas'?"

"It's a shower . . . see?" Sarah smiled. "You may even be able to get some of the women to bring cupcakes or cookies. Or you can order trays of goodies at the French bakery. Their pastries are fantastic. Wicked good, as a Mainer would say."

"You make it sound easy," I grumbled. "It sounds like a pain to me."

"Hosting a shower is one of the most important responsibilities of the maid of honor," Sarah said seriously. "At least it is in Australia. Isn't it here, too?"

"So I've found out. And I still have to find a dress for the wedding."

"You're on your own for that. But I'll bring cupcakes, if you'd like."

"Thank you. I accept. And I need to ask you, too, if you could find time to repair two of Skye's needlepoint pictures. Gram's killed the mildew, but missing threads need to be replaced."

"I can do that," Sarah agreed. "Not today or tomorrow, but later this week. I can work on them while I'm tending shop. It's still early enough in the season so I'm not busy every minute."

"Great! I have the panels in my car," I said. "Gram chose the ones of Second Sister Island and the moose in the field for you."

"No problem," said Sarah, finishing her wine and nibbling a last piece of onion. "I'll do what I can with the shower and the needlepoint. But the murder investigation? The arsenic poisoning? You're on your own there."

"I know," I said. "You don't have to remind me."

Chapter 24

From the manner in which a woman draws her thread at every stitch of her needlework, any other woman can surmise her thoughts.

—Attributed to Honoré de Balzac (1799–1850)

After delivering the first two needlepoint panels to Sarah, I hesitated. *What priority is next?*

I sat in my car and dialed the church office. Not surprisingly, no one answered. Probably the secretary was having lunch. Instead of leaving a message, I dialed Tom directly. I hoped Gram wasn't with him.

"Reverend McCully," he answered on the first ring.

"Hi, Tom, it's me, Angie. Is Gram there?"

"Hi! No, she said she had some chores to take care of. I suspect she was planning to do some gardening this afternoon. Beautiful day, isn't it?"

"It is. And I need to ask a favor of you."

"Ask!"

"This morning Gram told me she'd love to have a wedding

shower. You know—gifts and cupcakes and rejoicing, held sometime in the next couple of weeks before the ceremony."

"I'm familiar with the ritual." I could hear Tom smiling. "So you want me to keep her away from your house while you set up the event?"

"Not exactly. To begin with, she said you two had been thinking of creating a wine cellar of some sort. She wanted the shower to be gifts of wine."

"She said that?"

"She did," I said. "So I wondered whether you'd like to be there, too, since the gifts would be for both of you to share. We could make it a couple's shower."

"I suppose so," Tom said, hesitating. "It's very sweet of her to think of that. A wine cellar's always been one of my dreams, but on a minister's salary . . . "

"And would you mind if I contacted your secretary and got e-mails for the congregation so I could invite people? And perhaps held the party at the church?"

A long pause. "You could talk with Susan about addresses," he said. "But I don't think the church is the proper place for such an event. I suppose you could have it here, at the rectory. Charlotte might not expect that."

"Wonderful! How about next Saturday afternoon?"

Another pause. "My calendar is empty then. I'd planned to do some shopping . . . but you've given me an idea. Yes, Saturday afternoon would be fine. And I assume this is a secret from Charlotte?"

"I hope so. Although she said she'd like a shower, I didn't commit to anything."

"Good! Let me know what time would be best, and I'll make sure she and I are here whenever you say."

"Thank you, Tom!" I said, relieved.

"Not a problem," he answered. "And you just solved one I had. I hadn't decided what to give Charlotte for a wedding gift. Now I know. And, by the way, have you gotten a dress for the ceremony yet? Your grandmother's a bit concerned you'll show up in shorts and an ASU T-shirt."

"I'm working on that," I lied. Well, it wasn't a total lie. I was thinking about it. But when would I find time to go shopping? Elegant attire could be found in Maine, but not in Haven Harbor's outdoor apparel or gift shops. "I'll let you know about the time for next Saturday."

I put the phone down. It would work. Somehow it would all work.

When Gram had convinced me to stay in Haven Harbor and make it my home again, I'd agreed to six months. Naively, I'd assumed it would be a relaxing period. I'd be home. I'd have my old bedroom to sleep in, and Gram to make my favorite maple bread pudding when I was feeling down.

Instead, I'd found myself the director of Mainely Needlepoint and the granddaughter of an excited bride.

Not exactly what I'd planned for.

Plus, although I had no interest in following Gram to the altar, at least in the near future, I'd always enjoyed a fairly active social life. Or, perhaps more correctly, a sex life.

At every corner in Haven Harbor, there were memories of what I shouldn't have done as a teenager, and what my unwed mother had done before me, all conspiring to keep me on the straight and narrow now. But, truthfully, I hadn't exactly been turning down offers from eligible—or even ineligible—men here.

Ethan Trask, my girlhood crush, was married to a woman serving in Afghanistan and had a young daughter. Pete Lambert? Single, yes, but I suspected he had something going on with the clerk at the police department. She could have him. No chemistry there. Patrick West? Now, he might have been a possibility, but Sarah had called dibs. These days I needed a friend even more than I needed a sex life.

I looked down at my "to do" list for today. Dave Percy was next.

Now . . . Dave Percy? He was single. Straight, so far as I knew. A needlepointer, which was why I was going to head in his direction. Ex-navy. Now taught biology at the high school. Despite his hobby of growing poison plants, he was more conventional than most of the men in my "earlier lives," which was how I was beginning to think of my life in Maine as a teenager (first stage) and then my life in Arizona (second stage).

Dave Percy. Who knew? He'd always seemed nice enough, and he'd backed me up at one very tense moment in the past month. A possibility? At this point my options were like a net in the Dead Sea. Wide-open, but no fish in sight.

I turned the car key. I had work to do.

Chapter 25

With my needle and my thread,
Which now appears so neat,
Before I was quite nine years old,
I did this work complete.
It still will show when I am old
Or laid into the tomb,
How I employed my little hands,
While I was in my bloom.

—Sampler worked by Martha Jane Reynolds, age eight, Homer, Ohio, 1819

Dave Percy was a few inches taller than I was—maybe five-ten—and his ten years in the navy working on submarines had left him with a passion for neatness and cleanliness that even Gram's coon cat couldn't surpass. No, he didn't groom himself constantly, as Juno did, but I'd never seen a trace of dust in Dave's house, or a dirty dish in his sink. And although he gardened in gloves because of his poison plants, I'd never seen a weed brazen enough to pop up there.

Not surprisingly, he lived in an immaculate yellow Cape surrounded by a white picket fence. Although I'd always felt comfortable with Dave, I suspect he would have been horrified to know that I sometimes wore the same pair of jeans two days in a row. Some nights I even hit my pillow before brushing my teeth.

He answered my knock almost immediately. "Angie! Good to see you. I've been so tied up grading exams and submitting final grades I haven't had a chance to keep in touch with anyone in the past couple of weeks. Come on in!"

I eyed the stack of papers he was carrying. "Is there hope? Will you get all that done in time?" He put the papers on a table and offered me a glass of iced coffee before I had a chance to say anything else.

"Of course. I just have to isolate myself until I've put my red pencil down and handed in my class rosters. We only have half days of school this week, so I'll have the afternoons to work. By tomorrow morning paperwork will be done. Wednesday is the last day of classes."

"And then you're free for the summer."

"Free of school, in any case. But I see you have a package in hand. A new needlepoint assignment?"

"It is," I said. "A little different from our usual customer orders." I started to unwrap the two needlepoint pictures Gram and I had decided would be best for Dave. Then I stopped. "You were at the house sale Saturday, so you know Skye West bought the old Gardener place, out near Ob Winslow's house."

"Couldn't miss an event like that! I noticed you and Sarah were pretty busy that day."

"We've been out there for the past week. We organized the sale for Skye."

He looked at me quizzically. "A new sideline for Mainely Needlepoint?"

"Sarah was hired to appraise and price what was in the house, and she took me along," I explained. I didn't mention how much we'd been paid, or that Sarah would probably have done it for nothing to get to know Patrick better.

"I'm new enough to town that I hadn't heard anything about that place before. I'd just seen it standing there, sadly decaying. My students filled me in on all the gory details. Did you see any of the ghosts reputed to live there when you were sorting through things?"

I liked his smile. "Not a one," I assured him. "But it is sad that Jasmine Gardener died there."

"And her mother was either crazy or a witch," Dave added.

"What?"

"According to certain of my more romantic-minded students, you understand," he continued, "she never left the house, and had three black cats."

"Interesting! She did stay there alone for years after Jasmine died, but she left the house at least occasionally until she was ill, at the end. The black cats? That's a wrinkle I hadn't heard until now. I suppose she could have had a cat to keep her company. But I didn't see any broomsticks around that might have been used for transportation."

"Ah, so the exciting story loses interest when confused with reality," he said. "But what has that to do with why you're here?"

"Mrs. Gardener may not have been a witch, but she was a needlepointer." I unwrapped the package I'd brought with me. "A lot of her work couldn't be saved, although some people bought it, anyway, on Saturday."

"Me among them." Dave smiled. "Prices were pretty low. I figured I'd try to repair one of her table runners."

"Good luck! But here's another opportunity for you. Her best work was ten scenes of Aurora—that's the name of the estate—and Haven Harbor." I held up one of them. "Skye West would like us to restore all ten panels for her. Gram's managed to kill the mildew, but torn or missing threads need to be removed or stitched over, depending on their condition. I've divided the work up, and hoped you'd be able to do these two."

Dave sat down next to me on the couch and looked at the panels we'd chosen for him: the one of the fountain, and one of Haven Harbor itself, from the lighthouse to the yacht club on the other side of the harbor. That one was elaborate, with boats in the water and even a few tiny people on the wharves.

Dave examined both carefully. "She was good with a needle. No doubt. But I can handle this if we have yarn that matches or is close in color."

I showed him what else was in the package. "Sarah and I tried to find remnants of the threads she used in the pictures in her stash of needlepoint materials. We didn't always succeed, but what we found is in here, along with some other floss and yarn Gram thought you might be able to blend in."

"This looks like fun," he said. "A good start for summer vacation. I don't think it'll take me too long, since I'll have days free of anything but gardening and enjoying the warmth of summer in Maine."

"Good!" I said. "Then I'll leave all of this with you." I got up to go before I remembered. "Oh, and you're coming to Gram's wedding in two weeks, right?"

"Wouldn't miss it," he assured me.

"Well, I'm having a shower for her and Tom on Saturday.

It's a surprise. Tom knows about it, though, and it'll be at the rectory in the afternoon. I'll let you know what time when I know for sure."

"A shower for both of them? Very modern." He nodded. "Sounds like fun."

"It's a wine shower. Something else to imbibe would be okay, too, but they want to start a wine cellar."

"Great idea! I was planning a trip to the Cellar Door Winery sometime soon, anyway. I'll move that trip up on my schedule. They're doing some wonderful work there. Whoever thought there would be wineries in Maine?"

"And now we have at least a half-dozen," I agreed. "Local wines, as well as those from California or France."

"Or Italy, South Africa, Australia, or—"

"Okay!" I laughed. "So there'll be lots of choices. I'll let you know about the time of the shower. See you then, if not before."

"Looking forward," said Dave, showing me to the door. "I'm hoping to see you often this summer."

I glanced at him. *Is that an invitation?*

"Especially if you bring me interesting needlepoint projects like the one today."

Well, not necessarily an invitation, but maybe an invitation to friendship? I could do with a few more friends, of either sex. "For sure, I'll see you Saturday, then." I waved as I headed to my next stop.

Chapter 26

Dame Wiggins of Lee was a worthy old soul
As e'er threaded a needle or washed in a bowl;
She held mice and rats in such antipathy,
That seven fine cats kept Dame Wiggins of Lee.

—Anonymous, Nursery rhyme, 1823, said to have been written by a 90-year-old woman

Katie Titicomb didn't answer her door, but I knew she had a garden. I followed the brick path around her house into her backyard. As I suspected, Katie was there, kneeling on a gardening pad in the dirt, setting out tomato plants. She wore gardening gloves and a large straw hat, and, other than her face, her pale skin was covered from head to toe.

"Katie?" I said softly so as not to startle her.

"Yes?" She looked up. "Angie! It's you. I couldn't imagine who'd be calling on such a beautiful afternoon." She got up slowly, testing her knees as she stood. "I'm glad you're here. I'm ready for a break. I love gardening best in January and February, when I'm reading the Burpee and White Flower

Farm catalogs and planning for summer. Now that it's actually time to plant, my body rebels."

"Gram's at home, planting her tomatoes, too."

"And she won't even be living there in two weeks. Goodness, it's hard to believe her wedding is that soon."

"I'm planning a shower for her and Reverend Tom next Saturday afternoon at the rectory. Tom knows, but it'll be a surprise for her, I hope."

"Fun! I haven't been to a bridal shower since Cindy got married," said Katie. "You weren't here for that, were you?"

I shook my head. Katie's daughter, Cindy, had married while I was in Arizona.

"It was a lovely occasion. Balloons and umbrellas and lace baskets, and so many gifts! And a cake, of course, and pink punch."

Thanks to Sarah, at least I now knew about umbrellas. Somehow I didn't mourn missing Cindy's big day. "The shower's going to be for both Gram and Tom, and it'll be focused on wine. Turns out they've always dreamed of having a wine cellar."

"What a wonderful idea!" said Katie. "Can I help? I love showers."

"Could you help me decorate? I'm afraid I'm not a shower maven. But I do want it to be fun for Gram and Tom."

"I'd love to help! What's your color scheme?"

Color scheme? "Gram's wedding dress is pale blue. Pale blue and white?"

"That sounds elegant. Silk ribbons for Charlotte—she's too old for crepe paper. I'm going to Portland to do some errands tomorrow. Would you like me to pick up some decorations? Sophisticated ones. And nothing extravagant."

"I would love that," I said with relief. "I've never

planned a party like this. It sounds as though you know what to do."

Katie came over and patted me on the arm. "Don't you worry a bit about it, then. I'll take care of the theme and decorations. You just figure out the refreshments."

Food. Cake? Cupcakes? Or something a little more substantial? Cheeses. Breads. Crackers. And it was a wine shower. There should be wine. I certainly would want a glass. "I can handle refreshments," I assured her. *With Sarah's help,* I added silently to myself. Detective work I could handle. I was out of my depth at planning a bridal shower.

"So? Anything else happening?"

"Yes, actually. You've heard Skye West bought the old Gardener estate, Aurora."

Katie nodded.

"She's asked Mainely Needlepoint to preserve and repair ten needlework panels that Mrs. Gardener made. We're going to line and reframe them, but before then, they need some repair work. Would you have time to work on two of them?"

"Only two?"

"Several only need cleaning, and we're dividing the others among you and Sarah and Dave. That way we can get them all framed and back to Ms. West as soon as possible."

Katie agreed. "I have time. I finished three more lighthouse pillows for Harbor Lights last week, and I've practically finished the headboard Nautical Decorators in South Portland asked for. I'll be glad to finish that one up. I've been working on it, off and on, since February."

"I'll let them know they'll have it soon," I said, nodding. "Shall I get you the two panels for Skye West? They're in my car."

"Thank you. That'll be fine."

I turned to go, when she called out, "What do the panels picture?"

"The Congregational Church," I called. "And fireworks."

By the time I got back, Katie's hands were clean and she was sitting on a dark green lawn chair. I handed her the package containing the panels.

"The fireworks," she said, looking at that one. "They're the ones they used to have at Aurora."

Fireworks were fireworks to me. "How can you tell?"

"See how they're high in the sky, and gold?"

I looked.

"And over in this corner are three pine trees, and a lone pine on the other side is silhouetted against the sky."

"Yes."

"Every year the Gardeners ended their fireworks display at the end of their big Labor Day party with a fantastic group of explosions at once, almost all of them gold. It had something to do with the name of their house, Aurora. And if you sat on the back hill, looking out at the harbor where the fireworks were, you would see those pine trees, exactly as they are in the needlepoint."

"You went to their parties, then."

"Every year. My mother didn't like the crowds, but I'd beg, and my father would always take me."

"Were you at the last party?"

"The night Jasmine Gardener died? Oh, yes. I was only eleven, you understand. What I remember most is, despite what my father warned me about, I ate too many hot dogs and cotton candy and felt horribly sick. It was right before the fireworks started. I didn't know what to do. My father was talking to some friends. He'd told me to stay on the old green army blanket we'd brought to sit on during the fireworks. But I felt so awful. I ran to the corner of the field, away from everyone else, and threw up, right there, outside." Katie paused. "I was so embarrassed. I thought everyone would know. But the only one who saw me was Jasmine. She took me inside the big house with her and washed my face and then sent me back to my father." Katie smiled sadly. "She was so kind. And she looked so beautiful in her bright yellow-and-orange jumpsuit. They were all the style then, you know. It happened so suddenly. My father didn't even know I'd been away. Later, when we were walking to our car, we heard about Jasmine. We thought she was just sick. We moved aside so the ambulance could get to her." Katie sighed. "The next day we heard she'd died. I begged to go to her funeral. Lots of people in town were going. But my father said I didn't even know her, and I was too young to start going to funerals. But I did know her. I must have been one of the last people to see Jasmine Gardener before she died."

Chapter 27

My life at best is but a span;
Few are the days allowed to man
To number here in pain.
Each moment clips the little space,
Contracts the span, cuts short the race
And winds the mortal chain.

—Sampler worked by Sarah Hupman, age eighteen, Mad River Township, Ohio, 1846 (Sarah never married and lived to be eighty-four.)

Katie Titicomb—she'd been on Skye's list of people who'd been at the Gardeners' last party. And she'd definitely seen Jasmine.

"Did Jasmine seem drunk to you that evening?" I had to ask. The answer to that question seemed key to understanding what happened that night of September 5.

Katie shrugged. "I was young. Only six years younger than Jasmine, though. I was focused on being sick . . .

and embarrassed. If she'd had a couple of drinks, I didn't realize it. She certainly seemed in control. She realized what had happened to me, she took charge, and she helped me. If she'd been drinking heavily, which a lot of the young people were doing, then I doubt she'd have been able to do all that."

"That makes sense." Katie had only been eleven. She might not have noticed. But when I was younger than that, I'd known when someone had drunk too much. I'd seen and smelled my mother after a late night, and I'd watched from my bedroom window as a few of her "gentlemen friends" stumbled from our door at odd hours. Eleven-year-olds were young, but they weren't oblivious.

I thanked Katie for sharing her story and, needlepoint panels delivered, decided to stop and visit Ruth Hopkins. She was probably tired from her two weeks of tending Sarah's shop. In the past year she'd started using a walker instead of a cane, afraid her knees or hips would give out and she'd fall.

Ruth's house was in the shadow of the church steeple.

I gave her plenty of time to answer her door.

"Angie! I didn't expect company this afternoon," she said when she finally saw me. "Come in! Come in!"

Ruth's living room was arranged so she could easily maneuver her walker to the chair with the highest seat, where she was most comfortable. "I have some lemonade in the refrigerator. If you'd like a glass, feel free to go in and pour yourself some. I'm a bit weary today, so I'm giving myself a day off."

"No, thank you. I'm not thirsty. And you deserve more than one day off! It was kind of you to help Sarah and me out for the past two weeks."

"I'm glad Sarah called. Shopkeeping for her was fun. I've gotten used to staying at home by myself, between the

'Arthur Itis,' as my aunt used to call it, and my writing. I should force myself out more often. I liked talking with the customers. I even managed to make a few sales."

"Which she was very pleased about. I'm sure she's told you."

"She has. And she even insisted on paying me for my time. At first, I wouldn't accept anything, but then I decided I would. I did lose writing time, and she would have lost sales if I hadn't been there. Plus, I missed three afternoon Red Sox games. That requires compensation," Ruth deadpanned.

"You're absolutely right," I said. Two weeks out of Ruth's schedule was a good chunk of time. "Have you a manuscript deadline soon?"

"Only one I set myself," she answered. "I'm doing my books digitally now. Saves the hassle of dealing with an agent and editor. After publishing for forty years, I know what I'm doing. Plus, a lot of my readers don't want the evidence of what they're reading to be sitting on their coffee tables. They love e-readers."

I was one of the few in Haven Harbor who knew seventy-nine-year-old Ruth wrote erotica. It wasn't something she advertised widely, except to her fans online. "I haven't downloaded one of your books yet. But I plan to do that. Soon. After Gram's wedding. Also, her wedding is one reason I'm here." I explained about the shower, and Ruth accepted her invitation quickly.

"That should be fun. And the rectory is close enough so I can walk there, unless we have a heavy storm that day."

"You know," I said, changing the subject, "Sarah and I spent the past week at the old Gardener house. People there talked about Jasmine Gardener's death. I understand you were there, at the final party they had, back in 1970."

"I was. Ben, my husband, and I were there together. It's

strange that some events in your life are forgotten, and others assume much more importance in memory."

"And that's one you remember?"

"Oh, yes. Because of Jasmine's death, of course, and because that was the last Gardener party. But also because Ben and I had been married about ten years by then. They weren't easy years. At first, we had so many plans. We wanted children, a house. I wanted to write . . . and Ben wanted to support me. He didn't want me to work. But life didn't work out that way. He was one of the first drafted and sent to Vietnam. Instead of starting our life together, I lived with my parents here in Haven Harbor. And then Ben was injured. Badly. He lost a leg, and we lost the possibility of ever having children together. I went out to Texas to stay with him while he recuperated."

"That must have been horrible."

"It was hard on both of us, for sure. I'd started writing and publishing while he was away, and he wasn't happy about that. But we needed the money. And we weren't sure he could get a decent job with his disability. In those days they didn't have the wonderful prostheses they have today. He'd always been an outdoor sort . . . fishing and camping and hiking." Ruth looked off into the distance, remembering. "It was a hard time. But we came back to Maine, and because of my writing, we were able to buy this little house in the summer of 1970. Our life was beginning to work out. I remember our going to the Gardeners' party, drinking wine, eating lobsters and corn, and laughing a lot." She paused. "That night was one of the best times we'd had in a long time."

"Do you remember seeing Jasmine there?"

"Oh, yes. When we arrived, she was greeting people, with her parents. Later on, I saw her handing out balloons to the children. She was laughing and joking with them. Everyone loved Jasmine."

"Was she drinking?"

"Heavens, Angie, don't look so moral. Everyone was drinking! She was at her own home. We were all outside, in a beautiful place, with people we knew and cared about. No one seemed to mind."

"Did you see Jasmine with anyone in particular?"

"She was with several people I didn't know. I assumed they were from outside Haven Harbor. And with young people from the yacht club. Someone told me Jasmine and Jed Fitch had been dating that summer." She shook her head. "If she hadn't died, I wouldn't have remembered. Truthfully, I didn't pay much attention. I was focused on Ben and on our life, finally together and independent of hospitals and parents and wars. I remember making sure we didn't sit near where a lot of parents had small children. I was still dealing with the loss of the child I'd dreamed of having."

Nothing Ruth said clarified what happened that night, or what happened to Jasmine. But I'd learned a lot more about Ruth. What would it have been like for so many of your dreams to be destroyed by a war that half of America didn't believe in? I couldn't imagine.

My phone sounded. I glanced down at the text. It was Sarah Byrne: Call me ASAP re: needlepoint panel.

"I'm tired. You go and answer your call," said Ruth. "I can't remember any more. I think I'll lie down for a bit."

"Can I help you with anything?" I asked. "Get you something?"

"I'm fine, dear. Thinking about the past sometimes wears me out more than living in the present. One of the many frustrating parts of old age, I'm afraid."

I smiled. "You know I'd be happy to help you anytime. Groceries, mail, drive you somewhere. Just let me know."

"Oh, heavens, dear, I'm not that feeble yet. One reason I want to lie down now is so I'll have plenty of energy to watch the Red Sox tonight. Can't miss a Red Sox–Yankee game, can I?"

"I'll be in touch," I said, getting up. "Enjoy the game. And thank you for sharing your memories."

"Nice to know there's anyone still interested in them," said Ruth. "I'll see you at Charlotte and Tom's shower on Saturday. I'll be the one with bells on!"

I smiled as I headed back to my car. Ruth was more than ten years older than Gram, but she was still working and taking care of herself. I hoped Gram would be able to do the same.

When she was my age, Ruth had been married to someone who'd been badly injured. Her life had changed, and she'd adapted. Would I have been as strong? I hoped so. But I wasn't sure. So far, I hadn't even had enough faith in myself or anyone else to make a lifetime commitment to another person. Would I ever feel that strongly about someone?

Before I thought about sharing my life with someone else, I had to figure out who I was and what I wanted. Then, if my life changed, the way Ruth's had, I'd have to rethink everything. That was a task I wasn't ready for. Not yet.

In the meantime I dialed Sarah's number. What could be so urgent about the needlework I'd dropped off with her a couple of hours ago?

Chapter 28

A fair little girl sat under a tree,
Sewing as long as her eyes could see;
Then smoothed her work, and folded it right,
And said, "Dear work, good night! Good night!"

—Richard Monckton Milnes, Lord Houghton (1809–1885), "Good Night and Good Morning," 1859

"Sarah? What's the problem with the needlepoint?"

"Has anyone else looked at the panels? Looked closely?"

"Gram cleaned them and left them in the sun to kill the mildew. She and I looked at them. I left panels today with you and Dave and Katie. That's it. Is there a problem?"

"I don't know. Probably not. Just something curious."

"Curious?"

"After I got home, I decided to take a good look at the panels you gave me. To check colors and flosses—those you gave me and any I might have—because once I take something to the shop to work on, I don't like to leave. Even if I do just live upstairs."

"Yes?" I was getting a little impatient.

"I had the panel over by the window, to get the best light. And I found something strange."

"What?"

"Along with the embroidery floss Mrs. Gardener used, she stitched in strands of hair. Not a lot, you understand. But once in a while, I could see one. I got a magnifying glass out to check."

"Hair? Are you sure?"

"Pretty sure. I'm not an expert on hair. But it definitely isn't silk floss, or yarn, like the rest of the panel."

"Mrs. Gardener was getting older. Maybe her hair was thinning and a few pieces fell out. Maybe she didn't notice and stitched them into the pattern along with the floss."

"That's a lot of 'maybes.' And I found more than one or two pieces of hair."

I sat back in the car. "You're right. That's weird. I can't imagine why anyone would stitch hair into needlepoint intentionally."

"They did in the nineteenth century," said Sarah. "Not needlepoint exactly, but people, usually women, collected hair from those they loved, especially ones who'd died. They wove the strands into flowers and swirls and made them into jewelry or wreaths."

"Sounds creepy," I said.

"Here in America, weaving with hair was especially popular during the Civil War and after, during the Victorian period. Both men and women wore mourning jewelry made of, or holding, hair of deceased loved ones. The wreaths some women made were incredibly elaborate. They often included hair from many friends and family members so they could work with different colors."

"Interesting. But I'm not sure how that's relevant to the needlepoint."

"Maybe Mrs. Gardener took some of her daughter's hair and wove it into the pictures."

"I suppose that's possible," I said. "It would mean she planned those pictures before Jasmine was buried, though. I thought she'd made them years afterward."

"But we don't really know, right?" said Sarah.

"Right," I agreed. "It would be cool if Jasmine's hair was in the panels. We could check DNA to find out if it was hers."

"So we need to find someone who could test for DNA," Sarah said excitedly.

"Even if we could get someone to agree to do a DNA test, we'd need to have something of Jasmine's, or at least of her mother's, to compare it with. We threw out almost everything at Aurora. We didn't exactly leave a toothbrush to be tested for DNA."

"You're right." Sarah's voice went down.

"Why don't you work on the other panel first," I said. "Let me think about this a little longer. Maybe there's some way to get a DNA sample." *It doesn't seem likely,* I thought as I headed for home. Plus, police labs took weeks to analyze DNA. They wouldn't do it out of curiosity. Finding hair in the needlepoint was interesting. But I didn't see how it would help figure out how Jasmine Gardener died. Or who killed her.

And that was what Skye and Patrick and I were trying to do.

Chapter 29

Beautiful fireboards [boards covering the opening to fireplaces in warm months] can be made of silk, linen, or any of the woollen goods which come for decorative purposes, and embroidered in silk and crewels. Of embroidery it should be urged that for effectiveness it is necessary to adhere to one kind of stitch, as well as to insist on tones in choosing color, rather than contrasts.

—Laura C. Holloway, *The Hearthstone; or, Life at Home: A Household Manual,* L.P. Miller & Co., 1888

Somehow I managed to get my laundry done, talked with Gram without revealing anything about the proposed shower, and still got to bed before midnight.

My mind was still turning circles. But my body was exhausted.

By dawn I'd decided what to do next. First I called Sarah; then I called Dave Percy.

Admittedly, Sarah looked at me a bit strangely when I arrived to collect a couple of the hairs she'd promised to pull out of the needlepoint. But she handed me an envelope. "Be sure to let me know what you find out," she said. "I have a feeling about these hairs."

Then I turned my car toward Dave's house. He'd said classes were on a short schedule. But when would he have to be at school?

He was waiting at his door. "Come in! Come in!"

I handed him the envelope and followed him to his study. I'd never been in that room before. Papers were neatly stacked on top of an old oak office desk. Bookshelves were full of books on everything from protozoa to echinoderms, from birds and fish to humans, and, of course, poison plants. A human skeleton I hoped was a fake hung over the door.

Dave went straight to a metal table in the corner equipped with a microscope, test tubes, and bottles of chemicals.

"It will take me a minute or two to set this up and adjust it," he said, carefully removing one hair from the envelope, putting it on a glass slide, and then taking a piece of silk floss, separating out the strands, and also putting it on the slide.

I nodded and waited.

"Very interesting indeed," he said after a minute. "You're sure Sarah found these hairs woven into the needlepoint?"

"That's what she said."

He looked through the eyepiece again. Then he turned to me. "Here, take a look at this."

I peered through the eyepiece of the microscope. I'd never figured out how to use one of those things, although my high-school biology teacher had certainly tried to teach me. My eyelashes always got in the way.

"I'm sorry, Dave. I'm no good at microscopes. I see two lines, but they're blurry. Tell me what I'm supposed to be seeing."

"You're right. Two lines. One of them is a piece of silk thread from the lighthouse panel you gave me. The other is what Sarah found."

"But is what Sarah found also floss?"

"Definitely not. She was right. It's hair."

"Are you sure?"

"Trust me. I've seen a lot of hair under the microscope. It's one of the beginning microscope exercises I assign my classes."

"Maybe one of Mrs. Gardener's hairs fell out while she was stitching, and she never noticed and stitched it into her needlepoint."

"That would make sense, of course," said Dave. "It would make sense if the hair was human. This one is not."

My head spun. Sarah and I had wondered if the hair might be from Jasmine. Or, most probably, from Millie Gardener. Not human? "Then what *is* it from?"

"I can't tell right off. Hairs from different mammals are all different. I'll have to compare this hair to those from other animals."

"Can you do that?"

"Of course. Just not right now, because I have to get off to school." He looked at me. "Sorry to disappoint you, but I don't have the patterns for all mammalian hair in my head."

"Maybe Mrs. Gardener had a cat or dog," I suggested. "Those hairs could get mixed in with floss." I'd even heard of people knitting sweaters from their dog's hair.

"The hair isn't from a dog or a cat. Students often bring those to class. I'd recognize them."

"You'll let me know when you figure out what animal

the hair is from?" I said as we walked together toward his front door.

"Of course. I may even have time to do it later today." He hesitated. "Why is this so important to you, anyway?"

"I'm curious," I admitted. "It doesn't make sense. I like my world to be logical. Animal hair woven into an embroidery panel isn't logical. Or, at least it isn't logical until we figure out why it's there."

"I'm with you. That's why I love science," said Dave. "I promise to let you know as soon as I can. But right now I have to get to school."

Back in my car I realized I'd never reached Susan, the church secretary. That shower I'd been inviting people to attend wasn't officially "on" until we were on the church calendar. No one answered—it was only about seven-thirty—so I left a message for her to call me back as soon as she opened the office.

In the meantime I had plenty of time and nothing to do. I headed for the Harbor Haunts Café.

In the summer they opened for breakfast, and I'd been craving crabmeat eggs Benedict. Living in Haven Harbor had its challenges: solving crimes, digging up old secrets, even figuring out why an animal hair was in a needlepoint panel.

But fresh seafood (and farm-fresh eggs and cheeses and vegetables) was definitely one of the reasons I loved Maine.

In Arizona they hadn't even heard of crabmeat eggs Benedict.

Chapter 30

How fair is the rose, what a beautiful flower!
In summer so fragrant and gay!
But the leaves are beginning to fade in an hour,
And they wither and die in a day.

—Sampler by Lydia Frawley, age ten, Salem, Ohio, 1832 (Lydia was a Quaker, who married Hutchins Satterthwaite in 1846.)

Skye West was standing between two construction company trucks parked in Aurora's front drive. Roofers already had ladders up, and an empty Dumpster (how many of those had they filled already?) was standing at the ready. Few Maine homes had slate roofs. Slate cracked easily. I'd seen enough garden paths patchworked out of broken pieces to know that. Where had Skye found roofers able to repair the old roof? Replacing it would have been the easier, and less expensive, choice.

Then I noticed one of the trucks had New York plates. They might be experts on slate roofing, but Skye and

Patrick had just lost some of that local credibility they'd said was so important to them. Surely, there must have been someone in Maine who could deal with a slate roof.

How old was *the roof on the house that would soon be mine?*

Standing at the edge of Aurora's driveway I had a small wave of panic.

Am I ready to be a homeowner? To take responsibility for the house my family had built two hundred years ago?

True, I was next in line, and I loved the house. I loved that Mama and I and Gram always put our Christmas tree up in the bay window that had been added to the living room sometime in the early twentieth century. I loved that people walking by could see the shiny tinfoil star I'd made in kindergarten and we'd put on top of our tree ever since. I hoped Gram hadn't discarded it when I was in Arizona. But, no, she'd never have done that. That was our star. My star.

I loved the wide front porch overlooking the town green, where our Adirondack chairs caught breezes from the harbor and gave us a view up close of what was happening in town. I loved the old maple tree in our backyard, where my friend Frankie and I had built a rickety tree house the summer we were nine and kept records of the planes whose jet trails we saw high overhead. We'd dreamed of someday being on one of those planes and going somewhere exotic, somewhere far from Maine. A nor'easter had taken down most of our tree house one winter, but one stalwart board was still stubbornly nailed to the tree to mark the spot where our platform had been.

I loved my house. My home. But taking full responsibility for it? Grown-ups did that.

Was anyone ever completely ready to pick up the pieces

left by earlier generations . . . whether those pieces were genetic or clapboard?

Certainly, Skye West seemed capable. Of course, she was almost Gram's age. How many houses had she owned? Patrick had mentioned several. I watched her pointing at various places on the roof and the siding, while a burly man in blue overalls and a short-sleeved Yankee T-shirt listened and wrote notes on his clipboard.

Someone should warn him about being seen in town in an "Evil Empire" shirt. Haven Harbor was definitely part of Red Sox Nation.

A hand touched my back. I jumped.

"Patrick! I didn't hear you coming!" His hand touched off an electric circuit. I stepped forward.

His crinkly brown eyes laughed. "Not to worry. No murders here today, investigator lady. Talked with Mom yet?"

"Not yet. She seems pretty busy."

"A constant state with her, you'll find." Patrick agreed. "Mom's never bored. She's always got a project or seven to work on. This summer, of course, she has Aurora. And the carriage house."

"And the death of her friend," I added. "Did you know she planned to solve Jasmine's murder?" *Assuming she'd been murdered,* I added to myself.

"For years she's talked about the Gardeners. How they sponsored her scholarship at Miss Pritchard's, and later paid for her college, and helped her out when she was studying acting and only getting bit parts off-Broadway. But I didn't know about Jasmine's death, or the promise she made to Mrs. Gardener, until a few days ago." Patrick looked up at the old house. "I suspect Mom has always been fascinated by this house. After all, she saw it when it was at its height. It was here she learned what it meant to people of a certain class to summer in Maine, with all the possibilities inherent in those words. Maybe restoring the house is like bringing back the girl she was when she was here."

"Interesting," I said. "I hadn't thought of that. Then she's never restored another home?"

"Not like this one, for sure. Our New York place is a loft, converted before we bought it. The L.A. house is new, too."

"And you said the other day you had a place in Aspen."

"We did until a couple of years ago, but I never was fond of sliding down a mountain on two boards, and Mom's schedule didn't let her get there often. So we sold it."

"You don't like skiing. What do you like to do?" I guessed Patrick West didn't need to work. At least, work in the sense of being employed, or going to an office on a regular basis.

"I paint. I enjoy good music and good food and wine. I do some hiking. It feels good to be outside and not stuck in a building or car all the time, the way life is in L.A." Patrick looked around. "I'd never been to Maine before. I like it here. Low-key. Lots of artists and lots of galleries. A few good museums—I love the Farnsworth. And one day while Mom was busy with the contractor, I drove up to see the collection at Colby." He paused. "Impressive. I hadn't expected to find places like that in Maine."

"We're not the wilderness of Massachusetts anymore," I said.

"Not at all!" He smiled. "I've read reviews of restaurants in Portland and along the coast that sound amazing. Before I got here, I expected everyone to live on baked beans and lobster."

"Both good basic foods," I said, not mentioning I'd had both in the past few days—the lobster courtesy of his family. While we chatted, I kept an eye on Skye. She'd waved to let me know she knew I was waiting. "Also blueberry pie and haddock chowder and red hot dogs."

"Red hot dogs?"

"Next time you're in the supermarket, check them out. They're hard to find outside Maine. And, yes, they're red." Did Patrick go to the grocery store? Or did the Wests hire someone to do their shopping for them? "And fiddleheads. Don't miss the fiddleheads. It's the end of their season right now, but some restaurants still feature them."

He looked at me quizzically. "'Fiddleheads'? I assume you're not referring to a part of a stringed instrument."

"Ferns," I said. "Delicious."

"Sounds as though I have a lot to learn about Maine cuisine," he said, looking into my eyes in a way that made me feel too good. And uncomfortable. "Maybe you could teach me."

"Sarah could, too," I said. "She's also new to Maine. Perhaps you could go exploring together."

"You don't eat? I was thinking of restaurants," he said.

"I eat," I acknowledged, trying hard not to be friendlier than I should. My mind kept repeating, *Sarah saw him first.* "But I'm busy now, with the needlepoint business, and the investigating your mom wants me to do. And my grandmother's getting married in less than two weeks."

"That's right. You told me," he said. "Sounds like fun."

He couldn't be finagling for an invitation, could he? "Here comes your mom," I said. "I need to tell her what I found out yesterday."

"You do that," he said. "I'm sure we'll stay in touch." He definitely winked that time.

Would we? Or is he just referring to my work for his mother? I squared my shoulders and walked across the drive. "Skye, I found out a few things yesterday afternoon," I said. "We need to talk."

Chapter 31

When wealth to virtuous hands is given
It blesses like the dews of Heaven
Like Heaven it hears the orphans cry
And wipes the tears from widows' eyes.

—Sampler worked by Elizabeth Rind Nicholls
(1810–1904), age nine,
Georgetown, Washington, D.C.
(She never married.)

Skye walked to meet me. "I've been thinking about that list of people at the September fifth party. People connected in some way to Jasmine."

"Good." I glanced back at the men in the construction crew, several of whom were paying more attention to Skye and me than to their work. "Could we talk somewhere private?"

"I hope I'm included in that discussion," added Patrick, who'd followed me from the drive. "I find this whole investigation fascinating."

I gave him a dirty look as Skye called back to the work crew, "I'll be in the carriage house if you have any questions."

"Yes, Ms. West," said the guy I figured was in charge. He sounded a bit patronizing. I wondered how much the Wests were paying him.

"My copy of the list is in the carriage house, anyway," Skye added. "So, what happened yesterday, after you left here?"

"I spoke with several people who were here at Aurora the night Jasmine died," I said quietly. "They all remembered different parts of that evening. It would help if we began keeping a timeline of everything people say happened that night. Maybe some of the pieces will fit together."

"Excellent idea," Skye agreed as we approached the carriage house.

"I was surprised to find out how much people did remember," I admitted. "But Jasmine Gardener's death, and the fact that it was the last party here at Aurora, helped people pinpoint where they were then."

Skye picked a burgundy leather folder up from the coffee table. Then she and Patrick and I sat around an old country pine table stained with blue paint. I remembered Sarah once saying old red or blue paint made country furniture more valuable—the paint should never be removed. I looked at the table again. Something about it was familiar. Had it come from Sarah's store? I didn't remember seeing it here yesterday.

"Who did you talk with?" Skye asked as she looked through her folder.

"My grandmother, Charlotte Curtis. Ruth Hopkins. And Katie Titicomb. They were all at that last party, and all have slightly different memories of it."

"Did any of them have specific memories of what Jasmine was doing or who was with her?" Skye had found her list of the people she wanted questioned.

"Gram remembered Jasmine serving punch in the afternoon. Gram was newly engaged, and focused on her fiancé. She remembered hearing screams after the fireworks. Katie was only eleven then; she ate too much and got sick before the fireworks. She said Jasmine found her at the edge of the back lawn, throwing up, took her into Aurora and helped her clean up before the fireworks started. Then Katie went back to her father. Jasmine seemed very grown-up, and very kind, to her."

Skye made a note. "Did this Katie mention whether Jasmine was with anyone?"

"I didn't ask her that specific question. I suspect Jasmine was alone, or Katie would have mentioned that."

"The fireworks started a few minutes before nine o'clock that night. Since you said Katie was back with her father before they began, she must have been with Jasmine at about eight forty-five. It would take a few minutes to get from the edge of the field to the house, and then inside. And she said Jasmine cleaned her up."

"Washed her face is more like what she said," I remembered.

"No bathrooms are on the first floor, so either she took Katie upstairs, which she might have mentioned to you, or she used one of the kitchen sinks," Skye continued. "The kitchen would have been closer. And all the cooking was finished by then."

"I'll double-check that with Katie," I said, adding to the notes I was making.

"So Jasmine was alive and sufficiently sober to help a little girl at eight forty-five. But by the time the fireworks were over, about nine-thirty, she was dead." Skye looked down at her paper. "Good work, Angie. Now all we have to do is figure out where Jasmine was and who was with her during those forty-five minutes. Or even less, since we don't know when she fell or was pushed into the fountain."

Forty-five minutes to cover. And about two hundred of people on the estate, forty-five years ago. It didn't sound simple to me.

"I was impressed that everyone I spoke to remembered Jasmine that night. So if we go down your list, maybe they'll help us close that time period."

Skye looked at me, a slight smile on her lips. "I'm sure all the people on my list will remember Jasmine. They were all people close to her at the time. And most of them could have benefited from her death."

♦

Chapter 32

Wave after wave as rivers flow
And to the oceans run
So minutes after minutes go
And are forever gone.

—Alphabet and flower basket sampler
stitched by Julia Ann Dellaway
Georgetown, Washington, D.C., 1832

"One more minor mystery's come up," I put in before Skye started talking about the people on her list. "It may not mean anything, but it's interesting."

"Yes?" asked Patrick, who'd been listening.

"Last week my grandmother removed the needlework panels that Mrs. Gardener worked on from their frames. She's managed to eliminate the mildew."

"That's good news," said Skye.

"Yesterday I took several of them to people who work at Mainely Needlepoint, for them to replace the broken and rotten threads, and basically restore the actual work."

Skye nodded.

"Last night Sarah began looking at the two I gave her. She found something interesting."

Patrick and Skye both looked at me. "Interesting, how?" Patrick asked.

"She found hair worked into some of the stitching. Deliberately worked."

"Hair?" That got Skye's attention.

"Dark hair," I confirmed.

"Jasmine had dark hair," she said immediately. "Long, dark hair."

"That's what we thought of first," I confirmed. "Sarah wondered if Millie Gardener had used some of her daughter's hair in the needlework as a memorial."

"Interesting idea. Strange, but possible," Patrick said.

"But this morning," I continued, "I took a piece of the hair Sarah found to Dave Percy. He's another of our needlepointers, and he's also the biology teacher at Haven Harbor High. He doesn't have equipment to identify DNA. But with the equipment he does have, I hoped he could tell us whether the hair was human." I paused. "It wasn't."

"But if it wasn't human?" Skye looked at Patrick questioningly.

"I wondered if Mrs. Gardener had a dog or a cat—an animal whose hair might have, intentionally or unintentionally, gotten into her stitching. But Dave said the hair was from another mammal, not a dog or a cat."

"Stranger and stranger," Patrick said almost under his breath.

"That's for sure," said Skye. "Because Millie Gardener was allergic to animals. I remember Jasmine complaining she never was allowed to have a pet. She couldn't even take riding lessons with her friends because her mother was afraid she'd bring some of the allergens from the horses back with her into the house." Skye shook her head. "I remember thinking her mom must have really bad allergies." She took a sip of her coffee. "It was a long time ago. I hadn't thought of that in years."

"Dave told me some of his students believed Mrs. Gardener had three black cats," I shared. "If she was allergic, then I think we can put those stories down to rumors."

Skye rolled her eyes. "People are amazing."

"If she was allergic, then why would she have used mammalian hair in her work? It doesn't make sense." Patrick frowned.

"No, it doesn't. Knowing Mrs. Gardener was allergic to animals makes it even stranger," I agreed. "Dave's going to figure out what animal the hair is from. He's at school today, but it's the last couple of days before summer vacation. He'll let us know when he has a chance to work on it."

"Thank him for us, won't you?" Skye asked. "It's not exactly a mystery on the level of Jasmine's murder, but it's intriguing."

I nodded.

Skye turned to her papers. "The two people on the top of my list are, of course, the two possible fathers of Jasmine's child, Sam Gould and Jed Fitch."

I'd expected to hear those two names.

"Jed's sisters, Beth and Elsa, were also around that summer." She looked down at the list she'd showed me earlier. "And Carole Simpson. She's local, and she was dating Jed before Jasmine was."

"How many of those people were here Saturday?" I asked, thinking of the poor hummingbird. "I saw Elsa Fitch and her sister going into the house."

"Jed and Carole were here, too, for sure," Skye pointed out. "Jed, of course, was also our real estate agent."

"So all the Fitches were here Saturday." I made a note.

"They were."

"I'm sure he's not a suspect, but Ob Winslow was here Saturday, and he was at the last party," I added. "He was only ten then, but maybe he saw something. Or can suggest someone else in town who could help us with those missing forty-five minutes."

Skye was silent. "That's fine. You ask him."

I read the list over to myself. Considering the number of people said to have been at Aurora that night, I'd expected more people to contact than the two boyfriends, Jed's sisters, and a rival for Jed's attention. Sam Gould might have been involved—if he was, indeed, the father of Jasmine's child. But Jed had been local. The three women who'd known him well should be able to tell me more about him. "I don't know Sam Gould, so I wouldn't have recognized him Saturday."

Skye brushed that aside. "If he was here, I didn't recognize him, either. But it's been forty-five years. He could have been here and I didn't recognize him."

"Maybe someone else did," I said.

"And there's one more name," said Skye. "It's an important one. Although, like Sam, I didn't notice her at the sale Saturday. Putting her on the list might create problems for me, so I hope you'll be particularly discreet about finding out about her."

"Yes?" I knew how to be discreet. That was one of the first skills an investigator had to have.

"Linda Zaharee."

I'd remembered the name from Skye's list Monday. "Zaharee the artist?" If she was the one I was thinking of, Linda Zaharee, known professionally by her last name, was one of the best-known artists in Maine. I knew next to nothing about art, and even I'd heard of her. Her paintings of the sea were said to rival Winslow Homer's. She'd won international awards, and exhibited in galleries in New York and San Francisco and Europe. As I remembered, her home was down the coast.

"In 1970, Linda Zaharee was a young hippie with a camera waitressing at an inn in Camden to make ends meet. She'd met Jasmine somewhere—most likely through Sam, since he came from Camden. I don't remember. But she knew Jasmine's family had money, and Linda was saving to study in Paris. She flattered Jasmine. She said she had fantastic bone structure and could be a model. That it would be an honor to photograph her."

"So Jasmine posed for her?"

"In July." Skye hesitated. "Jasmine got self-conscious at the last minute. She didn't want Linda to take the photographs. So Linda asked me to come along, to encourage Jasmine."

"Did she photograph you, too?" I asked.

"She did. That's what makes this a bit embarrassing." Skye glanced at Patrick, who was listening intently to the conversation. "She photographed both of us. In the nude."

Chapter 33

No cord nor cable can so forcibly draw, or hold so fast, as love can do with a twisted thread.

—Robert Burton (1577–1640),
The Anatomy of Melancholy, 1621

"And Linda was at the party?"

"She was. Someone told Mrs. Gardener she was a good photographer. I think she'd done a wedding for one of Millie's friends. Millie asked her to come and photograph the party. I think only Linda, Jasmine, and I knew she'd taken the earlier photographs. I saw Linda with her camera at the party, but I never saw any photographs she took there. I'd hoped when you and Sarah were collecting all the photographs in the house you might find the ones Linda took that night, and they might give us some clues about what happened. Unfortunately, all the pictures you found were taken earlier."

I must have missed something. "So the reason you want

to contact Linda Zaharee is that she might have kept negatives or pictures taken at a party forty-five years ago?"

"That can be our excuse for contacting her," Skye said, "but I consider her a suspect, too. After Linda took those earlier pictures, the nude ones, Jasmine panicked. What if her parents saw them? Or our friends? Jasmine called Linda and asked for both the prints and the negatives—everything she had. She promised to pay well."

"And, of course, she had the money to do that."

"Not as easily as you might think. She certainly lived in a style that said 'money,' but her parents paid her expenses. Jasmine was on an allowance. A generous allowance, of course, by most people's standards, but an allowance, just the same. They wanted her to learn to manage money. Jasmine didn't have access to as much money as she promised Linda."

"How was she going to get it?"

"She talked about that for days. She debated calling her father's lawyer and seeing if he would send her money privately. Maybe stealing one of her mother's checks. She even considered taking a few pieces of the silver at Aurora—pieces they rarely used—and pawning them." Skye shook her head. "None of her ideas sounded good. Her parents weren't oblivious. They'd know she needed money for something."

"So, what happened?"

"I don't think Linda thought much about the photos until Jasmine panicked. Then she realized how valuable they might be, to the society press in New York or to Jasmine's parents, who might pay to keep the photos private. She refused to give Jasmine the photos or the negatives."

"And?"

"Jasmine threatened her. Remember, she'd just found

out she was pregnant. She knew her parents would have to find out about that eventually. She didn't want them discovering anything else foolish she'd done."

"Photographs, even nude photographs, aren't exactly the same as pregnancy," I said.

"Maybe not to you. But despite her pregnancy, Jasmine wasn't a free spirit, like some young people were then. People think of the late sixties and early seventies as free love. Peace to the people. Drugs. If Jasmine had been more into all that, she might not have been so upset. But she was desperate. And she focused on those pictures rather than on her pregnancy." Skye bit her lip.

"So, what did she threaten to do?"

"She planned to talk to Linda at the party. Threaten her, that if she didn't give us all the pictures and negatives, then she'd tell her parents, and the police, that Linda was a lesbian. She'd say Linda had forced us to pose for her, and planned to publish the photos as pornography."

I frowned. "Were the photos . . . sexual?"

"We didn't think so at the time. Most of them were taken when we were skinny-dipping in a small, private cove. No one else was around. But there were a few where she posed us touching each other. We'd had a little wine to loosen us up before the shoot. We didn't see any harm in it at the time. But the photos might look different to someone else."

"What happened?"

"I don't know," said Skye. "I don't even know for sure Jasmine talked to Linda at the party. I never saw Linda after that night, and I never saw the photographs. But if Jasmine threatened Linda, and Linda got angry—"

"Linda might have killed Jasmine."

"It's possible. That's why her name is on my list of possible suspects."

"And I assume you wouldn't want those photographs, if they still exist, to get out. Say, to the press."

"Exactly. I don't know if Linda kept the photos, or if she knows I became Skye West. She may have destroyed them all after Jasmine died. I hope so. But I don't know."

"So we have three reasons to talk with Linda. See if she still has the photographs she took of the party that night. See if she has the photographs of you and Jasmine."

"And see if she's a murderer," said Skye.

Chapter 34

'Tis useless that the fingers learn to draw
And soaring reason scans all nature's law
If innate virtue's not a welcome guest
And pure religion glows not in the breast.

—Stitched by Betsey Hathaway, age fourteen,
Freetown, Assonet Village, Massachusetts

I looked down at the list of possible suspects. "I can contact most of these people," I said. "I know the Fitch family, at least slightly. They attend the same church my family does. I'd also like to talk with Ob Winslow again, and I'll call Katie Titicomb, as you suggested, to check on the timeline."

Skye nodded. "I'll trust you on that. But what about Linda Zaharee and Sam Gould?"

"We could both talk with them. They should remember you if you tell them you're Mary North. And having two of us there would mean there'd be a witness, in case the meetings turn out to be important."

"I'd be happy to go with you on any of your interviews, Angie." Patrick leaned forward. "That way you'd always have a witness."

As though anyone in town would talk to me when Skye West's son was hanging around in the background. "I don't think that'll be necessary, Patrick. But thank you. If one of these people did kill Jasmine, we don't want to alert them." I turned to Skye. "I'll say you're curious about the history of the house you've bought, and you're trying to document it. Jasmine Gardener's history is part of that."

"Excellent," agreed Skye, standing up dismissively. "When can you start?"

"I'll make a few calls this afternoon," I suggested.

"I'll call Sam Gould and Linda Zaharee. Both of them," Skye volunteered. "I'll make up some story. My acting skills may come in handy. I'll let you know when we can go to see them."

I hoped Skye wouldn't get her hopes up too high. If there was a killer, he or she had managed to keep quiet all these years. Why would the murderer suddenly open up to me or Skye now?

I stopped at Ob's house, across the street from Aurora. No one was home. He and Josh were probably out on the *Anna Mae.* Anna could have been anywhere.

A wave of exhaustion hit me. I'd been working long hours for over a week, and had now taken on an investigation. What I needed more than anything else was quiet—and time away from everyone.

I drove to Pocket Cove Beach. I didn't even get out of the car. I put my windows down and looked out at the sea.

Three lobster boats were working the pots in the harbor, and one sailboat was visible farther out. By next week, with schools ending and tourists arriving, there'd be more activity here. There'd be small sailboats, kayaks, and skiffs.

Waves broke over the rocky beach and below Haven Harbor Lighthouse, farther down the harbor. Those waves looked as they always did. Like snowflakes, no two were alike, but swirled in an endless pattern. I'd seen those waves when I'd come here as a child with Mama and I'd played in the sand. Even after Mama'd disappeared, they'd still been here, reminding me that life, and time, went on. And here they were again. They still calmed me. I felt my breaths coming easier.

Jasmine Gardener had been an unwed teenager, like Mama. Maybe she'd come to this same spot to watch the waves. Maybe she even dreamed of bringing her son or daughter here someday.

Had someone ended that dream? Skye West thought so.

I didn't know. But I understood why Skye needed to know.

Jasmine's death, like Mama's, had been sudden, and undeserved.

I'd demanded justice for Mama. Skye wanted justice for her friend.

I sat for a while more, watching the waves break on the shore. Then I picked up my cell and called Mane Waves, Elsa Fitch's salon, and made an appointment to have my hair trimmed.

It was time to start talking with the people on Skye's list.

Chapter 35

Man for the field and woman for the hearth:
Man for the sword and for the needle she:
Man with the head and woman with the heart:
Man to command and woman to obey:
All else confusion.

—Alfred, Lord Tennyson (1809–1892)
The king's soliloquy from
The Princess: A Medley, 1847

I slipped into a chair at Mane Waves Beauty Salon, Haven Harbor's finest of its kind. (And *only* salon, too.) "Thank you for taking me on such short notice, Elsa," I said. "I only need a trim."

She picked up a piece of my hair and scrutinized it. "I'd suggest more than a trim, Angie. You need to let me cut off these split ends. They're hiding the whole shape of your cut. That will mean taking off a couple of inches."

I swallowed. Hard. It had taken me a while to grow my hair long enough to pin it up during the summer. But those had been Arizona summers. This was Maine. And my hair did look out of control.

"I use lots of conditioner," I said, a defense I knew was lame.

"Maybe a little too much," declared Elsa. Her own hair was cut short. I suspected it was never out of place. Messy hair wouldn't have been good for business.

I gave in. "Then take off the ends. And reshape it."

Elsa walked a couple of steps away and looked at my head. "A little layering would help."

I nodded. "Do what you have to do. But not too short, please."

"I've been doing your grandmother's hair for thirty years. She never complained. Got her appointment all set for the day of the wedding. I suppose you'd like me to fit you in that day, too?"

"I haven't decided yet."

Gram's hair looked okay, but Gram wasn't me.

"Don't be taking too long to make up your mind. This time of year, with all the summer folks wanting to be streaked and blown out, my time's tight," she reminded me.

"I'll let you know," I assured her.

I spent the next few minutes under the tap, being shampooed and (lightly) conditioned. I tried to think of a way to bring up a party forty-five years ago. But it turned out I didn't have to; Elsa did.

"I was over to the old Gardener place Saturday." *Snip. Snip.* "Saw you there, hobnobbing with that actress."

"Sarah Byrne and I helped her run her lawn sale."

"*Humph.* Not much of a sale, so far as I could see. A lot of junk. Nothing there worth buying." *Snip.*

"Sorry you didn't find any bargains."

"Got a couple of things. But Millie Gardener's been gone years now. You'd think someone would have had the sense to clean that place out before now. Millie always kept her home spotless. She'd turn over in her grave if she knew what it looked like now."

"Then you knew Mrs. Gardener?"

"Did her hair all the years she lived here. At first, she'd come into the salon, like other folks. But at the end, when she was poorly, I went over to her place. Did her hair in her own bathroom. She was sweet. And generous."

"Did she ever talk about her daughter?"

"Didn't talk about much else." *Snip.* That strand of hair that just hit the floor was longer than two inches. "She had nothing else on her mind I could see. She'd watch the news on the television and *Jeopardy!*—she did love that *Jeopardy!*—and she thought about better times, when her Jasmine was little." *Snip.* I couldn't see what hit the floor that time.

"Did you know Jasmine?"

"Oh, Lordy, I did. Course, she was older than I was, by a couple of years. But she spent a lot of time with my brother, Jed, that last summer, and with me, and with Beth, after she got home."

"What was she like? Jasmine?"

"Millie, may she rest in peace, didn't see it, of course, but Jasmine was a rich tease. She knew she had more than the rest of us. She wanted Jed because he was a star. That year he was handsome, and good at football. But he wasn't the brightest in the family. I wasn't surprised he went for Jasmine."

"So, who was the brightest in your family?"

"Well, Beth did well enough. Complete ride for college. She was only home for a month that summer before she headed to Guatemala in the Peace Corps. Taught English there a few years before she came back home and started teaching second grade. She wasn't dumb. Not by a long shot. But I was the smartest back then, if I do say so."

"You must have been fourteen or fifteen that summer, right?"

"Fifteen. Had won first place in the county science fair two years running. I couldn't decide whether to be an astronaut or a marine biologist back in those days." Elsa paused between clips. "Funny to think of that. It was so long ago."

"But, instead, you decided to open your own business."

"Went to beauty school down to Portland. I've done fine."

"I don't remember when there wasn't a Mane Waves. Mama brought me here to have my hair done before my First Communion."

"I've been here over thirty years now. I saved, and then I inherited a little. I've worked hard and made do." She backed off a bit. "See how nice your hair's falling now? A little more layering on the side and you'll be ready for a blow-dry."

"Were you at that party? The last party at Aurora?"

"I was."

"What was it like?"

"Big and expensive, like every year. Nothing special or different about that last time."

"Did you see Jasmine that night?"

"She was there, greeting people with her dad and Millie. Later she went with a group of us who took plates of food down to the back lawn to eat."

"You were with her, then?"

"There was a whole crowd of us. Some friends of Jasmine's I didn't know, and Jed and Beth and Cindy and me."

"Was she drinking?"

"I don't tell tales. But we were all pretty happy that

night. Jed and Jasmine, they'd had an argument earlier. But by the end of the evening, they seemed pretty cozy."

"So you were with them the whole time?"

"When they were eating. Then Jed and Jasmine went for a walk, and Beth was talking to someone she'd gone to high school with. Carole tried to get me to talk about how Jed felt about Jasmine. Carole'd been his girl the year before that. But I didn't think it was her business. I decided to go for a walk of my own."

"Where did you go?"

"Around that back field. Waited for the fireworks to start. And they were right on time."

"Did you see Jasmine after that?"

"Why're you asking all these questions? Jasmine's dead forty-five years now." She pulled the black cape off my shoulders. "And your hair's done."

I looked in the mirror. My hair was a little shorter, about chin length, but it was no longer straight. Instead, it fell in loose waves around my face. I touched my hair lightly, to see if the curls would stay. They did. Not bad!

"Thanks, Elsa. You did a good job."

"I do the best I can."

Chapter 36

May your bobbin always be full.

—Anonymous saying

Gram had outdone herself for dinner. Pan-fried scallops (in panko, light Japanese bread crumbs, to cut down on calories), homemade (of course) tartar sauce made with bread-and-butter pickles, and a salad. And, most important, generous slices of strawberry-rhubarb pie for dessert. "It's the season," she announced. "Fruit is healthy, right?"

"Absolutely," I agreed, serving myself another slice.

Gram looked at me sidewise. "I like what Elsa Fitch did with your hair. It was getting a little straggly."

I nodded, mouth full of pie.

"Elsa's a mite strange, but she's a good hairdresser."

"You've been going to Mane Waves for years."

"Ever since she opened her own place. She cut my hair before that, too, when she was at another salon. I can't even remember the name of that place now."

"She and her sister, Beth, my second-grade teacher,

came to the sale Saturday," I said. "And she told me she was at that last party the Gardeners had."

Gram nodded absently. "Lots of people in town were there that night."

"Do you remember seeing Elsa, or anyone in her family?"

Gram thought a minute. "Her brother, Jed, was a little younger that I was. He and Jasmine were together a lot that summer. I saw them at the yacht club. Beth was older than I was. She'd been away at college. Then she left for the Peace Corps. I didn't really know her until after she came back and started teaching in town."

"Jed went to college?"

"The next year. University of Maine. Football scholarship. He'd hoped to go to a Big Ten school, but the Black Bears offered him the best deal. He didn't stay all four years, though. I vaguely remember hearing he'd lost his scholarship. Flunked out. For a while he went back to working for his dad as a stern man, but then he started doing small repairs for people in town. He still paints rooms and fixes drains and such for folks. But about ten years ago, Cindy, his wife, convinced him to get a real estate license, so now he sells real estate, too."

"Those jobs go together. Help someone fix their house up to get it in shape to sell, and then do future repairs for the new owner."

"True," Gram acknowledged. "He'll never make a fortune, but he's a good, steady worker. Same as Elsa and Beth."

"Elsa said she'd wanted to be a marine biologist or an astronaut," I shared. "I wonder why she changed her mind and became a hairdresser, instead."

"Simple answer to that," said Gram. "Her mother was sickly. Migraines and stomach problems and such. Enough complaints to keep her to her bed a lot of the time. Today someone might say she was depressed. I'm no doctor. But she never seemed to get her life together. Elsa was the youngest. With Beth in the Peace Corps and Jed in college, their father expected Elsa to stay home and take care of their mother and the house. There was some talk about it at the time, but Elsa agreed to commute to beauty school in Portland instead of going to college. Once she got started in that direction, she didn't turn around."

"She seems to have done well enough."

"True. Sometimes life interferes with the plans people have."

I could tell she was thinking of other people, not just Elsa. Of Mama, who'd gotten pregnant too young? Or herself, who'd been widowed early? Or me, who'd had to cope with the fallout from Mama's disappearance and never considered college? (Unless you counted the couple of courses I took at Arizona State, which bored me to death.) Would I have made different choices if I'd had a father, as well as a mother? Or if Mama hadn't been murdered?

Maybe. But maybe not.

Gram finished stacking plates in the sink to wash and turned toward me. "Does your friend Skye really think she can find out about Jasmine all these years later?"

"She isn't sure," I said. "But she hopes so. It's her house now, and she's curious about what happened there."

"Well, I have nothing more to add except what I told you the other day. I saw Jasmine earlier in the evening. She was playing with some of the toddlers at the party, handing out balloons and balls." Gram stopped and smiled. "She had a dozen or so Hula-hoops, and she tried to show some of the six- or seven-year-old girls how to use them. I remember thinking it made a pretty picture—Jasmine with all the little girls and the Day-Glo Hula-hoops. In fact, I remember a woman taking pictures of them."

"Did you know the woman?"

Gram shook her head. "It could have been anyone. I remember the flashes of Hula-hoops in the sun, and someone with a camera."

Linda Zaharee, perhaps? Children and Hula-hoops might be a scene she'd have photographed.

"Then Jasmine wasn't with her friends all the time."

"I think one friend was with her. Another girl." Gram frowned, trying to remember. "It was a long time ago, Angel. Jasmine was usually at the center of a group of young people. She wasn't one to stay alone for long. Most of the time that summer she was with Jed Fitch and his friends." She hung her dishcloth on a hook near the sink. "I told you. I wasn't paying much attention to other people then."

I nodded. Gram had remembered something new from that evening: Jasmine playing with Hula-hoops. And a photographer. But that wouldn't have been in the last hour of the party. It would have been getting dark by eight-thirty at the beginning of September.

If Jasmine had been drinking heavily, she would have started earlier than the last hour of the party, though. Would she be playing with children and Hula-hoops if she was high? Who knew?

Too many unanswered questions.

Chapter 37

Useful and ornamental needlework, knitting, and netting are capable of being made, not only sources of personal gratification, but of high moral benefit, and the means of developing in surpassing loveliness and grace, some of the highest and noblest feelings of the soul.

—*The Ladies Work Table Book,* 1845

I slept in a little the next morning. When I got up I found two messages waiting for me. Susan, the church secretary, said she had the names and e-mail addresses of the church members and would be happy to send out shower invitations to everyone. Was two o'clock on Saturday a good time?

I hadn't thought of inviting everyone, but she was right. Reverend Tom's church family would be Gram's family soon, if it wasn't already. Including everyone would be the right thing to do.

Even better, she'd be sending out the invitations, not me. I texted her back, thanked her, and told her to go ahead and send the invitations. Short notice, but I hoped people would understand. Then I called the patisserie in town, threw myself on their mercy, and ordered all the cupcakes and cookies and éclairs they could bake and deliver to the rectory late Saturday morning. I still had to deal with punch (for those who didn't choose to imbibe spirits) and wine (for those who did). But I was beginning to feel the shower would happen. Thank goodness Katie Titicomb had volunteered to decorate.

The second message was from Ob. I'd called him late last night, hoping to reach him, but hadn't. He said he had an afternoon charter, but he would be home this morning if I wanted to drop in.

I did.

No word from Dave Percy about the hairs woven into the needlepoint panels, but I hadn't expected to hear from him quickly.

Today my plan was to talk with Jed Fitch and his sister Beth. Beth wouldn't be through with school until afternoon, but Jed might be in his office this morning. I'd risk dropping in.

When I got downstairs, Gram was looking through a thick paperback. From a distance it looked like a tourist guide. She put her hands over the cover and dropped the book into her lap as I came in.

"Honeymoon planning?" I asked. "Why such a secret?"

"No real need for it to be secret. Not from you, anyway. Tom doesn't want everyone in the congregation knowing exactly what we're doing."

"I can understand that. It *is* your honeymoon," I agreed. "And I promise not to call his cell number unless it's a real emergency." Gram didn't have a cell. I suspected that was a temporary situation.

"I certainly hope you do call, should there be any

emergencies or problems," Gram said immediately. "We're not disappearing. We're . . . Oh, you might as well know." She picked up the book hidden in her lap and held it up so I could read the title: *Quebec City.*

"You're going to Quebec!" I said. "I've heard the old section of the city is like a bit of Europe in North America."

"Neither of us has ever been there," Gram confided. "We wanted to go someplace new to both of us. And Quebec's only about a five-hour drive from here. The guidebook says the old part of the city is full of French restaurants and galleries and shops and museums."

"You don't speak French," I pointed out.

"No. But Tom speaks a little. And the book says people in the tourist industry speak English. We'll be fine. Tom's made us a reservation at one of the small hotels."

"Isn't Quebec the place with the castle-like hotel?"

"The Frontenac," she agreed. "We thought about staying there, but decided we'd rather spend money on food and wine, and maybe buy something to bring back as a remembrance of our trip."

"I see listings of antique shops," I said, looking over her shoulder at the guidebook. "They might have old Ouija boards."

"I'm sure we'll check that out," said Gram. "Adding to Tom's collection would be fun for him, but I'd rather bring home a painting or something made by a local craftsman as a souvenir."

I suspected they'd do both.

"Sounds wonderful! I look forward to hearing about your adventures after you get home," I said. "And I promise not to tell anyone where you've gone."

"Thank you, Angel. I feel more comfortable with your knowing what direction we're heading. Although it is fun to keep our destination mysterious for most people we know."

"You deserve your privacy," I agreed.

I left Gram researching Quebec restaurant menus on the Web, French dictionary at hand, and headed to the Winslows' house.

Men were swarming over Aurora's roof and four construction trucks were parked in the driveway there when I drove past. Ob's farmhouse, ell (the rooms connecting the house to the barn) and barn itself were a good size, but not on Aurora's scale.

Anna answered the door almost immediately. "Angie! Good to see you. Although we've seen your car across the street a lot recently."

No secrets in Haven Harbor. Plus, of course, Ob had worked at Aurora last week, too, pointing out the idiosyncrasies of the place, and then acting as part tour guide, part guard during the sale Saturday.

"Sarah and I were helping the Wests set up their lawn sale. That's over now. I can get back to focusing on Mainely Needlepoint and Gram's wedding. Did you get a call from the church or an e-mail? We're having a shower for Gram and Reverend Tom on Saturday afternoon."

Anna hadn't heard, but she immediately volunteered to bring oatmeal-raisin cookies. I accepted her offer. We couldn't have too much food or drink, and I had no idea how many people would show up. (Especially now that we were inviting the entire congregation.)

"Is Ob around?"

"He's out in the barn, painting some buoys for a friend," she said. "You go on and find him there. He mentioned you might stop in."

Ob was, indeed, painting buoys. Usually a winter obligation, but when a friend needs a hand . . . "Orange and light blue?" I commented. "I didn't think lobstermen went for blue buoys. Too hard to see."

Ob shrugged. "Said they were his kids' favorite colors. Whatever the man wants. And no one else has."

I nodded. "Didn't get to talk with you Saturday. We were all wicked busy."

"True enough," he agreed. "All those folks looking to capture a long-gone past."

"The Wests seem to want to bring the place back."

"They're spending enough to bring back Abe Lincoln," he said. "But they're not taking the time to do it right. Authentically. The way the Gardeners would have wanted."

I suspected he was right. "At least they're trying."

"Trying." He nodded.

"You told me you were at the party in 1970, that you knew Jasmine."

"Yup. I knew her. Course, she was seven years older than me. Don't think she would have said she knew me."

"What was she doing at the party?"

"Being seventeen, far as I could see."

"I mean, did she spend time with her parents? Her friends?"

"She was there to greet guests, like her folks expected her to be. They'd put her in charge of the kids' activities. Balloons, a clown or two, Hula-hoops. She did that for a while. Then she partied with people her age."

"Eating and drinking with them?"

"She was Jasmine Gardener. If she wanted anything to eat or drink, someone would bring it to her."

"You mean the staff?"

"Not always." He shrugged, a little embarrassed. "Once I overheard her say she'd like another drink, and I took her a glass of wine."

"So you were close by."

Ob looked at me almost shyly. "She was the prettiest girl I knew. Sometimes I hung around near her when I could." He shook his head. "Crazy, I was."

"That doesn't sound crazy. It sounds sweet."

"Mebbe so. But my father caught me watching her, and he told me off. Said she was none of my business. I should stick with kids my own age."

"But you got her a glass of wine . . ." I suddenly thought about that. "How could you do that? You were only—what—ten? The bartender served you wine?"

"Nah. I went over there, but, you're right, they wouldn't give me any. Then I saw Elsa Fitch. You know her—she's a hairdresser now. Anyway, she looked older than she was. Hell, Jasmine wasn't old enough to drink legally. But it was a private party. Elsa got me a glass of wine and I gave it to Jasmine. Spilled a little on the way—I was so excited. I was afraid my father would see me with the glass and take it away before I could give it to her."

"When was that?"

"About the time the fireworks began. Nine o'clock or so. It was dark, so I figured no one would see me with the wine."

"Had Jasmine been drinking much before that?"

"She'd been holding a glass most of the time. I don't know how much she'd had to drink. What does a ten-year-old know about such things?"

A ten-year-old knows when someone's drunk, I thought.

"Who was Jasmine with then? At nine o'clock?"

"Jed and Beth Fitch, and another guy I didn't know. And her friend Mary from New York. Carole Simpson was there, too. Maybe other people. I was watching Jasmine, not her friends." He rubbed his chin, as though that would bring back the answer. "It was a while ago, you know."

"Do you think Jasmine had so much wine she slipped and fell into the fountain?"

Ob stood up straight. "I don't. If I believed that . . . If I believed the wine I gave her had somehow ended up with her death . . . then I couldn't live with myself. I've gone over and over it in my mind, all these years. And I walked over that property hundreds of times when I lived on the estate, and after. Never did figure what Jasmine was doing in the front of the house at that time, anyway. Everyone was on the back lawn, watching the fireworks. To get to where they found her, she would have had to leave in the middle of the show. If she did, then someone was with her. She wouldn't have left on her own. At nine o'clock she was laughing with her friends. Half an hour later she was dead." He stared at the wall in back of me, remembering. "I still have nightmares about that night."

"She fell into the fountain."

"Jed Fitch found her there." Ob leaned toward me and lowered his voice. "Between you and me, I figured he was with her all along."

Chapter 38

May heaven to thee her bliss impart
And be your guide in every art.
May learning be your chief delight
And learn to live and act aright.

—Sampler worked by Fanny Abrams, age ten, Monhegan Island, Maine, 1821

Jed Fitch. His name kept coming up. Gram and Skye had said Jasmine spent a lot of time with him that summer. Skye thought he might be the father of Jasmine's child. Jed had been with Jasmine at the party, at least some of the time. And Ob was the second person who'd said Jed was the one who found her in the fountain.

I'd planned to go to the elementary school this afternoon to see Miss Beth Fitch, sister of Elsa and Jed. School wouldn't be out until two-thirty.

But I had time before then. I headed for the real estate office where Jed Fitch worked.

I was lucky; he was there.

"Angie!" he said, coming around the desk and shaking my hand with both of his. "I heard you were back in town. So good to see you!"

Although I knew who Jed Fitch was, I was pretty sure I'd never spoken to him before.

He was a big man. But the muscles he might have had as a young man had turned to fat, and the stomach hanging above his belt was only partially covered by his suit jacket.

"I got back about a month ago," I answered. "It's good to be home."

"No place like Haven Harbor," he agreed. "So, what can I do for you today? Thinking of buying a place of your own? We've got some great deals on homes right here. Some even have ocean views."

He was smart enough to know I could never afford shore frontage. "Ocean view" was the second most expensive category of home on the Maine coast. "Not at the moment, no," I said. "Although if I'm ever in the market, I'll be sure to call you."

"That's all I can ask," Jed said, handing me his card. "Keep this for your files. Just on the chance."

I slipped his card into my pocket. "Actually, I'm here doing a little research."

"'Research'?" He frowned and ran his hand through the little hair he still had. "About what? Maine real estate?"

"Indirectly," I said. "I've been doing some work for Skye West. You were the one who handled her purchase of the old Gardener estate."

"True. Lovely lady, Ms. West."

And I bet a lovely commission for Jed Fitch.

"She's asked me to take on a project for her. She'd like to have a history of Aurora, which, of course, means a history of the Gardener family. I wondered if you could help me fill in some details."

"Me? Why not check the library? I'm no expert on the Gardeners." Jed's smile stiffened.

"Several people in town said you were a close friend of Jasmine Gardener's. I hoped you wouldn't mind telling me a little bit about her." I pulled a notebook out of my bag. "For Ms. West's project. She told me how wonderfully you were handling the sale. She said she'd recommend you to any of her friends interested in Maine real estate. She was sure you could help me."

Jed leaned back in his chair. "I knew Jasmine, yes. We were about the same age. But that was a long time ago."

"I'll bet you knew her better than about anyone else in Haven Harbor. That's what people have said. They've said she had a real crush on you back then."

Jed sat up and straightened his tie. "We were close that last summer, yes. Who knows what might have come of it if Jasmine hadn't died so tragically?" He looked into my eyes. "Her death was devastating. Just devastating. It took me years to get over. I kept blaming myself, wondering what I could have done differently that day."

"People say Jasmine was drinking at the party. Did you think she was drunk?"

"Drinking? Sure. We'd all had a few. No one was paying attention, and it was the last party of the season. But— drunk? I didn't think she was drunk. But she must have been. How else would she have stumbled into the fountain and hit her head and drowned?"

"Ob Winslow mentioned you were the one who found her."

"Ob said that?" Jed hesitated. "I suppose it's part of the police record, too. Yeah. The fireworks were almost over. Jasmine said she didn't feel well. Maybe what people said later was true, and she'd had too much to drink. But I didn't notice. She headed for the house. When she hadn't come back in a few minutes, I followed her. She wasn't inside. One of the maids said she'd seen Jasmine heading for the driveway. I found her, lying in the fountain, her head under the water. I pulled her out, shouted for help, and started CPR." He sat back again. "I'd been a lifeguard at the YMCA pool in the winter. I had my certificate. All I could think was 'Thank goodness I know what to do.'"

"So you gave her CPR. That might have saved her life."

"All I wanted was to get her to breathe again."

"Someone called an ambulance then?"

He nodded. "One of the cops the Gardeners had hired to direct traffic and check for drunken drivers wasn't far from the front gate. I yelled for help. He ran toward us, saw what I was doing, and radioed for an ambulance."

"Lucky he was nearby."

"It was. I was on top of her, giving her mouth-to-mouth, you know, the way they used to recommend. The sky was all lit up with the last firework display—the gold one that was always the biggest. It seemed to take forever for the ambulance to get there, but it must have been only a few minutes. The paramedics whisked her away."

"What did you do then?"

"Mr. and Mrs. Gardener went with Jasmine in the ambulance. Everyone was leaving the party. The word was spreading about Jasmine's being taken to the hospital. I didn't know what to do. I just stood there. Finally my friends found me and Carole drove me home." He stopped. "Mr. Gardener called me the next morning to thank me for trying to save Jasmine. He's the one told me she hadn't made it."

"You said you sometimes blamed yourself."

"I shouldn't have let her drink. She was little. Only

about five feet tall, maybe a hundred pounds. She shouldn't have been drinking as much as the rest of us. And I should have gone with her when she said she didn't feel well."

"How had you and Jasmine been getting along that summer?"

"We were close. Really close." He hesitated. "I'd even asked her to marry me." He hesitated, as though deciding how much he'd tell me. "She hadn't given me an answer. I'd thought she would that night. I asked her again during the party, but some little kids interrupted us. We were never alone. Never had a chance to talk."

"So if she'd said 'yes,' you wouldn't have gone to college?"

"Jasmine was more important to me than college."

Jed sounded sincere. I decided not to ask him whether he'd known Jasmine was pregnant. It would explain why he'd asked her to marry him. But she hadn't agreed. Was she waiting to hear from Sam Gould, the other young man Skye suggested was also a possible father-to-be?

"Did you know Sam Gould?"

Jed hesitated. "Sam Gould. That name's familiar. He may have a shipbuilding business up the coast. Years ago, Sam was a friend of Jasmine's."

"Then you did know him."

"Met him once or twice that summer. Jasmine and I tried not to talk about people we'd dated in the past. Now I see his ads in *Down East*."

"So you knew he and Jasmine had been dating in New York City."

"Sure. Like she knew I'd dated Carole."

"Carole Simpson."

"Right."

It was my turn to hesitate. I looked at the picture on the

wall, near Jed's computer, of Jed and his wife and their two sons. "When did you and Carole marry?"

"Several years later. It had nothing to do with Jasmine or the Gardeners." He stood up. "I've told you everything you need to know, everything I remember about back then." He hitched up his pants. "It was a long time ago. Life went on after Jasmine Gardener died. I went on."

Chapter 39

Virtue and wit, with science join'd
Refine the manners, form the mind,
And when with industry they meet
The female character's complete."

—Sampler stitched by
Sophia Catherine Bier, 1810

I stopped at home for a light lunch and checked my messages. Several questions had come in about Gram's shower, and there were two inquiries about Mainely Needlepoint. I answered them all and nibbled a sandwich of fresh lettuce and an imported tomato. Local tomatoes would be ripe in about a month. They'd taste better.

A little after two-thirty I pulled into the driveway of Haven Harbor Elementary School. My elementary school.

Yellow school buses were lined up and about a dozen parents were there to pick up students headed for Little League practices, music lessons, orthodontia appointments, or going to Grandma's for the afternoon.

I hadn't ridden the school bus until high school. I'd only lived seven blocks from the school. Most days, in fall, winter, and spring, I'd walked those blocks, often in snow or mud boots. But sometimes, if the weather was bad and she wasn't working the afternoon shift, Mama had been in one of those cars waiting to take students home. It hadn't happened often, but I'd always looked to see if she was there. Just in case.

I remembered one January afternoon I'd walked home. I must have been in third grade, because it was before Mama disappeared. Snow had been heavy all day. Haven Harbor schools rarely closed. That day blowing snow and sleet made it hard to see, and my boots were full of melted snow before I'd gotten two blocks. My feet were numb, and the wet boots rubbed against my bare legs beneath the dress I'd insisted on wearing that morning. But despite the cold I'd felt hot—so hot I'd taken off my hat and scarf and stuffed them in my book bag. And my head hurt. My ten- or fifteen-minute walk seemed to take forever.

When I finally reached home, Gram took one look at me and insisted on giving me a warm bath and putting me to bed. By the time the doctor arrived to announce I had a bad case of the flu, Gram already had lowered the shades and moved her radio into my room, tuned to soothing music.

When Mama got home, late that night, Gram hadn't let her see me. I was contagious, she said.

Mama called in to me, and then went to bed. Gram sat next to me all night, and all the next day, putting cold cloths on my forehead, reading *Little Women* and *Rebecca of Sunnybrook Farm* out loud, and bringing me bowls of chicken noodle soup and Jell-O with whipped cream.

I remembered thinking I was too old to be taken care of like that. I remembered luxuriating in the attention.

Were those old snow boots still in the attic?

Probably not.

The closing school bell brought me back to today. Dozens of boys and girls rushed out the front door, just as I had twenty years ago, heading for school buses or cars. Then there were the "walkers," as I'd been, running in various directions away from the school. Did any of them have single parents? Fathers who were absent or abusive? Mothers who drank too much? Childhood wasn't always a time of innocence. I hoped they all survived it.

As the stream of students became a trickle, I walked in the front door.

"I'd like to see Miss Fitch," I said to the school clerk.

"Sign in here. Miss Fitch is in Room 201."

Miss Fitch had always been in Room 201. I knew where it was without looking at the map of the school the clerk handed me.

Her straight back was to me. Miss Fitch (she'd never be "Beth Fitch" to me) was erasing the whiteboard at the front of her classroom. It had been a blackboard when I'd spent a year sitting at one of the small desks evenly lined up to face the front of this room.

"Miss Fitch?"

She turned around. She had a few more lines around her mouth and eyes, and the brown hair I remembered as long and straight was now short and streaked with gray, but she still favored sweater sets, slacks, and loafers. She was still Miss Fitch.

"May I help you?" She stared at me a moment longer, as though searching her mind's index to identify and label me correctly. "Angela Curtis?"

I nodded.

"I was so sorry to hear about your mother's death. I

would have come to the funeral, but it was during school hours. Come in. I'm so glad you stopped in."

She'd recognized me, after all these years. She'd seen me in the hallways of this building until I went to high school, but not after that. I'd changed a lot since then. But maybe not as much as I'd thought.

She hadn't.

"What can I do for you, Angela? Or is this just a friendly visit?"

A visit after twenty years?

"I'm doing some work for Skye West."

"The actress who bought the Gardener place?"

I nodded. I felt like the second grader I'd been in this room. Nervous. Afraid to make a mistake.

"How does that bring you to Haven Harbor Elementary?"

"You knew Jasmine Gardener."

Miss Fitch sat down at her desk, and gestured that I should sit down, too. The student desks were obviously too small. I perched awkwardly on top of one, feeling as though I'd been kept after school.

"Your brother, Jed, dated her the summer that she died."

"He did. But I only knew her slightly. That summer I was taking a course required for Peace Corps volunteers. I was assigned Guatemala. I had to learn Spanish quickly, and study the country and culture I'd be working in. The course was in Rhode Island. I was only home a couple of weeks, maybe a month, at the end of the summer."

"So you didn't know Jasmine well."

"I met her a couple of times. But I wasn't pleased Jed was so involved with her. Jasmine seemed flighty and childish and demanding. When I got home, I'd expected Jed to be practicing with the high-school football team. If he had any chance at a football scholarship at a good school, he should have been working out on his own all summer, and then attending early football practices. Instead, he was hanging around the Gardener estate, mooning over that girl. I told him he was making a big mistake. He was going to be a senior in high school and he had to grow up. Plan for his future."

"What was his reaction to that?"

"He laughed. Said I'd been away, that I didn't know him anymore. That being with Jasmine Gardener would get him further than any football scholarship." She paused. "I was furious."

"He meant . . . because she had money?"

"That's what I assumed. He told me her father had gone to Yale. Jed was planning to ask him for a recommendation."

"Would that have worked?"

Miss Fitch shrugged. "I suspect not. Jed's grades weren't as good as his football plays. I knew how hard it was to go through college on scholarships and grants. I'd done it. And Jed wasn't heading in the right direction, so far as I could tell. I told him he should be more like Elsa, our little sister. She was working like mad, studying, working on science projects. She was going to be president of the math club at the high school in the fall."

"How did he react to that?"

"He said Elsa was a boring brain. He'd never be like her." Miss Fitch shook her head. "I was worried about him. And then, of course, Jasmine died, and took all his high hopes with her."

"How did he react then?"

"I left for Latin America a few days after her death, so I don't know. He didn't write often. When he did, it was about school or problems with our parents."

"What problems?"

"Our mother wasn't well, and our father wasn't much help with her. I don't think Jed was, either."

"And you were thousands of miles away."

"As I think back, everything fell on Elsa. But at the time I was proud to be the first in our family to graduate from college. I was excited about being in the Peace Corps. I thought if I'd been able to leave and go to college, Jed and Elsa could, too. But they didn't. By the time I got back here, Elsa was going to beauty school. Jed had flunked out of U Maine and was married and picking up odd jobs around town. We'd all changed."

"That night . . . the night Jasmine died, do you remember what she was doing? Who she was with?"

"She was flitting about. Drinking. They all were. She'd be with her parents' friends for a while, and then with Jed and Carole and her little nebbish of a friend from New York. She spent a lot of time playing with children, as I remember. Jed wandered about, watching her, like he was her puppy. I couldn't take it anymore, watching him make a fool of himself. I left the party with a high-school friend I hadn't seen in years and went down to Pocket Cove Beach to watch the fireworks and talk. By the time I got home Jed and Elsa were in bed. I learned what had happened to Jasmine the next morning. Horrible, no matter what I thought about her. Just dreadful."

"Jed tried to save her. He gave her CPR."

"He told me that. It didn't surprise me. He'd have done anything for Jasmine that summer."

I got up. "Thank you, Miss Fitch. I appreciate your honesty. And your memories."

"Nothing I said couldn't have been said by someone else," she said. "How are you doing, Angela?"

"I'm fine. I'm back, for at least six months. I'm now the director of my grandmother's Mainely Needlepoint business."

"I mean, how are you *really* doing? Not what are you doing."

"I'm all right," I answered, standing a little straighter. "Doing well."

"You were always a tough little girl," said Miss Fitch. "Too brave, I thought sometimes. You don't always have to be brave, you know."

I felt tears well up at the back of my eyes. I blinked quickly. "I know, Miss Fitch. Thank you."

I was back in my car within a few minutes. I started the few blocks toward home, and then changed direction.

I headed out of town. Toward Aurora.

Chapter 40

Virtue should guard the tender fair
From man's deceptive flattering snare.

—Anonymous American sampler, 1828

Most contractors worked from seven until four o'clock. Some of those under contract to the Wests had been working longer hours. By the time I reached the gates of Aurora that afternoon, all the trucks but one were gone. I drove to the carriage house.

Patrick and Skye were enjoying an early cocktail. It only took one invitation for me to decide to join them. "Beefeater and tonic with lime," I requested, noting that they'd now installed a full bar in their tiny new kitchen.

With drinks in our hands, we sat out on a small brick patio I hadn't remembered from my visit the day before. Money could certainly equal progress. At least it did at Aurora.

"I thought I'd check in and let you know who I'd talked with today," I said.

"Good. I was going to call you tonight, anyway," said Skye. "I've made appointments for us to visit Sam Gould and Linda Zaharee tomorrow. Sam in the morning, and Linda in the afternoon." Skye sat back and raised her glass to me, looking more confident than I felt.

"How did you manage that?" I asked.

"Since Sam now owns the shipyard his father built up years ago, I told Sam who I was, that I'd bought a place in Maine, and I might be interested in buying a boat. He bit right away. Plus, it turns out his wife is a fan. I promised a personalized autograph."

The power of fame! "And Linda Zaharee?"

"I just moved to Maine and was thinking of having my son's portrait done. Or mine. I admired her work and wanted to talk with her." Skye raised her eyebrows. "Presto! Doors opened."

"Congratulations. I'm afraid my accomplishments don't rank with those," I said, sipping my tall drink. "I talked with my grandmother and with Ob Winslow, and with all three of the Fitch siblings—Elsa yesterday, and Jed and Beth today."

"Good. Any news on the mysterious hairs in the needle-point?"

"No. Dave was at school today. I wouldn't expect to hear from him until tomorrow at the earliest."

Patrick nodded. "I'm assuming no one you talked with confessed to killing Jasmine."

"Afraid not! But I can add a few things to our timeline."

"Good!" said Skye. "Tell us."

"Ob was only ten in 1970, but he had crush on Jasmine, and spent a lot of time watching her. He even got her a glass of wine once. But he said he didn't think she was drunk. He said, and it was confirmed by others, that Jasmine greeted guests with her parents and spent some of the time at the party playing with the children there—giving out balloons and teaching kids how to use Hula-hoops." I looked up from my notes. "My grandmother remembered a woman taking pictures of Jasmine with the Hula-hoopers. That might have been Linda Zaharee."

Skye nodded. "Good."

"I learned a bit about the Fitch family, too. Beth, the oldest, wasn't home for most of the summer. But she didn't like Jed hanging out with Jasmine. She thought he wasn't working hard enough to earn the football scholarship everyone seemed to think he might get. She thought he was hitching his wagon to Jasmine's money and influence. And she might have been right. Jed told me he'd proposed to Jasmine late in the summer, but she hadn't given him an answer."

"Did he say anything about her being pregnant?"

"No. And I didn't bring it up, because he'd wonder how I knew. But why else would he have asked her to marry him?"

"Unless it was for her money," Skye said, thinking. "Interesting. And interesting that she hadn't said 'yes' or 'no' to him."

"The family sounded troubled to me. Their mother was sickly, and sometimes demanding, and their father ignored them all. Beth had been away at college and was leaving for the Peace Corps. She'd basically removed herself from the family. Jed was expected to go to college, but his situation with Jasmine could have helped him or hurt him, depending on how you looked at it. Elsa ended up being the one who took care of her mother and went to beautician's school in Portland."

"Ouch! Sorry about Elsa. I don't remember much about her except that she kept to herself and always seemed to have a book with her." Skye paused. "When you're seventeen or eighteen, fifteen seems very young and unimportant."

"As for the timeline . . . Jed said Jasmine didn't feel well in the middle of the fireworks and headed back toward the house. He followed her, found her in the fountain, pulled her out, and tried to resuscitate her. Everyone I spoke with said Jasmine had been drinking, but no one seemed to think she was drunk, except Jed, who said he could have underestimated how much she'd had."

"Did you get the feeling anyone was hiding anything?"

"No," I said. "They were surprised when I asked so many questions. Jed, especially, seemed genuinely sorry about Jasmine. He said he blamed himself for her death. He shouldn't have let her drink so much, and he should have gone with her back to the house. If she hadn't been alone, he said, she might not have died."

Chapter 41

When this you see, remember me
Though many miles we distant be
Remember me as you pass by
As you are now, so once was I
As I am now, so you must be
Prepare for death and follow me.

—Sampler stitched by Maria Wise,
age sixteen, Pike Township, Ohio, 1837

Skye and Patrick and I each had several drinks, poured generously. Somehow there was always something to talk about.

Skye told funny stories about her adventures in Hollywood. Patrick shared what it was like growing up with a famous mother. Skye finally suggested dinner.

Or, rather, she suggested Patrick and I go out for dinner.

"You young people go out and enjoy yourselves. You've been working hard for the past week. Get something good to eat. Enjoy the evening. I'm weary, and we have salad makings in the refrigerator. I'll be fine here. I'm too tired to eat a big meal."

If I hadn't had as much to drink, I might have hesitated. But we were all pretty relaxed by then, and Patrick was charming. I agreed. It was nothing serious, I'd tell Sarah, if she found out. I just happened to be here.

The thought of a quiet dinner with Patrick was very attractive.

We left my car at the carriage house and headed for Damariscotta in his. He'd read a review of the Damariscotta River Grill and wanted to try it. I'd never been there, but had no objections. It had been a while since I'd eaten at any restaurant other than the Harbor Haunts Café or the Lobsterman's Co-op. Both decent places, but neither contenders for the label "fine dining."

The Damariscotta River Grill, on the other hand, had tablecloths and a wine list. We were seated upstairs. The walls were covered with local artists' work. Tables overlooked either Damariscotta's main street or its harbor, or were close to a large fireplace. That fireplace would be a big plus in January. Tonight we chose the harbor view. Before I opened the menu, Patrick ordered a bottle of Merlot and two glasses. I didn't object.

"But no more, Patrick. We have to drive back to Haven Harbor."

"We'll drink and eat slowly," he answered, raising his glass to meet mine. "To a lovely evening, and an even lovelier lady."

He did have a way with words.

We ordered mussels in wine as an appetizer to share. Then I ordered the duck (not a common choice on a Maine summer menu) and Patrick ordered scallops.

He asked me about my years in Arizona, and I told him about Mama and why I'd left: a story I didn't share with everyone. I didn't tell him about how I'd used the carriage house when I was in high school.

He talked about private school and prep school, and how he'd first wanted to be a set designer and had studied at the Rhode Island School of Design. It was there he'd realized he was essentially a loner. He wanted to do his own art, and not be part of a production company, even though his mother's name could have opened doors for him.

We talked through the appetizer and our main courses and continued talking while we sipped espresso and shared a piece of chocolate lava cake.

I found myself laughing at his jokes—and looking into his eyes. I hadn't had a dinner like that in . . . a while.

On the way back to his car, he took my hand. A little sappy, but I liked it. The night was beautiful, and it was getting late. As Patrick had promised, we'd eaten slowly, savoring our food and being together. We were one of the last couples to leave the restaurant.

On the way home Patrick focused on the road and I considered where, if anywhere, this evening might end up.

We returned to Aurora. After all, I'd left my car there.

Patrick saw the flames first.

He slammed on the brakes, almost swerving his car into a tree, and jumped out. "Call 911! I'm going to find Mom!" The roof of the carriage house was burning.

It took me a split second to connect. Then I pulled out my cell and dialed the Haven Harbor Fire Department. They were all volunteers; it would take a few minutes for them to arrive.

The smoke and flames from the roof were increasing.

I got out of the car and watched as one section of the roof collapsed.

Patrick and Skye were inside. Would he get her out? Instinctively, I touched my gold angel pendant. But the angel was meant to keep me safe. Who would help the Wests?

I ran across the street, toward Ob's house. Ob must have a hose, even if he only had well water.

Before I got to his barn, Ob ran toward me. Skye was with him, dressed only in a long nightgown.

"Skye! Thank goodness. You're all right!"

"I'm a light sleeper. The smoke woke me. I ran downstairs and out and stupidly left my phone inside. I came over here so Ob could call for help."

She looked at me as we headed back toward the carriage house. "Where's Patrick?"

Chapter 42

Tis religion that can give
Sweetest pleasures while we live
Tis religion must supply
Solid comfort when we die.

—Sampler stitched by Mary Muir (1805–1881),
age twelve, Alexandria, Virginia,
taken from poem attributed to English poet
Mary Masters (1694–1771), published in 1733

"Patrick! He went inside the carriage house to find you."

Skye screamed as she and Ob and I ran faster, back toward the carriage house.

The first firefighters, arriving in pickups and jeeps as well as fire engines, got there when we did. A police car pulled up seconds later.

"There's a man inside!" I yelled to the first firefighter on the scene. He took one look at me and at Skye, who had stopped screaming and was staring at the burning house. He pulled on his mask and gestured to his partner. They pushed their way through the large door, which had once led to where the horses, carriages, or cars had been housed.

I held my breath, trying not to breathe the smoke, trying not to think about what was happening in the carriage house.

Anna arrived, carrying a bathrobe. She draped it over Skye's shoulders. "You poor dear. Don't want no one taking pictures of you looking like that," she said. Skye didn't seem to hear her. Her eyes were blank, focused on the house.

Firefighters were pointing their hoses at the roof, which increased the smoke. In the dark the only light was from the moon and the spotlight on one of the fire engines. It was hard to tell whether the water was making a difference.

An ambulance pulled in behind the trucks. The EMTs ran out, checked with the policeman, and then stood. Waiting.

Just as Skye and Ob and Anna and I were.

Another section of the roof crashed in. Had Patrick been under it? What about the two men who'd gone in after him?

Sparks from the fire ignited branches of a tree nearby. It started to smolder.

Finally, through the smoke, we could see figures emerging from the house. The two firefighters were carrying someone.

Skye and I ran toward them, but we were stopped by the policeman. "He needs medical attention. Don't get in the way."

Skye sobbed and covered her mouth. I felt in shock. I'd had an almost-romantic evening with a handsome man. How could Patrick be that limp form the EMTs were putting on a stretcher? I put my arm around Skye's shoulder, but she didn't seem to feel it. Her body was tight.

"They'll take him to Haven Harbor Hospital," I said. "I'll drive you there."

Then I realized my car was blocked in by all the emergency vehicles. I ran over to the policeman. "Please, can his mother ride to the hospital in the ambulance? My car's blocked."

He hesitated, but then he looked at Skye. "Make it quick, then. In the front, not the back." Skye nodded and climbed into the front seat of the ambulance. A second or two later, it pulled away, sirens on and lights flashing.

They were gone.

"Was that the actress?" asked the cop.

"Yes. Skye West," I answered. "The injured man was her son, Patrick."

I stood watching. The firefighters did their best, but they couldn't save the carriage house. It burned to the ground.

"Under construction," I heard someone say. "Maybe flammable materials left inside."

"Could have been electrical."

"Nah. Seemed to be centered on the stairway to the second floor. Spread faster than it should."

"They'll be calling the arson guys in on this one, for sure."

When only one truck was left to oversee the carnage and put up barriers so no one would get near the fire site, I was finally able to reach my car. The sun was beginning to come up. It was going to be a beautiful June day.

I drove to the hospital.

Chapter 43

Whoever thinks a faultless piece to see
Thinks what ne'er was, nor is, nor e'er shall be.

—Stitched by Abigail Currier, age nineteen,
Newbury, Massachusetts, 1830,
taken from Alexander Pope's (1688–1744)
An Essay on Criticism, Part II.
(Abigail's hands were deformed.
She pulled every stitch through
the linen with her teeth.)

By the time I got to the hospital half the media outlets in Maine had trucks outside. I went in the emergency room door and tried to explain who I was to the guard posted there.

"I'm a friend of the West family! I was with them last night. I just left their home. Please let me in to see Patrick. Or at least to wait with Skye."

I got nowhere. But when I was walking back to my car

through the now-dispersing media, I heard Patrick had been airlifted to the burn center at Mass General.

So he was alive. But, I assumed, not in good shape. Skye would have gone with him.

Gram was sitting at the kitchen table waiting for me when I got home about six-thirty. She took one look at my smoke-marked clothes and hair and sniffed. "You were at that fire. Angel. I've been up all night listening to reports. They said someone was hurt in the blaze. I thought . . ." Her face crumpled with relief.

"Oh, Gram," I said, putting my arms around her. "I'm so sorry. I should have called. Really. I'm fine. Just exhausted and dirty. Skye's son, Patrick, was the one hurt. At the hospital people are saying he was taken to Boston."

She nodded against my chest. How could I have forgotten to call her? I hadn't even told her I was having dinner with Patrick. She'd probably waited dinner for me, too. How could I have done that to her? Yes, I was used to living on my own. But I knew very well I was now home, and Gram kept track of me.

She sat back up. "I called Sarah. I thought you might be with her. Now she's worried, too. You'd better call her."

I nodded. "I will. I should never have disappeared." (That word we seldom used at home.) "I should have let you know where I was."

"Thank goodness you're all right." Gram dried her eyes. "We both need to get some sleep. Mustn't spend all our time blubbering. I should have known you could take care of yourself."

She left the kitchen and walked slowly upstairs, leaving me feeling guilty, as well as exhausted. How could I have forgotten to call home? Such a simple thing.

Now I'd have to call Sarah. It wouldn't be a secret I'd

spent the evening with Patrick. Nothing more, heaven knew. But Sarah wouldn't be pleased.

And today? Skye had made appointments for us to see Sam Gould and Linda Zaharee. Should I cancel them?

I put my head down on the kitchen table.

Why couldn't I do anything right? I'd upset Gram, and no doubt Sarah, too. The two people closest to me in Haven Harbor.

Maybe I should give up and go back to Arizona. There I'd had a job, and my own apartment, and no one cared where I was or when or with whom.

Some days I'd been lonely.

I wanted people to care about me. I did. But sometimes that wasn't easy.

I picked up my phone and dialed Skye West's number. She didn't pick up. I hadn't thought she would. "Skye, this is Angie. When you get a chance, please let me know how Patrick is doing. And how you are. I'm going to go ahead and talk to Sam and Linda today. I'll keep in touch. And, please, know I'm praying for you and Patrick."

Praying. I hadn't done that in a very long time. This seemed the right time to start again.

Chapter 44

Next unto God dear parents I address
My self to you in humble thankfulness
For all your care and charge on me bestowed
The means of learning unto me allow'd
Go on I pray and let me still pursue
The golden art the vulgar never knew.

—Sampler stitched by Sarah Fabens, age fourteen, Salem, Massachusetts, 1807

I called Sarah. She didn't pick up, so I left a message. Yes, I was all right. I'd been with the Wests. Skye and Patrick were both now in Boston. (I assumed.)

Then I went to bed. I didn't even stop to shower. I needed the escape, and rest, of a couple of hours of sleep. I set my alarm for nine. As I'd promised Skye, I was going to keep our appointment with Sam Gould at ten-thirty.

His office was in a big brick building outside Gould's Shipbuilders and Marine Services, on Camden Harbor. The sky was blue, and a flotilla of sailboats was in the harbor, along with two three-master ships, several lobster boats, and dozens of recreational vessels.

Gould's specialized in building small yachts. Not the Aristotle Onassis– or Bill Gates–sized vessels (if Gates had one), but the size that said, *"I'm important even if you've never heard of me."* The kind bought or chartered by people who moved in circles far above Haven Harbor.

The slim young man seated outside Gould's office was dressed in tan slacks and a pale blue golf shirt. Or yachting shirt. I wasn't sure of the difference. "May I help you?" he asked in an accent that hadn't originated Down East.

"Skye West and I have an appointment with Sam Gould at ten-thirty. Ms. West is having some personal problems today. I'm Angela Curtis; I'm keeping her appointment for her."

He arched his eyebrows at me. "I'll see if Mr. Gould is still interested in meeting with you." He shook his finger at me as though I were a disobedient child. "You should have called ahead when Ms. West had a change of plans."

My mind wanted to say something inappropriate, but I held my tongue. Being rude wouldn't help me keep the appointment.

How was Patrick? I hadn't heard from Skye. I didn't want to hear news about him from an entertainment reporter.

Then I realized . . . no wonder Skye hadn't called. She didn't have her telephone. She'd left it in the carriage house. That's why she'd gone to Ob Winslow's to call the fire department. She hadn't gotten my message.

Drat!

Would I be able to reach her at Mass General? I suspected not.

I'd have to wait for her to think of contacting me. And I probably wasn't high on her priority list right now.

I'd always thought Hollywood people had personal assistants or secretaries, or both. Skye had never mentioned having either, but I suspected that, somewhere, she had people on call who could do her bidding. Today was a day she'd need them.

"Ms. Curtis? Mr. Gould will see you. Briefly." The simpering young man was back, pointing at the room he'd just left.

If Jasmine Gardener had admired men of a certain type, you couldn't tell it by looking at Jed Fitch and Sam Gould forty-five years later. Jed was a big man, now given to fat, but (according to Skye) was muscular in his teens. In contrast, Sam Gould was small—not much taller than me. Although his face had the permanent tan of a man who spent many hours outdoors, probably at sea, I wouldn't have trusted him to have the strength to hoist a sail. He might weigh less than I did.

One thing he and Jed Fitch lacked in common was hair. Sam Gould was not only completely bald, but even his eyebrows were gone. Age? Chemo? I had no idea. But his smile was genuine.

"Ms. Curtis? Welcome. I heard on the news this morning about that horrible fire in Haven Harbor. Tell me, how is Ms. West? I didn't expect either of you to show up for your appointment this morning."

"She's fine. She's with her son at Mass General," I said. "I let her know I'd be coming this morning in her place." Although, of course, she didn't get the message I had left.

"I'll be thinking of them both. What a horrible situation. You know, it brought back a lot of memories for me when she called yesterday and told me that she'd bought Aurora. I spent some time there when I was a young man."

"You knew Jasmine Gardener."

"Yes, I did." He looked at me closely. "How did you know that?"

I decided to plunge right in. "Because that's what Skye wanted to talk to you about today."

He started to speak, but I interrupted him. "I know, she said she wanted to talk about your building her a boat. And she may indeed want you to do that. I can't speak about that. But, you see, Skye knew you forty-five years ago."

He frowned. "I'm sure I would have remembered her."

"Her name wasn't Skye West then," I said, brashly going on ahead. "She was Mary North."

"Mary!" The name rang a bell. "The Mary who was Jasmine's friend?"

I nodded. "So you do remember her."

"Mary North. Skye West. Amazing." Clearly he remembered Mary. "That certainly explains why she decided to buy Aurora. Mary loved that place. Maybe she loved it more than Jasmine did. Jasmine took it for granted."

"Mary/Skye is trying to figure out what happened at Aurora that last day, the day Jasmine died. She wanted to ask you what you remembered."

Sam Gould was quiet. "It's been a long time. I've tried not to think about Jasmine, and what happened that summer. But Mary deserves to know."

"She said you and Jasmine had dated the previous winter, in New York."

"Yes. A mutual friend introduced us. I was going to Columbia, and we met at a party and started talking about Maine. Her Maine, of course, was very different from mine. I grew up here in Camden, and was definitely a local, even if I was lucky enough to have a father with a prosperous business. She was a summer visitor. A 'summer complaint,' we used to call them."

I smiled. I hadn't heard that phrase recently, but I certainly recognized it.

"We started going places together. You could call it dating. We usually were with girls she knew, and some students I knew. Girls in the prep schools were always looking for 'presentable college men,' as Jasmine once put it." He smiled, remembering.

"And you were presentable."

Sam shrugged. "She must have thought so. Jasmine and I did a lot together that winter. It was a turbulent time, even though it was two years after Columbia students had gone on strike, protesting the Vietnam War and Columbia's taking over a park the students wanted to keep part of Harlem. That all happened before I was there. I was a sophomore when I met Jasmine. Everyone was against the war, but I didn't want to get as involved as some of my friends did. I didn't protest or march. My father would have had a fit if I'd been arrested, even for a good cause." He pushed his square glasses back on his nose. "Thinking back, I was kind of a wimp when it came to taking social risks. Jasmine was like me. She just wanted to have fun. If someone was burning a draft card and that meant a party, she was for it. If it meant a demonstration, she'd rather stay home." He stopped. "We had more in common than I like to admit."

I decided to be blunt. "When she died, Jasmine was pregnant. Were you her child's father?"

Sam Gould shifted backward in his chair. "However did you know? . . . Oh. Of course. Mary would have known."

"And?"

"About a week before she died, Jasmine told me she was pregnant. At first, I didn't believe her. Then I accused her of sleeping with a Haven Harbor guy she'd been seeing while I was working in Camden. I'll admit I didn't take the news well."

"Jed Fitch?"

"I don't remember his name. I was angry, and felt betrayed, when she told me about the baby. And I panicked. I told her I'd help to pay for an abortion, so she wouldn't have to tell her parents."

"What was her reaction? What did she want to do?"

"I don't know. She said she could take care of herself—that she didn't need me. I remember where we were. It was a bright day, and we were down at that little beach in Haven Harbor."

"Pocket Cove Beach."

"Right. And she walked off. She said she didn't even need a ride back to Aurora. She'd get there, and anywhere else she wanted to go, without me. Truthfully, I was relieved."

"Did you see her at the party Labor Day weekend?"

"No. I'd been invited, before she'd confronted me about the baby. At first, I decided it would be best if I didn't go. Then I changed my mind and drove to Haven Harbor. I got a drink and looked for Jasmine." His eyes darkened. "She was with another guy, probably that Jed. So I turned around and left." He sighed. "When I heard she'd drowned, my first thought was that she'd killed herself. Because of the pregnancy, you know. But no one ever said that. I kept wondering if she would have lived if I'd talked to her at the party, despite our problems. Instead, I went to her funeral."

"Thank you for taking the time to talk to me," I said, standing up. "I'll tell Skye—Mary—what you said."

"Tell her I hope her son is all right. And that I'd love to see her when she's back in Maine. See her as a friend, even if she isn't a customer."

"I'll tell her," I said.

I turned on my telephone again when I got into my car.

I had four messages. Sarah was glad I was all right, and wanted to know about Patrick. She didn't ask what I'd been doing with the Wests last night.

Skye said Patrick had burns on his arms and hands, which were concerning because of his art. Although he'd be in the hospital for a while, his lungs looked all right, and he would recover.

I felt as though someone had given me a full-body hug. Relief. He'd be all right.

The next call was from Dave Percy. "Angie, I stayed up late last night, but I figured it out. Those hairs Sarah found in the needlepoint? They're from a moose. And, Angie, I'll admit I was curious. The hair didn't seem normal to me. So I tested it. If I didn't have such a background in poisons, I might have missed it. That hair was soaked in arsenic."

Arsenic! The same poison the hummingbird had died drinking.

And one more call.

"Angie, Sergeant Pete Lambert. We've got the state fire marshal's people out here at Aurora with a black Lab named Amy. I'm assured she can sniff out gasoline or kerosene or any other substance that shouldn't have been in the carriage house. No conclusions yet, but indications are that there were accelerants here in several places. That would indicate a strong probability that last night's fire was set. You were here, with the Wests. They're in Boston and not available. I'd like to talk with you as soon as possible."

Chapter 45

The up-to-date bridal linens will include at least one breakfast set, and to be quite choice, it must be trimmed with lace, preferably hand-made filet. And there must be tassels or pendants of some sort dangling from the corners of your breakfast set. At least there will be if you have a truly feminine way with you, because they are fetching and up-to-date.

—*The Modern Priscilla, Home Needlework and Everyday Housekeeping* magazine, May 1918

Arsenic? Arson? But Patrick is going to be all right.

My brain, still foggy from lack of sleep, chose to focus on the (relatively) good news.

Patrick will be all right.

I sat in my car a moment, taking in the view of Camden Harbor. Two boys in kayaks shouted to each other. A black-backed gull screamed. The scent of ocean breezes and salt water filled my car and my consciousness.

My visit with Sam Gould had been interesting, but it

hadn't given me any clues to Jasmine's death. He'd known she was pregnant. She'd told him the baby was his. (Did that explain why she'd rejected Jed's proposal?)

I didn't know. I pulled out the little notebook I'd been carrying and jotted a few notes. Who hadn't I talked to who'd been on Skye's list?

Carole Simpson—now Carole Simpson Fitch, Jed's wife—and Linda Zaharee. I had an appointment (or Skye did) with Linda this afternoon at four o'clock.

Meanwhile, Pete Lambert wanted to talk with me. I dialed his number.

"I don't know what I can help with, Pete. The fire started before Patrick and I got back from dinner."

"That's what I thought. But so much was going on last night, I wanted to check with you. So you're certain Skye left before you got back to the carriage house?"

"She'd gone to the Winslows' house across the street to report the fire."

"But you didn't know that when you arrived at the carriage house."

"Patrick and I assumed she was still inside. She hadn't gone to dinner with us because she was tired. She'd planned to go to bed early."

"You didn't see anyone else around the place?"

Pete was checking off possibilities.

"Contractors' trucks have been around both the big house and the carriage house during the day. But last night the only cars there were mine and the Wests'."

"So when the fire broke out, Skye West was the only one at the carriage house."

"She said she'd fallen asleep, and that the smoke woke her up."

"She was lucky," Pete commented. "Did you smell anything at the fire?"

"Smoke. Fire. Wood burning. I wasn't paying attention to specific odors." The place was burning down! Why would I have been sniffing?

"I've tried to reach Skye at the hospital. She's the only one who might have seen or heard anything unusual before the fire started, but right now she isn't thinking about the fire. She's thinking about her son."

"Have you any ideas?"

"That's still being investigated. It doesn't seem electrical. Did Ms. West smoke?"

"I never saw her smoking. Do they think she set the fire?"

"They're covering every angle, from accidents to arson."

"She loved the estate. She was planning to fix it up and live in it."

"So I've been told."

"Pete, if that fire was set, then it's the second time in a week that someone tried to kill Skye."

Our connection went silent. Then, "You're talking about that dead hummingbird? I can't see a dead bird has anything to do with a fire. By the way, what're you doing in Camden this morning? I thought you'd be home, recuperating from last night."

I hesitated. Then I told him. "Skye's convinced Jasmine Gardener was murdered forty-five years ago. She's asked me to talk with Jasmine's friends who were at that party in 1970. I was in Camden talking with one of them."

"You mean, for the past few days you've been running around town dredging up past history, getting people excited about that old Jasmine Gardener story?"

"That's right."

"You realize that, on the slight chance that girl was murdered, you've been turning over rocks covered for years? That if she was murdered, you may have alerted her killer? That what you've been doing could have driven someone to make sure Skye West and her family leave town . . . permanently?"

Shit.

"Then may I request . . . no, order you to stop playing amateur detective, and forget 1970? Experts on fires are investigating what happened here. The Wests are in Boston. You need to go home. Go work on your needlepoint or plan your grandmother's wedding. Leave the crime fighting to people who know what they're doing."

"Yes, Pete." There was no sense in arguing with the man. But if Skye and I had started a ball rolling downhill, I wasn't going to stop it just when it was picking up speed. "But you'll keep in mind what I said? If you find the arsonist, you may also find a killer."

"If you should talk with Skye West, ask her to call me, please?" Pete asked.

"I will," I promised. That was all I promised.

I sat back, thinking about that telephone call. *Arson? Who would have started a fire in the carriage house?*

Dave's message was strange, too. Moose hair soaked in arsenic? What's that about?

I left a message for Sarah about Patrick and headed back to Haven Harbor. My appointment with Linda wasn't until midafternoon. I could fit in visits to both Carole and Dave before that.

Chapter 46

She fares the best whose every virtuous deed
With truth is registered in realms above
Eternal happiness shall be her need
Crowned by the blessing of th' Almighty's love.

—Stitched by Betsy Warren, age fourteen, at a young ladies boarding school in Portland, Maine, 1805 (Embroidery was often taught at such schools.)

An hour later I turned into the driveway of the Fitch home.

I was lucky. Carole Fitch answered the door. I wondered what she'd looked like in 1970, when she'd dated Jed. Now she was heavyset, with straight hair cut so short none of it touched her round face. Maybe she'd been on her way to the Y to work out. Yoga pants might be in style in some places, but Carole hadn't attempted to be stylish. Her sweatpants hung loosely around her wide hips, although the Common Ground Country Fair T-shirt she was wearing was a size too small.

"Yes?" She looked at me, obviously trying to remember who I was. That happens when you've been out of town for ten years. "Angie Curtis?"

"That's right. Do you have a few minutes?"

"I'm sorry about your mother. I went to her funeral last month. I wasn't a friend of hers, but I wanted to pay my respects to your grandmother. How's she doing?"

"She's fine, thank you."

She was puzzled, I could tell, by my being on her doorstep. I suspected her husband hadn't mentioned my visit to his office the day before.

"May I come in?"

She opened the door and gestured toward the living room. "I was on my way out. But you're welcome to stay a few minutes."

"This won't take long." I smiled.

Carole Fitch sat on the edge of a wide armchair. Her husband would have fit comfortably on the large seat. Carole wasn't tiny, but the chair still looked too big for her.

"I'm sorry to bother you. You know Skye West bought the old Gardener place."

She nodded. "I've known that for a while. My husband was her agent."

"You may have heard she's interested in compiling a history of the estate. She asked me to help her. I've been talking to people around town about what they remember about Aurora, and about the Gardeners."

"I'm afraid I can't help you. I have nothing to contribute to your project." She started to get up.

"But you were about the same age as Jasmine Gardener. You and your husband both knew her through the yacht club."

She sat down again. "We did. But my husband knew her

much better than I did. Of course, that was years before we were married."

"Of course. So you didn't spend any time with Jasmine?"

"Sometimes. As you said, we were in the same group of friends. We all went places together. But she wasn't a special friend of mine."

"What did you think of her?"

"Please don't put this in your history, but I always thought she was a spoiled bitch. She wanted what she wanted, and she was used to taking it. She thought of herself first. She didn't care about other people unless they helped her get what she wanted."

"That's a pretty strong statement," I replied.

"I know. We shouldn't speak ill of the dead. But it's always driven me crazy how people who hardly knew her talked so much about her after she died. She was seventeen and she died. That should have been the end of it. Here it is forty-five years later, and you're asking me about her. She should rest in peace. Her life was over years ago. People should focus on the living, not the dead."

"You were at that last party, at Aurora."

"Everyone I knew was."

"Was Jasmine drinking that night? Heavily?"

"She was drinking more than she should have been. I didn't notice at the time, but later, when people said she'd been drunk and fallen and hit her head, I believed it. We were all drinking that night. Or smoking. Or both."

"So you don't question how she died."

"She drowned. That was all there was to it."

"Your husband was the one who found her."

"And it's given him nightmares for years, I can assure you. Jed was one of those under her spell that summer. He followed her around. I swear, he would have done anything that girl told him to do. Stay up so late he didn't show up for his job the next morning. Drink too much. Miss football practices when he should have been preparing for his senior year. He missed out on major scholarships because of that girl. If it hadn't been for her, there's no telling what he could have become."

"You loved him then, didn't you? Someone told me you'd dated Jed before Jasmine did."

"That's no secret. And I was better for him than she was, despite her money and her fancy clothes. I loved him. Jasmine only knew what she thought was best for herself." Carole looked over at a wedding picture of herself and Jed taken many years ago. He was still young and handsome; she was beautiful, looking at him as though she couldn't be happier. "It took Jed a while to figure out I was the best woman for him. But we've had a good life together. I don't often think about Jasmine anymore. Jed was young then. He had dollar signs in his eyes. He liked Jasmine, of course. But he also thought being with her would be a lot easier than sweating on the football field and studying 'till all hours."

"So he was dating Jasmine for her money."

"That's what I thought then, and that's what I think now. No matter what he, or anyone else, says, Jasmine's death was the best thing that could have happened to him."

Chapter 47

And for the gate of the court shall be an hanging of twenty cubits, of blue, and purple, and scarlet, and fine twined linen, wrought with needlework: and their pillars shall be four, and their sockets four.

—Exodus 27:16, King James Version

I thanked Carole Fitch for her thoughts.

She hadn't been a Jasmine admirer.

Could she have been her murderer?

She'd been a jealous girlfriend. And Elsa and Beth, Jed's sisters, had agreed with what she'd said about Jasmine's influence on Jed: it left him unprepared to compete for the football scholarship his friends and family were hoping he'd earn.

But that didn't make Carole a murderer. Despite what everyone had said about Jasmine, I didn't see anyone as a killer.

Maybe she had drunk too much and drowned, just as the police had determined at the time.

Next stop: Dave's house.

He was right where I'd suspected he'd be: in his poison garden. I assumed the plants he was pulling up (with his gloved hands) were weeds. "Dave? I got your message."

He stood up, brushing the earth off his long pants and long-sleeved shirt. He'd once told me he had to "suit up" to take care of his garden. Some of the plants, like poison ivy, no one would want to touch. "Glad you got my message," he said. "I called as soon as I confirmed my tests."

"I was in Camden."

Dave left his garden and walked toward me. "I'm ready for a sit-down. Some iced tea or coffee?"

"Iced coffee would be great."

"You sit, and I'll bring us each a glass," he said, indicating two red Adirondack chairs under a maple tree.

I sat, glad to have a few minutes to think. It was still early in the season, but some of Dave's plants looked as though they could take over the garden. In one corner lilies of the valley had almost finished blooming. I remembered his warning about them. If you picked the flowers and put them in water, the water could kill a child or an animal who drank it. I couldn't imagine a child drinking out of a vase. But a cat or a dog? Sure.

And now he'd detected arsenic in or on moose hairs. Not any moose hairs, but moose hairs that had been stitched into a needlepoint picture. Arsenic? Moose hairs? Just one of those would be strange enough.

Dave came back with two frosty glasses.

"I remembered you didn't take sugar in your coffee. I hope that's true of iced coffee, too," he said.

"It is. You have a good memory." I took a good sip of the drink. I hadn't realized I'd been thirsty.

"Let me tell you about the moose hair," he said.

"Please."

"The hair was mammalian, of course. Natural hair is always mammalian, although I wondered for a few minutes whether I'd looked at what you'd given me too quickly. That maybe it was a fiber of some kind, not a hair."

"But it was hair."

"Definitely. I did some more research and found it was from a moose."

"Which makes no sense. Why would Millie Gardener have stitched moose hair into her embroidery?"

Dave nodded excitedly. "That's what I thought. It made absolutely no sense. But hair, even hair from a moose, is usually flexible. Even soft. This hair was stiff. Of course, it must have been flexible when it was woven into the embroidery. But I couldn't figure out why it was now hard. So I put it in a little water to soften it. At first, I tried cold water, but that didn't help. Then I put it in warm water and . . . presto! It became soft."

"I can't believe you spent so much time on a piece of hair that might have gotten into the panel by mistake," I said, a little amused at how seriously Dave had taken this.

"I had a hunch. A crazy one, but a hunch. Some substances dissolve more easily in hot water than in cold. One of them is arsenic. And I remembered hearing students saying Mrs. Gardener thought her daughter was poisoned."

"True," I said, sitting up a little straighter. Should I tell Dave about the hummingbird? I decided not to. At least not yet.

"Arsenic is one of the easiest poisons to test for." Dave

nodded as he spoke. "So I did, and, sure enough, there was arsenic in the warm water I'd soaked the hair in."

"It can't have been a lot of arsenic," I said. "In one hair?"

"Not enough to kill anyone, if that's what you're thinking. But moose hairs don't come one at a time. If there were more hairs, and they were all soaked in arsenic . . . arsenic is very potent. It only takes a hundredth of an ounce of arsenic to kill someone."

"I know arsenic was an important poison historically. But you hardly ever hear of anyone being poisoned by it today."

"You can't buy it at a hardware store anymore. But it's still used in some manufacturing. And since it occurs naturally, traces of arsenic are even in our drinking water. Here in Maine, and other eastern states, especially in rural areas where there were family graveyards in the nineteenth century, arsenic, which was used as a preservative for bodies of men killed in the Civil War, has sometimes leached into the ground, and then into the groundwater."

I shuddered. But Dave was on a roll.

"During the nineteenth century, arsenic was used as a basic preservative. Angie, are there any mounted animals at Aurora? Or were there, before you cleaned the place out?"

I stared at him. "Yes. And, yes, one was a moose head."

He nodded with satisfaction. "I don't have to test those to know one place the arsenic could have come from. Beginning in the eighteenth century, arsenic was a basic tool of taxidermists. They mixed arsenic with plaster of paris and rubbed it into the skin and hair of animals or birds they wanted to preserve, or sometimes dipped whatever they were preserving into an arsenic solution. Either way, the arsenic prevented decay. Even moths wouldn't harm their work. It would kill the moths or other insects."

"So . . . you're saying . . ."

"Someone could cut a small piece of a preserved animal, or even its stuffing, so no one would notice, soak it in water, and get an arsenic solution that could kill someone."

Elsa Fitch had bought two of those preserved heads at the lawn sale. I hoped she knew they contained poison.

Chapter 48

Cleaning Woolwork: If the woolwork is not much soiled, stretch it in a frame and wash it over with a quart of water into which a tablespoon of ox gall has been dropped. If much soiled, wash with gin and soft soap, in the proportions of a quarter of a pound of soap to half a pint of gin.

—*The Dictionary of Needlework: An Encyclopaedia of Artistic, Plain, and Fancy Needlework,* London, 1882

"So the moose hair may have been from a preserved moose head, because of the arsenic. But that still doesn't explain why Millie Gardener was using moose hair—poisoned moose hair, at that—in her embroidery," I said, trying to put it all together.

"I have no idea what the connection is. Except, as you've said, that Mrs. Gardener suspected her daughter had been poisoned with arsenic."

"Maybe she left it as a clue? But a clue to what?" I turned the information over and over in my mind.

"Maybe knowing the poison would help identify the killer," Dave suggested.

"If she set it up as a puzzle, she's succeeded. I have no idea where she's trying to lead us," I admitted. "But this isn't the first time this week arsenic has shown up."

I had Dave's attention immediately.

"Where else was there arsenic?"

"Late Saturday afternoon a hummingbird sipped lemonade out of Skye's drink at the lawn sale and died. The police tested the glass and found it contained arsenic."

"Are the police investigating who poisoned the glass?"

I shook my head. "They don't seem concerned about it. They even implied she might have added the arsenic herself to call attention to Millie Gardener's accusations about Jasmine."

"Maybe you should nudge them a little."

"I did remind Pete Lambert, this morning. But I don't think they want to hear from me right now. They're busy trying to figure out whether the fire was arson."

"Fire? What fire?" Dave asked, putting down his glass.

"The carriage house at Aurora burned to the ground last night. Patrick West was injured. He thought his mother was inside, and he tried to find her."

"Is he going to be all right?"

"Last I heard, he'd live, but take time to heal. He and his mother are at Mass General now."

"And the police think it might be arson?" Dave leaned toward me, clearly concerned.

"They called in the state fire marshal to investigate. When I talked with Pete earlier today he said arson was likely."

"Then there've been two attempts on Skye West's life in the past week."

"I agree. Maybe it's because she's investigating Jasmine Gardener's death." I paused. "Or . . . she hired me to."

Dave stared at me. "She did what?"

"She'd planned to investigate by herself. She'd started by having that lawn sale, hoping it would attract people she felt had motives to kill Jasmine Gardener back in 1970. Then she realized I'd be in a better position to do some sleuthing, since I lived in town, and I'd worked for a private investigator. She gave me a list of people to talk to."

"So you could be in danger, too."

I shrugged.

"Have you found out anything?"

"Nothing significant. I've rounded out details about people close to Jasmine Gardener the summer she died. So far I haven't come up with anyone with a strong enough motive to kill her."

"Have you talked with everyone yet?"

"All but one—" I was interrupted by my phone. "Excuse me, Dave. Yes? Sarah. Did you get my voice mail? I don't know any more than when I called earlier. Skye left me a message. Her cell phone was lost in the fire, so I can't easily get hold of her. It sounds like he'll have a rough recovery, but he'll be all right." I kept listening. "That's strange. I'm with Dave right now. We'll look. And that hair you found in the needlework? It was from a moose. And it had been soaked in arsenic." I put my hand over the phone. "Sarah wants to know if she's in any danger from the poison, since she was working with the needlework panel."

"Tell her I don't think so. Only trace amounts of arsenic were on the hair."

"Did you hear that, Sarah? Dave and I will look at the

panels he has. Even if the numbers are there, they're probably just notes about what order they were hung on the dining-room wall. But I'll get back to you." I clicked off.

"What numbers?" asked Dave. "I assume that was Sarah Byrne."

I nodded. "She's been working on her two panels. She says she's found small numbers embroidered within the designs. She wanted to know if anyone else had seen them."

"I've hardly had time to look at the two you gave me," said Dave. "School ended yesterday. I'd planned to start stitching in a day or two."

"Let's look at your panels. Just to see," I said. "Sarah suggested examining them with a magnifying glass. The numbers she found were small, but distinct. And they were Roman numerals."

"The ones you gave me are in my dining room. I keep my needlepoint stash in an old pine captain's trunk there."

Dave's two panels—the fountain at Aurora and the wide view of Haven Harbor—were on top of his threads and needles and canvases. We spread them out on his dining-room table.

"I don't see any Roman numerals," I said.

"I have a box of magnifying glasses in my study," said Dave. "I use them in my classes. I'll get us each one."

I examined the fountain panel, inch by inch. Had Sarah imagined numbers? Or were they only on her panels?

But that wouldn't make sense. On the other hand, not a lot was making sense right now. And being up most of the night at the fire was beginning to catch up with me.

Dave returned and handed me a large glass. "Have you found anything?"

"Nothing."

We were both silent as we examined the embroidery. "I feel like Sherlock Holmes looking for a clue," I said in a few minutes, straightening up. "I don't think there's anything here."

Dave kept looking. "Wait! I found one!" He pointed to an *X* on one of the sailboats in the harbor. "It's the number ten. Sarah was right. I wouldn't have noticed an *X* as a number if she hadn't alerted us."

"'Curiouser and curiouser,' as Alice would have said. And you're sure it's not just an *X*?" I looked down at the tiny, but perfect, numeral. "Okay. Now we have to see if there's one in my panel."

My eyes were weary. Dave found the number on the other panel, too. An *IV* was hidden in the folds of the statue of Aurora's cape.

Chapter 49

Happy the child whose tender years
Receives instructions well
Who shares the sinners Path and fears
The road that Leads to hell.
When we devote our youth to God
'Tis Pleasing in his eyes
A flower when offered in the bud
Is no vain sacrifice.

—Sampler worked by Williamina Robertson, age nine, Alexandria, Virginia, 1827

We called Sarah to tell her we'd found numbers in the needlepoint Dave had, too. Then, despite Pete's warning and my exhaustion, I headed down the coast to Linda Zaharee's home and studio. I kept thinking about the mysterious numbers on the needlepoint.

There were ten panels. We'd found four numbers. Chances are the other panels had numbers, too. But why?

Could they be more important than instructions about how to hang the panels?

If Millie Gardener had wanted to leave directions about something like that, why not write the numbers on the back of the frames? Why go to the trouble of stitching them into the pictures? And why Roman numerals?

Too many unanswered questions.

A teenager with her hair in dreads and wearing tight jeans and a flowered T-shirt answered the door of the strikingly modern home. Most of its outside walls were glass. I could see behind the girl that at least some of the inside walls of the home were granite.

"Yes?"

"I'm here to see Ms. Zaharee."

"Okay." The girl took two steps into the house and yelled, "Grandma! Someone's here to see you." I followed her inside. The granite walls were partially covered by immense paintings—some of the sea, some portraits.

"Keisha, tell her I'll be there in a minute. Be polite!" came a voice from the second floor. Aurora's carved oak staircase was dark. The wrought-iron stairway here pulled the outside light in.

"Come in and sit down," said Keisha. She gestured at a white couch near a massive fireplace. The couch could have seated six comfortably.

"Do you mind if I look at the view for a moment?" I walked to the glass wall facing the ocean. "What a spectacular place to build a house!"

"Grandma and a friend of hers planned it. She says it brings the rhythms of the sea into her life."

"That's exactly what I say, Keisha." A tall, graceful woman, her long gray hair braided and pinned in a high circlet, came down the spiral stairway into the living room. "When I'm home, I like to feel as though I'm at sea."

"You have a beautiful home, Ms. Zaharee." I put out my hand. "I'm Angela Curtis. I'm afraid Skye West couldn't be here today."

Linda Zaharee frowned slightly, gesturing that I should sit down. "She could have called me to reschedule."

"Perhaps you haven't heard what happened on the news today?" I asked.

"I try not to listen to the news. What did I miss? And, Keisha, could you get us some iced tea?"

The girl didn't look thrilled, but she left the room.

"My granddaughter is visiting for a few weeks. Summer vacation, you know. She used to love visiting Maine, but I'm afraid it's getting a little boring for a young teenager whose friends are in North Carolina."

I smiled. I remembered all too well being a restless teenager. But today I had to focus on business, not memories. "As she may have told you, Skye West has bought and is restoring the old Gardener estate, Aurora, in Haven Harbor. While work is being done on the house, she and her son have been living in the estate's carriage house. Last night the carriage house burned down."

"Oh, no. Is she all right?"

"She is. But her son was injured. He's at Mass General now, and she's with him. That's why she couldn't make this appointment."

"Well, I certainly understand that. Ms. Curtis, are you her personal assistant?"

I hesitated. Wasn't that what I'd been doing for the past couple of weeks? Helping Skye organize her life and taking care of unwanted chores? "Not exactly. But she's asked me to take care of some of the details of her life."

"And hiring me to paint a portrait is one of those 'details'?"

Keisha returned, put tall glasses in front of each of us, and left.

I'd used the wrong word. "No. Not at all. If Ms. West wants you to paint a portrait, then she'll be in touch with you as soon as her son is well. But she also wanted to contact you about another matter."

"Which was?"

"Forty-five years ago you took photographs of her. She was wondering whether you still had copies of those pictures."

Ms. Zaharee shook her head disbelievingly. "I'm sure I don't have the pictures she's looking for. I was a photographer for only a couple of years. It was a way to make money until I had enough experience to be recognized as a painter. When I left to study in Paris, I put all those photographs and negatives in a storage unit. Unfortunately, I didn't choose the location of the unit well. While I was away, it was flooded in spring storms. All my photographs were destroyed."

"Then you don't have any. No photos or negatives?"

"Truthfully, I only kept one photograph from that period of my life. It was a photograph of a girl. Not of Skye West. Somehow I managed to capture that moment exactly the way I'd wanted to." She smiled. "About ten years later I painted a portrait based on that photograph. Would you like to see it?"

"I'd love to. You have it here?"

"It seemed a part of Maine, and of my early life. I've kept it for sentimental reasons. Come, I'll show you."

I followed Linda into her office. A wide plank desk dominated the room. The walls were lined with bookcases holding books on art and artists and photography. But my eyes went immediately to the portrait she'd hung in front of books of photography. Jasmine Gardener was nude, standing in water almost up to her waist. Her head was thrown back in a laugh that never ended, and her long hair was dripping.

"Jasmine," I said quietly, walking over to it.

"You recognized the girl?" Linda stared at me. "But, of course. You come from Haven Harbor. You must have seen pictures of her somewhere."

I couldn't take my eyes off the painting. "I saw pictures of her at Aurora. Pictures of her and her friends." I turned around. "I told you Skye West bought Aurora."

"You did. But this was a girl who lived there long ago. I didn't think anyone would recognize her."

"Skye would." I finally stopped staring at the portrait. "She was Jasmine's best friend. Her name then was Mary North. You took pictures of them together."

Chapter 50

Precept 1: How To Get Riches
In things of moment on thy self depend,
Nor trust too far thy servant or thy friend.
With private views thy friend may promise fair.
And servants very seldom prove sincere.

—Lines stitched on a 1773 sampler, taken from Nathaniel Low's *An Astronomical Diary, or Almanack for 1772*

"Jasmine's friend. I remember," said Linda Zaharee. "She was shy. She didn't want me to take her picture, but Jasmine insisted. I wish I did still have those pictures. They were some of the best I took in those years. I loved that one." She pointed at the portrait.

"The Gardeners hired you to take pictures at their big town open house that Labor Day weekend," I continued. "Those pictures are gone, too?"

She shrugged. "Gone long ago. That summer I was staying in Camden. I didn't know what had happened to

Jasmine. I mean, I knew she'd been taken to the hospital the night of the party. But I didn't know it was anything serious. I was taking pictures of the fireworks when it all happened. About a week after that, I called the Gardeners to tell them their proofs were ready. Mr. Gardener told me they'd just gotten back from Jasmine's funeral. They didn't ever want to see the pictures. They didn't want to be reminded of that night. He sent me a more-than-generous check for my time, and I threw out the negatives and proofs. Who else would have wanted pictures of a party?"

"Skye was hoping you'd still have them."

"Well, you tell her I'm sorry, but no. They've been gone a long time."

"Skye also told me Jasmine was angry about the pictures you took of her. She asked for them, and you wouldn't give them to her. She threatened you with blackmail, Skye said."

Linda sat down at her desk. "Skye West, or whatever her name was then, seems to have remembered a lot about that summer. Yes, Jasmine was a little upset about the pictures. She didn't have any problem the day I was taking them. And, as you can see from my portrait, which is all that is left of that day, she was beautiful. Young, exuberant, full of life! But later she had second thoughts. She was afraid of what her parents or her friends would say if they knew she'd posed in the nude." Linda Zaharee looked at the portraits and then back at me. "She was so innocent. So naive. She wanted all the pictures and the negatives. I refused. They were some of my best work at that point. I wanted to keep at least the one for my portfolio. Keep in mind, in those days I made my living as a photographer. And she'd already signed a release. I was young, but not stupid enough to take nude pictures of an underage girl without getting her permission. I should have had her parents' permission first, I know now . . . but I didn't. The idea of nudity came up suddenly when I was taking other pictures of Jasmine and her friend. But I did have her signature on that form."

"So you didn't give her the photographs."

"I was going to. Not all the negatives, but the photographs. But then she died. And I didn't know how to contact her friend—I didn't even remember her name—except by going back to Mr. and Mrs. Gardener. Out of respect for Jasmine, I didn't want to do that."

"What happened to the pictures?"

"I kept the one, as I told you—the one I based the portrait on. The others were in those files that were destroyed."

I looked at the portrait again. "Skye would love to see that."

Linda Zaharee stood up. "When her situation is more relaxed, tell her to call me again. I'm here year-round, except when I have commission work that I have to do somewhere else. Or sometimes in January or February, I go to Sanibel Island in Florida. I have a small home and studio there."

"I'll tell her. She'll like hearing about the portrait. She'll be calling you."

"I look forward to that."

On my way back to Haven Harbor, I passed fields of purple and pink and white lupines. Lupines grew wild. When I was a child, the woman who lived next door would plant lupines every year. They'd never come back. Lupines grew where they chose to grow. Their independence was one reason Mainers loved them so much.

My sleepless night was catching up with me. I'd also skipped lunch. I stopped at a Dunkin' Donuts for a large black coffee and a bagel.

All I wanted to do was get home and go to sleep.

Our house was still, except for Juno's meowing welcome.

Gram had left a note. She was having dinner with Reverend Tom.

I was glad. I didn't want to eat or talk with anyone.

I went to bed and fell asleep almost immediately.

Sarah's call woke me four hours later. I looked at the clock. Only eleven.

"Yes, Sarah?"

"I called Katie. She's checked. Her panels have numbers on them, too. Hers are *VI* and *IX*. What about the panels your grandmother kept?"

"I haven't checked. I was exhausted. I was up all last night."

"Why?"

Oops. I hadn't told her about the dinner with Patrick. "Yesterday afternoon I met with Skye about the investigating that she wants me to do. The meeting went on into the early evening. She was tired, but Patrick wanted to go out to eat. So the two of us went."

Sarah was silent.

"Have you heard anything more about how he is?"

"Nothing since this morning."

"Did you have a nice dinner together?"

Darn. "All we did was eat together." *Or was it a date?*

"He's at Mass General, right?"

"Right."

"Shall we send flowers?"

"Why don't you check with the hospital? The burn center may not allow flowers. But if they do, sure. Go ahead. I'll reimburse you for my share."

"The numbers in the needlepoint are important, Angie."

"I know. I'll check the panels that are here. Promise."

"And you'll let me know?"

"I will." Her silence hurt. "Sarah, it wasn't a date."

"I understand. Be sure to let me know about the numbers, okay?"

"Okay."

I fell back asleep. Visions of fighting Roman numerals filled my dreams. Roman numerals that ran, like people did. And they were entwined in every tree and cloud.

Hallucinations. And I hadn't even had a drink in twenty-four hours.

Chapter 51

Merit should be forever plac'd
In Knowledge Judgment Wit and Taste.

—Stitched by Sarah May Horwell, age eight, Alexandria, Virginia, 1807, taken from the poem "Cadenus and Vanessa," 1713, written by Jonathan Swift (1667–1745)

"Gram, do you have a magnifying glass?"

It was morning, and Gram was pouring orange juice. I was sipping black coffee and looking to see if any of Gram's cranberry muffins were left in the freezer. There weren't.

"Angel, even with a magnifying glass, you won't find any more muffins. And we won't get any blueberries for another month."

By which time Gram would be living at the rectory and I'd be on my own for muffins. Which reminded me I still had work to do for her wine shower tomorrow. I'd had a text from Susan at the church office that over fifty people had RSVP'd. Katie was going to decorate. I'd ordered éclairs (my favorites) and cookies from the patisserie on Main Street. But I still needed to get a gift—not to mention that maid of honor dress that wasn't hanging in my closet. *Yet.* I closed the freezer door.

"The magnifying glass isn't for the muffins. Yesterday, Sarah and Katie and Dave found Roman numerals in the needlework panels I asked them to work on. We wondered whether there were numbers on the panels still here."

"Roman numerals?" Gram poured herself a cup of tea and pointed at the bread box. No muffins this morning. Toast.

I put two slices in the toaster and found a jar of wild-blueberry jam. It was the closest to Maine blueberries there'd be until late July. "Tiny Roman numerals. That's why I thought a magnifying glass would help. And something else is strange. Sarah found strands of hair in her panels, and Dave checked them. They're moose hair. Soaked in arsenic."

"Arsenic!" said Gram. "However could that be?"

"He said they could have come from a moose prepared by a taxidermist." I shrugged. "It sounds crazy, but Skye was almost poisoned by arsenic. The police found it in her glass at the house sale. And she says Millie Gardener suspected Jasmine was killed with arsenic—that poison caused her to fall in the fountain and hit her head."

"I remember hearing rumors about that," said Gram, looking through the drawer near the back door that contained anything and everything that didn't have another place in her house. She held up a magnifying glass. "I knew there was one in there somewhere. I used it to check the panels for mildew after I had them in the sun for a few days." She handed it to me. "Arsenic found in two places? Sounds strange to me."

"I agree," I said, buttering my toast before I topped it with jam.

"I don't know whether it's what you're looking for, but when I was checking the panels, I did notice a couple of marks on the top of the Haven Harbor Lighthouse. I thought they were shading, but they might have been a Roman numeral."

"We'll check after breakfast," I said.

"Have you heard from Skye again? I've been thinking about her, having to stay down at that hospital, waiting to see how her son is." Gram took a bite of her own toast. "Not to speak of her losing the carriage house. Thank goodness it wasn't the big house. Maybe one of the construction people left behind some combustible materials, or a wire was left ungrounded. When work is done as fast as she wanted it finished, sometimes it's not done as carefully as it should be. And I heard some of those construction people were from New York."

Because, of course, New York contractors would be more careless than Mainers.

"I talked with Pete Lambert yesterday. Inspectors from the state fire unit were there. Pete said it looked as though the fire was set."

"Set? You mean intentionally?"

I nodded. "'Why' would be the question."

Gram shook her head. "Horrible. Who would do such a thing? The Wests just arrived in Haven Harbor. I wouldn't be surprised if they packed up their money and moved back to California after this."

"It's lucky no one was hurt worse than they were. Patrick was burned, but from what his mother said, he'll eventually be all right. And Skye wasn't hurt at all."

"I'm glad you've been able to help them, Angel. They

should know not everyone in Haven Harbor is the sort who'd set fire to their home."

"Or put arsenic in Skye's drink," I added.

Gram took a last sip of her tea. "We're not accomplishing anything sitting here talking about it all. Let's take a look at those needlepoint panels."

Gram focused the magnifying glass on the marks she'd remembered seeing in the stitches of the Haven Harbor Lighthouse. "You take a look. See if it's a *II*," she said.

I agreed. It was definitely a *II*.

"Here," said Gram, handing me another of the panels and the magnifying glass. "Check the eagle flying over the yacht club. Your eyes are younger than mine."

I didn't tell her I hadn't yet found one of the numbers. Sarah and Dave and Katie had been the ones with the good eyes.

While I was looking carefully at every stitch on the yacht club building and the shore, Gram got a piece of paper.

"So the lighthouse panel is number two," she said. "I assume there are ten numbers, since there are ten panels." She listed the numbers one through ten.

"Sarah found the number five in the panel of the moose," I said. "And a seven on Second Sister Island."

Gram wrote that down.

"And Katie said there was a six on the fireworks panel, and a nine on the panel of the church. When I was at Dave's house yesterday, he found a four on the statue of Aurora, and a ten on a sailboat in the harbor."

Gram stared at the list she'd written as I continued staring at the panel she'd given me.

"Wait! I've found a one," I said. "It's woven into the feathers on the eagle's back. You look."

"You may be right," said Gram, after taking the panel

close to the window and adjusting the glass. "But the Roman numeral for one is just *I*. That shape could be in a lot of designs."

"Let me look at another of the panels, then," I said.

She handed me the one of Aurora's main staircase. That one I saw immediately. "I think it's the three . . . but, like the one, it's hard to tell. It's a part of the staircase," I said. "If Sarah hadn't seen the seven and the five, I don't think we would have seen the one or two or three."

"Agreed," said Gram, writing down what we'd found. "But if we're right, the last panel we have, the one of the town pier, has to have the number eight."

This time she looked. "And, yes, it does. *VIII* is on the ramp."

I picked up her list and added the pier:

1 – Eagle
2 – Lighthouse
3 – Staircase
4 – Aurora statue
5 – Moose
6 – Fireworks
7 – Island
8 – Town Pier
9 – Church
10 – Haven Harbor

"But why the code? Why the Roman numerals?" asked Gram.

I stared at the list. "She was trying to tell us something. But she didn't want it to be obvious. Maybe Arabic numerals would have been too easy to see."

"Maybe," said Gram. "It's a puzzle, though."

We were both staring at the list when my telephone

rang. "Good morning, Sarah! Gram and I are looking at her panels. We've found the rest of the numbers. No, I haven't heard from Skye or Patrick." I hadn't expected to hear from Patrick—not while his hands were badly burned, not unless he used a speakerphone. "Among all of us, we've now found the numbers one through ten. But, of course, we've always known there were ten panels. We don't know why the numbers. Gram and I were wondering why Millie Gardener chose to use Roman numerals instead of regular Arabic ones. What has Rome to do with Haven Harbor?"

I put Sarah on speakerphone. Her voice came through clearly. "I've been thinking about that. Aurora was a Roman goddess, wasn't she?"

"Of course." I looked over at Gram. "Aurora was the Roman name for the goddess of the dawn. And the name of the Gardeners' house. So that's it. She chose to honor Aurora by using her number system."

Sarah's voice was sure. "Aurora was also the place Jasmine died. And Mrs. Gardener was determined to prove she'd been murdered."

"True," I agreed. "Skye told me Millie Gardener was sure she'd figured out who'd murdered Jasmine. But she didn't have proof."

"She didn't tell Skye who she suspected?"

"No. If she had, Skye wouldn't have needed me to talk to so many people about Jasmine's death. Although after talking with everyone on her list, plus a few more, I'm no closer to knowing what happened in 1970."

"Well, if you figure it out, let me know. I'm beginning to think Millie Gardener sent us a secret message."

"That's what Gram thought, too," I answered.

"I have to go and open the shop. If you hear any news from Boston, call me."

I turned to Gram, who'd been studying the list we'd made. "You heard. Sarah thinks there's a code in the panels, too." I said.

"She's right," said Gram, staring at the list she'd made. "I've even figured it out. But I have no idea how anyone could prove the person Millie's named killed her daughter. Or why."

Chapter 52

Finger: A measure of length, employed for every description of textile for wearing apparel or upholstery, etc. It comprises 4½ inches and is much in use by needlewomen.

—*The Dictionary of Needlework: An Encyclopaedia of Artistic, Plain, and Fancy Needlework,* London, 1882

Gram pointed to the list. "Look at the subjects of the panels. That couldn't be a coincidence."

I looked at where she was pointing. All those Sundays doing the acrostic puzzles in the newspaper had paid off. Gram had seen something where I'd seen nothing. But once she'd shown me where to look, it was all clear.

"The first letters of the words spell a name," I said, incredulously. "And that person was at the party in 1970, and at the house sale. And had access to Aurora while Millie Gardener was alive."

Gram nodded. "I can hardly believe it, though. Why

would Elsa M. Fitch kill anyone? I've known her for years. She's a decent hairdresser. But other than a few haircuts people might have wanted to kill her for, Elsa's a sweetie. Took care of her mother for years. The needlepoint panels may say who Millie Gardener believed was guilty. But that doesn't mean she was right. Elsa was younger than I was in 1970, and you said Mrs. Gardener couldn't prove anything. Maybe Millie Gardener was losing it a bit in her later years, living all by herself in that big house." Gram shuddered. "Putting Elsa's name in the needlework doesn't make any sense."

"No. But I talked with Elsa, and with her brother and sister. So she knew Skye was trying to reopen the investigation of Jasmine's death. To stop the investigation, she might be trying to kill Skye. That would explain the arsenic in the cup, and the fire in the carriage house."

"I'm not convinced Elsa's the one you're looking for. But if anyone did those things, then Skye is still in danger," said Gram.

"She's probably safe so long as she's in Boston. But she could decide to come home at any time." I thought a few minutes. "The local police didn't listen when they found the arsenic in Skye's cup. But now there's been the fire, too. And these clues. Could be they'll finally listen." I dialed Pete Lambert's number. "Pete? Angie Curtis. I need to see you as soon as possible. It could be a matter of life or death." I hoped he checked his messages often.

"A little melodramatic?" Gram remarked.

"Absolutely," I agreed. "And very serious. If Pete doesn't call back in half an hour, I'm going to call Ethan Trask. He's with the homicide unit of the Maine State Police. But first I'm going to talk with Ob and Anna Winslow. We might need their help."

I left Gram staring at the pad of paper on the coffee table.

Pete called back in ten minutes. I needed to talk with the Winslows first, so I agreed to meet Pete at the station in forty-five minutes. In the meantime I called my old high-school friend Clem Walker, who worked at Channel 7 in Portland. I'd need her help.

The Winslows hesitated, but they agreed. And Clem said she'd do what she could.

It was all set.

I just needed to get Pete on board.

Luckily, the Haven Harbor Police Station was a short drive.

Pete's desk was covered with stacks of papers and binders. I sat in the chair opposite his. "Paperless society?"

He winced. "Not exactly. No one here trusts computers, so everything is in duplicate. Or triplicate. Or whatever comes after that. And I'm always behind. But you didn't come here to talk about paperwork."

"I'm pretty sure I know who tried to poison Skye West, and who set the fire in the carriage house two nights ago. And I know how we can prove it."

"I'm listening." Pete leaned toward me.

"And Jasmine Gardener was murdered, just as her mother thought."

"Angie, that's an old rumor," Pete said, shaking his head. "Stick to what's happening now."

"Listen to me! When that hummingbird died at Aurora, you didn't think it was important. But I'm convinced someone wanted to get rid of Skye. Kill her, or scare her enough so she'd leave town."

"So you figured this out while you've been going around town, asking people questions about what happened forty-five years ago?" Pete did not look happy.

"I have. And I've found out a lot. I think the person who killed Jasmine Gardener in 1970 is trying to kill Skye West now."

"For sure you've stirred up everyone's memories, good and bad. But can you prove that this mysterious person—I've noticed you haven't named anyone—is guilty of all these things?"

I hesitated. "I'll admit my suspect doesn't sound likely. But she fits! Millie Gardener thought she was guilty. She left clues in her needlework. I even think this person might have killed Millie Gardener after she knew Mrs. Gardener suspected her. Or at least she contributed to Mrs. Gardener's death. Was Mrs. Gardener's body ever tested for arsenic?"

"So far as I know, the old lady was never autopsied. She lived alone. She died. No one had a reason to question her death."

I nodded. "That's what I thought. But she'd figured out who killed Jasmine. When she couldn't find proof, she got discouraged. She told the Haven Harbor Police Department what she thought, long before your time on the force. She wrote to Skye and told her she suspected someone. What if she told someone else in town, or what she told the police got back to the killer?"

"You're off base there," said Pete. "No one in the police department would have talked." He looked at me. "And isn't it time for you to tell me who this serial killer and arsonist is?"

"Elsa Fitch."

"What? That old woman who runs Mane Waves?" Pete laughed out loud. "Angie, I can't think of a more unlikely murder suspect. Elsa Fitch would scream if she saw a mouse."

"I'm not so sure. She deals with women all day long. She's got to know all the gossip in town. My impression has been that the police didn't take Mrs. Gardener and her fixation on her daughter's death seriously. Maybe they even joked about it sometimes. I don't know. If the suspect found that out . . . but that's not critical now. What's critical is identifying who tried to poison Skye and who set the fire two nights ago."

Pete looked incredulous. "Elsa Fitch's feet probably hurt from standing all the time. That's her only problem I can think of. And that doesn't make her a murderer."

"Please! Listen to my plan. If it doesn't work, you've only lost one night. If it does work, you'll have solved at least two cases."

"This plan of yours better be wicked smart, Angie. 'Cause right now, nothing you're saying makes any sense to me."

"I have a friend at Channel 7 in Portland. She's already talked with her boss, and they've agreed to help out, on the condition we give them credit if our plan works."

"'Our plan'?" said Pete. "I haven't heard the beginning of a plan yet. All I've heard is a crazy story."

"You'll issue a press release to the *Haven Harbor News* and Channel 7, saying you're close to an arrest for arson at Skye West's carriage house. Say that on the night of the fire an older man who lives across the street from Aurora saw someone entering the carriage house carrying something, and then running out. This man can identify the person and their vehicle. Of course, everyone in town will know the only person who matches that description is Ob Winslow."

"You already got this Clem person to agree to broadcast this?"

"She says the station will broadcast anything about Skye West. She promises it'll be on the air when I tell her the plan is a go."

"And what about Ob Winslow? Is he in on this, too?"

"He's agreed. On the condition that his son and wife not be home tonight, and that you and I and Ethan Trask, whom he's known for years, be with him at his house."

"You're assuming that whoever is guilty will try to get to Ob," said Pete.

"And silence him," I agreed. "One way or another."

"We'd have to get the state fire folks on board," said Pete, getting up and pacing the four or five feet across his small office. "And I don't feel comfortable with your being there."

"Ob insisted. It was my idea, and he wants me there."

Pete stopped pacing. "Angie, this is basically a crazy idea."

I nodded.

"But it just might work."

"If it doesn't, all that's happened is you've lost a night's sleep. And you might catch a killer and arsonist."

"I'll call Ethan. Six o'clock at Ob's house sound okay?"

I stood and smiled. "I'll bring sandwiches. It may be a long night."

Chapter 53

Fresh in the morn the summer rose
Hangs withering ere tis noon
We scarce enjoy the balmy gift
But mourn the pleasure gone.

—Stitched by Lucy Perkins, Liverpool,
Nova Scotia, 1792

June nights are the longest. Certainly this one was.

The bag of sandwiches was almost empty; we'd finished one pot of coffee and were working on a second. Half-empty bowls of potato chips and popcorn seemed to have sprouted from every table at Ob's house.

After sympathetically making an enormous batch of chocolate chip cookies for us, Anna had taken Josh, under protest, to her sister's house for the night. Ob was calmer than the rest of us. When he hadn't been eating, he'd been playing video games.

Luckily, his barn was big enough to hide two police

vehicles and my little car. Ob had closed the barn doors, as he did each night. An observer would think all was as usual.

Pete and Ethan, who'd reluctantly decided to join us, were dropping crumbs as they took turns watching out both the front window and the back. The front gave them a view of the road, including Aurora, and Ob's driveway. In back were acres of woodlands that would be challenging to cross, especially at night—especially for someone old enough to have been at a party in 1970.

I sat on the couch, watching the local news (Channel 7 did announce the impending arrest) and then CNN, hoping neither Pete nor Ethan would notice the gun I was wearing under my loose sweater.

You had to be a Maine resident for six months to qualify for a hidden-carry permit. I'd only been home two months. But my boss at the detective agency in Arizona had insisted I learn to shoot, and I felt comfortable carrying. I'd only pull my weapon in an emergency, but tonight it made me feel safer.

A murderer might show up at any moment.

Could Elsa Fitch shoot? Many women in Maine could. Or would she arrive bearing arsenic-laced libations or a can of gasoline? The women varied her methodology. I gave her credit for that.

I nibbled another handful of popcorn. In addition to my tuna sandwich, I'd already had three cups of coffee and several cookies. It was only a little after nine o'clock. The combination of caffeine and sugar kept my nerves on edge.

Ob left his computer and sat next to me. "Anything good happening in the world?"

"Middle East chaos, Internet fraud, political maneuvering, and a few murders."

"Same as usual."

"Yup." I took another handful of popcorn.

"How long do you think we'll have to wait?" he asked. "I start heading for bed about this time of night. Elsa's a few years older than me. She's no spring chicken. I'd think she'd want to make her approach early in the evening."

"You signed up for the duration, Ob, same as us," said Ethan Trask. "If it's you she's after, you'd better be here. And awake."

"Bait. That's all I am. Bait!" Ob smiled and leaned back, clearly enjoying his role. "Most exciting thing that's happened to me in years. But you know what happens to bait that sits around for a while."

"It stinks," agreed Ethan. "This idea of Angie's is crazy, but we're all in it now."

"Hey, you guys agreed," I pointed out. "And think of the cases you'll solve if she does show up."

"Brandishing her shears and curling irons, no doubt," chortled Pete.

"Or she'll shampoo Ob to death," added Ethan with a grin.

"If you'd told me that was a possibility, I might not have agreed to all this," said Ob. "And no hair spray, either. Hate that stuff," he added, turning to me. "How do you women cope with all that?"

I rolled my eyes.

"Stabbing us all with her scissors is the simplest idea," Pete continued. "With all the cookies we've eaten, we'd burst like balloons."

"Right. If we don't get blown apart in the meantime," said Pete. They'd already checked the house for any explosives or incendiary materials. Country houses are full of possible fuels, and, after all, we were waiting for someone who hadn't hesitated to set the carriage house on fire when Skye West was inside.

"Should be dark by nine-thirty or so," Ethan said. "It's going to be a long night. We've committed to this foolishness. Now we have to wait until the sun comes up, to be sure."

We sat. Once in a while someone would take a bathroom break, or comment on a news story. At eleven o'clock, Ethan said, "Angie, I can't take hearing about UN peacekeepers for the umpteenth time. I like the idea of the TV being on. If anyone gets near enough to the house to hear, it'll explain the voices they hear. But couldn't you turn on *Law and Order* or something? CNN is depressing."

I nodded and switched channels. Reality TV. People being dunked in cold water. Cooking shows. A nature program about weasels. I left that on for a few minutes. Maine fisher cats were in the weasel family. They were active at night.

"Mean critters," muttered Pete, taking a break from his turn at the window. "Killed a couple of cats in my neighborhood last summer, until someone got their rifle out."

"Is that legal?" I asked. "Shooting in your neighborhood?" I didn't know where Pete lived; but unless you lived way out in the country, shooting was legally frowned upon.

"It was on their own property. Didn't hear no one complaining about the cat killer being eliminated."

I shivered. One of the reasons Gram's Juno was an indoor cat was the number of fishers who ventured into town.

Pete poured himself the last of the coffee. "Hey, Angie, why don't you make us some more coffee?"

"Make it yourself," I said. "I've had enough to keep me awake for the next week."

"A little touchy?" Pete reached for the coffee beans. The sound of grinding covered any noise from the television or from outside.

"Sh, can't you?" asked Ethan. "We're supposed to be on a stakeout, not at a dinner party."

Pete raised his eyebrows and poured the ground beans into the coffeepot.

I'd been on a lot of stakeouts—most of them by myself. But on most of those assignments, the only danger involved had been falling asleep, or missing a sighting of my target. My target to photograph.

Murder and arson were a little beyond my experience level.

And it would be embarrassing if my guess had been wrong. Nothing had happened so far.

I touched my angel, just in case.

My waistband holster was hitting me in an awkward place. "My turn for a bathroom break," I said, getting up and heading in the direction of the facilities. We were all pretty familiar with that room by now, and I could make a few wardrobe adjustments while attending to other business.

I reached to turn on the light. Then I stopped.

Was that a movement in the shadows outside? The glimmer of a light flickering? It appeared as if someone holding a flashlight was moving between the trees.

I went to the window.

Definitely a moving light. And it was too early in the season for fireflies.

"Ethan! Pete!" I called softly. Pete came immediately. "Someone is outside with a flashlight."

He nodded and gestured that I should stay in the hall. My bladder hoped either I'd been wrong, or that whatever was happening would be over quickly.

"Get Ethan," he whispered. He'd drawn his gun. I left mine where it was. For now, at least, I didn't need it.

I went back to the living room. "I saw a flashlight moving out back. Pete's watching it."

Ethan gestured that I should get down, below window level. Ob had dozed off on the couch.

If someone was able to get to the window . . . or had binoculars . . . or a rifle sight, she would be able to see him.

I hadn't considered all those possibilities. What if Elsa was a crack shot? What if she had a long lens on her rifle? It would be a long shot, literally, but she could fire through the window.

For now, she was out back. How had she gotten here? What was she thinking, seeing the lights on at this time of night? Most Mainers, like Ob, retired by eleven o'clock.

Pete came back into the living room, with his gun still in his hand. "She's gone in back of the ell. Maybe she'll come around the barn, toward the side of the house."

The barnyard door, the door most people used, was on the side of the house by the ell.

"Should we wake Ob?" I asked. If something happened, we'd have to stop to rouse him.

"Do that," said Ethan, joining us. He'd drawn his weapon, too. "Quietly. And you, Angie, stay down. You don't want to be another target."

He stood on the far side of the door they suspected the intruder might try to enter. Pete went into the nearby hall, out of sight of anyone entering through that door.

"Ob," I said quietly. I sat on the floor and reached up to touch Ob's arm gently. "Ob, wake up. Someone's outside."

His eyes opened. He understood immediately.

"Stay on the couch," Ethan whispered. "Ob, don't move. Don't get up unless we tell you."

An infomercial for a backyard trampoline was blaring on the television.

Just what we needed.

Ob nodded.

That's when we heard a knock on the door. No one moved.

What was the protocol?

Whoever was out there was looking for Ob. If Ob answered the door, he might be shot. Or stabbed, even with those hairdresser shears the guys had been joking about earlier.

No one was joking now.

Whoever was out there expected Ob, or perhaps Anna, or even Josh, to answer the door.

They wouldn't expect me.

I got up and walked to the door.

"Angie! No!" Ethan tried to grab my arm as I passed him. But I was too fast. If anyone was going to be hurt tonight, it should be me.

Someone had to open that door.

I'd gotten us all into this situation.

I braced myself, put my right hand on my weapon, and quickly opened the door with my left.

Standing in the doorway was my second-grade teacher.

Chapter 54

Fisher Fur: The Fisher is of the genus Weasel and is a native of America, whence upwards of 11,000 of their skins are annually imported to this country. They are larger than those of the sable, and the fur is deeper and fuller, and very beautiful. The tail is long, round, and gradually tapering to a point, and is employed for hats, as well as to form a decoration in the national cap worn by the Polish Jews. One skin of the fisher will suffice to make a muff, for which three Marten skins would be required.

—*The Dictionary of Needlework: An Encyclopaedia of Artistic, Plain, and Fancy Needlework,* London, 1882

"Miss Fitch!"

She looked almost as surprised as I was.

"What are you doing here?"

"I came to see Ob," she answered. "I know it's late. But it's important."

I looked to see if she had a weapon of any sort. I didn't see anything. To my side, but hidden, Ethan gestured that I should let her in. "Ob's here. He's watching television." The infomercial had changed, but the announcer's voice was droning on. "Come in." I stepped aside.

Ethan and Pete had somehow disappeared. Probably they were in the kitchen, the room on the other side of the doorway. They hadn't gone far. Why was Miss Fitch here? Where was her sister Elsa?

She walked ahead of me. Ob stood up. Then he turned and clicked off the television. Without that noise, the house was ominously silent.

"Hello, Beth. I didn't expect more company tonight. Angie and I were just talking business. She's the director of Mainely Needlepoint now. I work with them."

She nodded. "I know it's late. But after I heard the news report, I had to talk to you."

"Ah, the news," said Ob. "The broadcast that said I'd seen the person who set the fire over at Aurora. That I was going to tell the police what I knew. I'm not surprised you're here."

"That's right," said Miss Fitch. She looked over at me. "If you've finished your business with Angie, she could leave."

"Oh, no. We haven't finished," said Ob. "We still have a lot to discuss . . . about needlepoint. Lots of projects coming up."

"I'd rather not have anyone else hear what I have to say."

"I wouldn't worry about that," said Ob. "You can talk to both of us."

And to the two hidden cops, I thought.

Miss Fitch looked uncomfortable. She glanced at me several times. Then she looked at Ob and blurted, "You didn't tell the police right away because you figured I'd come crawling and beg you not to, right?"

Ob had done well so far. How far could he carry this and still sound believable?

"Is that what you think?" he asked.

"You expected me to come tonight. What do you want? Because I'm just a teacher . . . I don't have much money."

"Why did you do it, Beth? Arson's a felony. And you might have killed someone. Burned them to death, Beth."

"You think I didn't know that? That's what I wanted. I wanted Skye West to die. To disappear. Not to be here in Haven Harbor messing up all of our lives."

"Is that what she's doing?"

"Come on now, Ob. You know it. She's been opening sores that healed long ago. You were there—you know what happened."

Ob leaned back on the couch, away from Miss Fitch. I hoped he knew what she was talking about. I didn't.

"Don't deny it. You were a little boy. But if someone figures out what happened back then, you're liable, too."

"What could I be liable for?" he asked, his voice rising.

Miss Fitch glanced at me. "Angie shouldn't be here. This should be between you and me, Ob. No one else has to know. Only three of us are left who remember."

"I want her to stay."

She shrugged. "All right, then. How do you think your family will feel? Your friends? What will you tell them?"

Ob looked confused. "I don't know what you're talking about, Beth. I've done nothing wrong."

"You actually believe that? When you're the one who handed Jasmine that glass of wine laced with arsenic, the one that killed her?"

Ob's body froze. "Me?"

"You. No one else."

"How do you know that?"

"Elsa told me, of course. She said she'd given you the glass for Jasmine. That way she'd have no connection with Jasmine's death."

I remembered. Ob told me Elsa Fitch had given him a glass of wine to take to Jasmine that night.

"Elsa put arsenic in the glass?" I said.

"No one can prove that. It's been forty-five years. Only Millie Gardener suspected, after Elsa told her about our grandfather's being a taxidermist. Elsa was a smart girl, except when she talked too much. She tried to keep Millie quiet, too, but that time she tried too hard to make death seem natural. She only used a little arsenic." Miss Fitch shook her head, as though chastising a naughty child. "She was too smart for her age back in 1970. She was jealous of all Jasmine had. She wanted the money and the freedom and the college that Jasmine accepted as her due. Jasmine even accepted Jed as her due. Elsa and I knew Jasmine's pregnancy could end Jed's possibilities. He was so dumb sometimes. He was already skipping football practices. He figured if Jasmine had his baby, then her daddy would take care of them both. Would set them up and send him to college. Or maybe he wouldn't even have to go to college. Jasmine's family would pay their expenses." She took a deep breath. "He thought Jasmine was the answer to what he was going to do with his life. He wasn't willing to work and earn a future, the way I had. The way Elsa wanted to do it."

"So Elsa poisoned Jasmine."

Miss Fitch shrugged. "She was only fifteen, and she always had her nose in science books. She had the idea that arsenic would make Jasmine miscarry. Our grandfather had been a taxidermist. He'd told her about some of the traditional uses of arsenic. She'd cut a piece of moose skin out of an old head we had in the attic—our attic was full of junk like that—and soaked it. The day before the party, she'd tried to add the water to Jasmine's lemonade at our house, but Jasmine hadn't been thirsty. So the night of the party was Elsa's last chance. She managed to get a glass of wine, doctored it a little, and then gave it to you, Ob. She knew you were sweet on Jasmine. You'd be happy to deliver it to her."

"And then when Skye West arrived in town and started asking questions, Elsa got scared. She put arsenic in Skye's cup at the house sale," I said, hoping I hadn't missed anything.

"No," Miss Fitch said, looking at me. "You were never the brightest student, Angela. I poisoned that cup."

"And set the fire," said Ob.

"All these years Elsa's been paying for what she did. She was stuck in Haven Harbor, taking care of our parents, while I was abroad. Jed missed his chance to escape, but that was his own fault. He didn't work hard enough to get a scholarship, and Jasmine's family wasn't there to bail him out. I have no sympathy for him. But Elsa wanted so much to go to college, to get away from Haven Harbor. Father made her turn down the scholarships she got. He told her it was her responsibility to take care of Mother." Miss Fitch shook her head. "It wasn't fair. But I wasn't around to fight for her, and all Jed was doing was taking a few classes and drinking his way through those. Elsa accepted the responsibility to keep the family together. She paid in her own way for what she did. It wouldn't be fair for the town to find out what really happened back in 1970. That was forty-five years ago." She looked at me, and then at Ob. "I couldn't let that happen. It was time for me to take some responsibility. Elsa had nothing to do with what happened in the past week. She was too scared. She would have messed it up, like she did trying to poison Millie Gardener. This time I took care of everything myself. I had to protect my baby sister."

Chapter 55

Down in a greend and shady bed
A modest violet grew
Its stalks was bent, it hung its head
As if to hide from view.
And yet it was a lovely flower
Its colors bright and fair
It might have graced a rosy bower
Instead of hiding there.

—Sampler stitched by Francis Rebecca Cooke,
age twelve, Schenectady, New York, 1810

"So Elsa Fitch did kill Jasmine." Sarah opened the third box of éclairs and stacked them on a platter. Reverend Tom's house looked amazingly festive, thanks to the blue and the white balloons, the umbrellas, and all the ribbons fastened everywhere Katie could. She'd even hung a CONGRATULATIONS CHARLOTTE & TOM! banner.

She hadn't been able to cover all the Ouija boards. But if anyone consulted the spirits this afternoon, I was sure they'd say the signs were positive. Gram and Reverend Tom were going to have a wonderful life together.

I touched my gold angel. *Mama, Gram and I are all right. Life went on. And, Jasmine, we found the person who poisoned you. Justice has been done. Now you can rest in peace.*

I smiled to myself. Talking to the dead. Maybe being near Reverend Tom's collection of Ouija boards did bring out the spirits. Or opened my mind to them.

Sarah had found a perfect gift for their wine shower: a Victorian silver wine caddy. She and I were giving it from both of us. Gram would love it.

A large box in the corner (it was covered in pink paper—he hadn't gotten the message that the shower colors were blue and white) was Tom's gift to Gram. He'd whispered to me Friday night that it was a wine refrigerator, which would hold thirty-six bottles at different temperatures.

This house was getting ready to party!

"I still can't believe Beth Fitch would try to poison and burn Skye," said Sarah. Two éclairs toppled, and she started another platter. I may have ordered too much from the patisserie.

I shrugged. "I heard her say it. They're both in police custody now. Charges like murder and attempted murder and arson aren't minor."

"Speaking of arson . . . Patrick called me this morning," Sarah said.

He hadn't called me. But, then, I wasn't supposed to be interested in him, was I? Sarah was.

"He said another two or three weeks in the hospital and

he'll be released. He has to have therapy for his burned hands, but he's arranging for it to take place here in Maine." She smiled, clearly pleased. "He and Sky have decided to rebuild the carriage house. He's excited about designing it exactly the way he'd like. They're going to stay at Mrs. Chase's B and B when they get back to Maine. They've reserved both her rooms for the summer."

"That's good news," I said. "Then we can talk to Skye about how she wants the needlepoint panels framed. Last time I talked with her, she said she still wanted them, complete with clues and moose hair." I shook my head. "She said it would be a tribute to both Jasmine and her mother to have those panels in the house."

Sarah stood back and admired the dining-room table. The blue tablecloth we'd put down half an hour before was now covered with platters of cupcakes, cookies, brownies, and éclairs. There were two punch bowls—one of them was filled with sangria. ("After all, it's a wine party, and this is June!" Sarah had reminded me. "We need a summer drink.") For those who wanted a lighter drink, one punch bowl had pink lemonade.

We'd also used blue cloth to cover three card tables in the corner, for people to put gifts on.

Now all we had to do was wait for the guests.

I picked up an éclair to sample it. *Mmm.*

"So, have you gotten a dress for the wedding yet?" Sarah asked.

"Tomorrow," I promised. "Tomorrow, after church, I'm heading for South Portland and the mall. If there's nothing there, I have the names of several boutiques in Portland's Old Port. I'm not coming home without something to wear."

"Good plan," said Sarah, pouring herself a cup of

sangria. "And, after all, you have a whole week. Haven Harbor is a quiet place. Nothing could happen here to distract you."

I grinned back. "'Summer in Maine. The way life should be.' Well, at least most of the time."

Angie Curtis's Gram, Charlotte, loves to cook; her specialty is classic Maine dishes. In *Threads of Evidence* she cooks this elegant but comforting bread pudding made from northern New England ingredients. It's one of Angie's favorites.

Maple Bread Pudding

2½ cups light cream
4 eggs, separated
¾ cup pure maple syrup
Pinch of salt
Pinch of nutmeg
5–6 cups day-old French or Italian bread cut into cubes
Whipping cream (optional)

Preheat oven to 350. Heat baking pan (e.g. lasagna pan) half filled with hot water.

Scald cream. Cool.

Beat together egg yolks, maple syrup, and salt.

Stir cream into egg mixture. Beat egg whites to peaks. Fold into custard mixture.

Spread bread cubes in buttered 1½-quart baking dish and pour custard mixture over the cubes, mixing lightly. Sprinkle nutmeg on top.

Place baking dish in the pan of hot water.

Bake in preheated oven 40–45 minutes, or until knife inserted in center comes out clean.

May be served warm or cool. Gram prefers it warm, and often adds a bit of whipped cream to the top.

Serves 6–8

Acknowledgments

With thanks to everyone who's made my life easier, especially when I'm in "writing mode".

My wonderful husband, Bob Thomas, who believed in me before anyone else did, and cooks and does errands and takes time to listen to plot problems even when he's in the middle of painting for his next gallery opening.

My sister, Nancy Cantwell, who, along with Bob, is my first reader. My granddaughters Vanessa and Samantha Childs, who tease me, encourage me . . . and help address postcards to my readers.

My agent, John Talbot, who made this series possible.

All the wonderful people at Kensington Publishing who bring Angie and her friends to readers, especially editor John Scognamiglio who believed in this series, copy editor Stephanie Finnegan, who kept all the details straight, Morgan Elwell, publicist extraordinaire, and Robin Cook, production editor.

My fellow Sisters in Crime and friends at Mystery Writers of America, my wonderful readers, especially those at Malice Domestic, and fellow authors Kathy Lynn Emerson, Kate Flora, Barbara Ross, Vicky Doudera, Paul Doiron, Gerry Boyle, Jim Hayman, and Susan Vaughan, Mainers all.

The librarians and bookstore owners who've welcomed me and shared my books with readers.

I invite you to friend me on Facebook and Goodreads, check my website (www.leawait.com)for more about me and my books, including discussion questions for groups reading *Threads of Evidence*, and read www.MaineCrimeWriters.com, the blog I write with other authors who write mysteries set in the wonderful, and sometimes mysterious, State of Maine.

Lea Wait

Please turn the page for an exciting sneak peek of Lea Wait's next Mainely Needlepoint Mystery

THREAD AND GONE

coming in January 2016!

Chapter 1

The world, my dear Mary, is full of deceit
And friendships a jewell we seldome can meet
How strange does it seem that in searching around
The source of content is so rare to be found.

—Poem stitched by Lucy Ripley,
age thirteen, Hartford, Connecticut, 1802

The simple folded leather packet looked old. Old, cracked, and very out of place, as it lay innocently on the bright red Fourth of July tablecloth. A mystery from the past had interrupted my first Haven Harbor dinner party.

Before I'd seen that packet and its contents, I'd been feeling high on more than the Pouilly-Fuissé recommended by the owner of Haven Harbor's local wine and gourmet treats store. (Buying beer? No problem. Wine? That's a whole different world.)

I'd gotten up the courage to invite Sarah Byrne,

Dave Percy, and Ruth Hopkins, three other Mainely Needlepointers who were going to be alone on the holiday, to join me to celebrate the official start of the tourist season, and my first Maine Fourth of July in ten years. I figured all three of my guests would be understanding if my salmon was a little dry or my peas undercooked.

But until the packet arrived, everything had been perfect.

I'd pulled it off. My guests had made appropriate compliments and serious dents in the baked salmon, fresh green peas, and hot potato salad that made up my close-to-traditional New England Fourth of July menu. And I'd only had to interrupt Gram's Quebec honeymoon twice to ask for cooking advice and counsel.

As I looked around the table, I couldn't help smiling. Two months ago I hadn't known these people. Today I counted them friends as well as colleagues.

Gram had brought us together. She'd managed to gather an eclectic and talented group of Mainers to do custom needlepoint for her business, and as the new director of Mainely Needlepoint I was reaping the benefits of her choices. Not only could everyone in the business do needlepoint, but they'd all brought their own personalities and talents to their work.

Anyone meeting us for the first time would never guess that middle-aged Dave, navy retiree and now a high-school biology teacher, also had an extensive garden of poisonous plants. Or that Sarah, whose pink-and-blue-striped blonde hair and Aussie accent made her very noticeable in a small Maine town, was also a member of the staid Maine Antiques Dealers Association. Or that Ruth Hopkins, a sweet little old lady whose arthritis forced her to depend on her pink wheeling walker, wrote erotica.

And me, Angie Curtis. The most ordinary of the lot. As long as you understood that "ordinary" included ten years working for a private investigator in Arizona. I knew how to use the gun I now kept hidden under Gram's winter gloves and scarves in the front hall. I was also the youngest of the group—twenty-seven, a born Mainer, and a native of Haven Harbor. Most unusual in this crowd, I was just beginning to learn needlepoint.

I was also learning what it was like to live alone. Gram's wedding to Reverend Tom last weekend had been pronounced "a smashing success" by Sarah, and as soon as Gram returned from her honeymoon, she'd be moving to the rectory. True, I'd lived alone (nearly all of the time, anyway) in my Arizona apartment, but being alone in two rooms was different from being alone in a large, creaking house built over two hundred years ago.

But I'd grown up here, as my mother and grandmother and great-grandmother had before me. I couldn't imagine another family in these rooms. I'd get used to living here by myself. In the meantime my only full-time companion was Juno, Gram's large yellow Maine coon cat.

Juno looked up expectantly when anyone came into the house and then curled up in Gram's favorite chair, sadly waiting. She didn't understand about honeymoons. To make up for Gram's absence, I'd been giving Juno more treats than I'm sure Gram would have approved.

I'll admit I even slipped a piece of salmon into her dinner dish before I served my guests. And I suspected Dave had been passing her a few tidbits under the table during dinner.

The four of us had comfortably finished off two bottles of wine and were debating the virtues of strawberry-rhubarb pie now, or strawberry-rhubarb pie after the fireworks, when we heard a knock on the front door.

The young people standing there could have been any two Haven Harbor teenagers celebrating the Fourth.

But they weren't.

BOOKS BY LEA WAIT

Mainely Needlepoint Mysteries

1 – *Twisted Threads*

2 – *Threads of Evidence*

3 – *Thread and Gone*

Shadows Antique Print Mysteries

1 – *Shadows at the Fair*

2 – *Shadows on the Coast of Maine*

3 – *Shadows on the Ivy*

4 – *Shadows at the Spring Show*

5 – *Shadows of a Down East Summer*

6 – *Shadows on a Cape Cod Wedding*

7 – *Shadows on a Maine Christmas*

Historical Novels for ages 8 and up

Stopping to Home

Seaward Born

Wintering Well

Finest Kind

Uncertain Glory